In Sickness
and in Health

Essential Prose Series 215

Canada Council   Conseil des Arts
for the Arts   du Canada

ONTARIO ARTS COUNCIL
CONSEIL DES ARTS DE L'ONTARIO
an Ontario government agency
un organisme du gouvernement de l'Ontario

Canadä

Guernica Editions Inc. acknowledges the support of the Canada Council
for the Arts and the Ontario Arts Council. The Ontario Arts Council
is an agency of the Government of Ontario.
We acknowledge the financial support of the Government of Canada.

In Sickness and in Health

NORA GOLD

**GUERNICA
EDITIONS**
TORONTO • BUFFALO • LANCASTER (U.K.)
2024

Guernica Founder: Antonio D'Alfonso

Michael Mirolla, editor
David Moratto, interior and cover design
Guernica Editions Inc.
287 Templemead Drive, Hamilton, ON L8W 2W4
2250 Military Road, Tonawanda, N.Y. 14150-6000 U.S.A.
www.guernicaeditions.com

Distributors:
Independent Publishers Group (IPG)
600 North Pulaski Road, Chicago IL 60624
University of Toronto Press Distribution (UTP)
5201 Dufferin Street, Toronto (ON), Canada M3H 5T8

First edition.
Printed in Canada.

Legal Deposit—First Quarter
Library of Congress Catalog Card Number: 2023948158
Library and Archives Canada Cataloguing in Publication
Title: In sickness and in health ; Yom Kippur in a gym / Nora Gold.
Other titles: In sickness and in health (Compilation)
Names: Gold, Nora, author. | container of (work) Gold, Nora. In sickness
and in health | container of (work) Gold, Nora. Yom Kippur in a gym
Series: Essential prose series ; 215.
Description: Series statement: Essential prose series ; 215
Identifiers: Canadiana (print) 20230566294 |
Canadiana (ebook) 20230566340 | ISBN 9781771838658 (softcover) |
ISBN 9781771838665 (EPUB)
Subjects: LCGFT: Novels.
Classification: LCC PS8563.O524 I5 2024 | DDC C813/.54—dc23

For my baby grandson,
Asa Weissgold,
who already loves books.

Saturday

SICKNESS IS A foreign country. You are lost there, you don't know the language, no matter how many times you've visited before. Nothing is familiar. You're alone, but a different kind of alone than usual, because when you're sick, you don't have yourself. Your own body has turned against you—it is your enemy now, and no one can fight, and try to destroy, their own body—so you are defenceless.

Sickness is an alternate reality, its own existential state. In it you are lost. Lost not only like a mapless, hapless tourist, but in the sense of someone cursed, doomed, and consigned to hell. There is no hope or salvation for you. You live, when you are ill, in an underworld that healthy people don't even know the existence of. So there is no one, not even the most loving Orpheus, who can save you.

* * *

Once a month you are struck by a mysterious illness which transforms you from an active, busy, dynamic, productive, energetic, lively, cheerful person to a helpless body on fire, sweating, moaning, its eyes closed, lying in bed waiting passively for the fever to burn itself out. So far it has every time, and for this you count yourself lucky. You've never died from this illness. You always recover. Though over the past three years, these episodes have extended longer and longer. Originally, they lasted only two to three days. Then four or five, then six or seven, and twice in the past six months they have dragged on for eight or nine days. You worry now that eventually these attacks of illness will continue for ten, twelve, fifteen days, occupying half of each month. And after that, two-thirds, three-quarters, four-fifths, and before you know it, you'll be a full-time invalid.

Perry says not to think this way, to stop catastrophizing. Easy for him to say. He's not the one trapped in a burning body day after day. Be optimistic, be hopeful, he says, pointing out that so far this year the episodes have averaged out to only one week per month. "Only," he says. On the calendar magnetted to the fridge you violently blot out with a thick black marker all the days in that particular month that you have been sick: the lost, dead days. Each of these seven, or nine, calendar squares, if they were a frame in one of your comic books or graphic novels, would be an illustration of absolute darkness in the dead of night.

At other times you are more philosophical. Maybe losing one week out of four isn't so terrible. It almost seems reasonable since you and Perry are in a twenty-five percent tax bracket. You're accustomed to paying the Canadian government a quarter of everything you have, so why not be required to pay, as well, to some higher authority—fate, or some unknown god—a quarter of your life?

* * *

Your illness attacks either suddenly or gradually. Last month was one of the sudden attacks. In January 2000, the start of a new millennium, you were standing at the whiteboard in a classroom, teaching art students a fine point about illustration by sketching it in two frames of a comic strip. Out of the blue the marker in your hand was too heavy to hold, your shirt was drenched with sweat, and you were shivering with cold and also blazing hot. After muttering a semi-coherent apology to your students and then to your department chair's secretary, somehow you got yourself home. You crawled into bed, whimpering, and lay there for hours, feverish and nauseated, with your eyes shut and ears ringing. And that is how, and where, you were for the next nine days.

Yesterday, on the other hand, your sickness came upon you gradually, sneaking up from behind. It posed as—and you mistook it for—an innocuous fellow soldier on your side of the battlefield, rather than as someone from across the enemy line. You should have recognized it for what it was, your enemy in disguise, but this is hard to do because your illness often changes its spots and begins in a subtle and tricky way. All you noticed at first was a vague malaise, the sense that something was slightly off-kilter. Then life seemed too difficult for you, its demands impossible to meet, even in trivial matters. You went to open a new jar of strawberry jam—you tried and tried but couldn't. Defeated, you burst into tears. When Perry came home soon after, you yelled at him for leaving his boots in the hallway, and for the next hour found fault with every little thing he did. At supper you recited, sobbing, a litany of all the miseries of your life. Knowing you are not like this when you're well, Perry, not unreasonably, said, "It sounds like you're getting sick again." "I am not!" you screamed at him. "Why are you always trying to make me sick? There's nothing wrong with me! I'm just unhappy!" You lay on the living room couch with one arm flung over your eyes while he cleaned up from supper. For the rest of the evening, you were mean to him and the next morning you awakened so weak you couldn't sit up in bed. Your sweat-soaked pajamas smelled sour, you shook with fever but complained of freezing and could open your eyes only a slit. Perry said your face was as dead white as a corpse's, a sure sign of your illness. Before leaving for work, he brought you breakfast in bed but, grimacing, you pushed it away and immediately slid into a feverish, groaning sleep.

Now, an hour later, you are awake. *Here we go again.* Day One of this new round of illness.

***

No one knows what's wrong with you. Not one of the doctors you've consulted has a clue. All seven of them seem to you as medically insightful as the seven dwarfs might have been. Thanks to the lack of a clear diagnosis, you can't get a doctor's note from any of them when you are too sick to work, so even though it's only six months into the school year, you have already used up all the discretionary vacation days you're entitled to annually. Your boss Ned, the head of the fine arts department, is fed up with your being sick, and warned you last month that if you miss even one more class, he's going to cancel your contract and find someone to replace you. "I've been more than fair with you," he said. "I have to be fair to the students, too."

Today is Saturday, your next class is Wednesday, and you have to be well by then. You have to. You can't afford to lose this job. Financially—you and Perry have two kids in college and a mortgage —but in another way, too. Having a job means you're normal. This job of yours is a central pillar of the beautifully normal life you have painstakingly constructed, and without it everything will come crashing down around you like a house of sticks in a storm.

"What if I'm not okay by Wednesday?" you asked Perry anxiously this morning. "That's only four days away."

"We'll manage somehow," he said reassuringly, squeezing your hand. But you didn't miss the shadow of doubt behind his eyes.

* * *

You're as exhausted now as when you went to bed last night. You might as well not have slept at all. With this illness, you don't get refreshed by sleep. You've read online that this is a classic symptom of Chronic Fatigue Syndrome, one of the many syndromes, illnesses, and conditions that the doctors say you don't have. Even so, you've discovered that, as with CFS, all you want when you're sick is bedrest, and it's the only thing that helps you recover. (Recover: get well and re-cover yourself so you look normal again to the world.) Bedrest for several consecutive days is the magic bullet. You know that it's ridiculous to have the cure for a problem without first understanding what the problem is. How could you fix a bad drawing without grasping beforehand what is fundamentally wrong with it? It's nuts that you've figured out how to get well without knowing what makes you sick, but it's true, and it's fortunate. The only path back to health, once you're sick, is to spend day after day lying in bed, doing absolutely nothing. To the uninitiated, this may sound like fun, a string of days of laziness and leisure, just relaxing and goofing off. In fact, doing absolutely nothing is very hard. You can't sit up (you lack the strength), and you can't read or watch TV since both these activities necessitate keeping your eyes open, which requires a great deal of effort. All you're capable of is lying in bed, immobile, feverish, with your eyes shut. You endure endlessly boring, long, lonely, suffering days while the people closest to you are off at work or living their lives. You are in a kind of solitary confinement; with your eyes closed, you have closed out the whole world, leaving you no stimulation but what's in your mind. It's terrible lying here feebly like this, sweating through your clothes repeatedly like a baby wetting itself. But you have your thoughts, emotions, and memories—and these are your prison, yet also your freedom.

* * *

It feels like ten-fifteen at night, but it's only ten-fifteen in the morning, and you have no idea how you're going to get through the next twelve hours. Perry, after leaving you your breakfast tray, went to the basement, to work in his den. His den of iniquity. No, it isn't really that. It's just his office. He's an accountant and he works out of your home, it's cheaper that way. But sometimes you wonder. What if he finds another woman, someone healthier than you, who he doesn't have to climb two flights of stairs for, three times a day, to bring her her meals? Like his secretary Charlene, for instance, who is cheerful, young, and peppy, wears short skirts and tight sweaters, and is in her sexual prime. (Perry, though tall and attractive, is not.) You've heard them laughing together when you were in the living room, right above the office, and he never laughs like that with you. He's probably not doing anything wrong, and he is allowed to have a life, after all, even if you, at present, do not. It isn't his fault that you lose a week every month to a mysterious illness while he continues to work, play handball, and lead a full and vibrant life. It feels unfair and you're envious. But okay, let him have his health—it's good that at least one of you is healthy—and let him be happy, too. As long as he's not too happy (meaning happy with Charlene).

Ten twenty-five. You pick at a bagel. You sense, like a dark fog rolling toward you, the approaching boredom and isolation and the gears of your mind preparing to churn out hour after hour of anxiety, misery, and fear. You'll do anything to escape this—to get some real-life stimulation and connect with something outside yourself. So, although you know you shouldn't—it will delay your recovery by at least a day—you start to work. You are shaking with fever, your pajamas are drenched and cold (and getting up to change them now would be almost an impossible feat); but you need to prove you are still the person you were before: a capable human being, and not just a worthless blob of feeble, febrile, failing flesh.

Perry brought up your laptop with your breakfast—your computer as dessert. Lying flat on your back, your head tipped up just enough to see the screen through slits of eyes, you briefly answer a couple of emails. Ned asks if you'll be well enough to teach your class on Wednesday. You have only three days to recover, it's a gamble, but you tell him yes. You cancel your Monday appointment with a student. You reply laconically to a friend you don't like and to a cousin you do but who is a shyster. You shut your eyes, drained by all this exertion. When you open them, it's noon—you've slept. You decide to finish preparing your Wednesday class, but your eyes go blurry. You blink them, rub them, open and close them a few times slowly, and then a few times quickly. Nothing helps. You know from experience it will take an hour or so till your eyesight returns.

"Siug aan my aambeie en wag vir beter dae!" you yell. (Suck on my hemorrhoids and wait for better days!) (Afrikaans)

"Tofu no kado ni atama wo butsukete shine!" (Hit your head on a corner of tofu and die!) (Japanese)

"Ik laat een scheet in jouw richting!" (I fart in your direction!) (Dutch)

"Grozna si kato salata!" (You're as ugly as a salad!) (Bulgarian)

You are practicing your foreign language skills. Curses and insults from around the world are your hobby. Not all kinds interest you: not the "fuck your whore-mother" theme, on which there are many variations (fuck her up her ass, up her toenails, up her nose). The curses you appreciate are colourful, culture-specific, and showing originality or flair. You have no idea how to properly pronounce them, you are probably mangling all these languages terribly, but so what? "Na mou klaseis ta'rxidia!" (Fart on my balls!) (Greek)

You continue, your mood lightening with each curse:

"Go ndéana an diabhal dréimire de cnámh do dhroma ag piocadh úll i ngairdín Ifrinn!" (May the devil make a ladder of your back bones while picking apples in the garden of hell!) (Gaelic)

"Jebiesz jeze!" (You fuck hedgehogs!) (Polish)

"Me cago en la leche!" (I shit in the milk!) (Spanish)

You're laughing. Happily at first, then a little hysterically. You may be burning up with fever and so frail you can't sit up in bed, but still, you are powerful. You are a god, or goddess, because you can curse. You can rain down black magic, doom, and ignominy on anyone you want. You lack the power to bless or to heal—yourself or anyone else—but you can curse your illness, and yourself, and this whole sick and sickening world. An ugly salad of a world. A hemorrhoid, a farthole, of a world. You shout this out as loudly as you can: "A hemorrhoid, a farthole, of a world!" The sound that comes out is a pitiful squeak. You rasp out a few more curses, from China, Mozambique, and Chile, and feel like you have now travelled the entire globe and sampled the best (or worst?) of what each culture has to offer. Suddenly you are as tired as if you've literally walked the globe's circumference. And your eyes are heavy, like someone being hypnotized, and getting heavier by the moment.

⌣ When they open, it's three-thirty. You snack on the oatmeal cookie and crunchy apple slices (already turning brown) that Perry silently left on the floor near your bed—part of your lunch, while you slept. You ignore the rest of it: the tuna sandwich and cold cup of tea. You're not feverish anymore. Maybe there's nothing wrong with you, after all. Perhaps the doctors who think you've invented this whole illness are right, and it's time to stop malingering. You have three hours till Perry comes up with supper; put them to good use. Finish preparing Wednesday's class.

Using your elbows, you try to raise yourself to a sitting position, but you're too weak and quickly slide back down. You hear a cackle of mocking laughter: "So I'm only a figment of your imagination, you say? I'm not real? Well, we'll see about that!"

You recognize this curser, this jester with a mask. He is your friend and your enemy. The Sickness Monster, the Sickness God, is laughing in your face.

"How dare you deny me like this! Me—your only true friend. The only one who really knows who you are and tells you the truth. You want proof I'm real? Proof that you're genuinely sick? Here!"

Whammo! You're knocked out, dazed, as though someone has actually clubbed you on the head. You want to vomit, your ears ring like church bells, you can't open your eyes, and when you touch your face, it's so hot it singes your hand.

"Who do you think you are, to not believe in me? I am a god and you are nothing. Do you hear me? Nothing!"

⁓ You are a rational person. Just because you're an artist and an art teacher doesn't mean you are a fool or a flake. Obviously, you know there is no such thing as a Sickness Monster or a Sickness God, and that no one is trying to torment or punish you. Illness is not divine retribution; it is a random virus, parasite, or bacterium. It is germs, cells, biology—science, not religion. It just happens in nature that some trees wither while others thrive. There is no rhyme or reason to it. You know that no microbe is blowing through the air like a piece of dandelion fluff from the other side of the world, traversing half the planet and flying over four continents, an ocean, eight other bodies of water, and sixteen countries just to find, and land on, you—to infect you, and make you sick for one week per month. No microbe is hurtling toward you with your name plastered across its forehead like the sperm in Woody Allen's film: a microorganism designated specifically for you. No biological element or evil force is seeking to hurt you—you, out of the whole universe. You know this with certainty.

And yet, with equal certainty, you know that this illness of yours is a punishment, chosen and designed specially for you—that the microbe, or poisonous mosquito, or snake, or virus, or whatever, indeed has a bull's-eye of you in its crosshairs. And you even know what you are being punished for.

Hubris.

***

You aren't normal. You never were and never will be, and you shouldn't be pretending that you are. Your deceiving of others and your self-deception have angered the gods. So once every month, as regular as getting your period ("The Curse"), the Sickness God visits to remind you who you really are. A sick little girl. Defective. Disabled. Second class. Or third, or tenth.

Perry, of course, doesn't hold with any of this. He says it's poppycock. Illness, he declares, is not a moral category; it is a physiological one, and getting sick is only a matter of bad luck. For some reason he thinks that believing in bad luck is more rational than believing in a supreme, uber-powerful being. But what is so rational about believing in luck, which is merely the conviction that life is random and unpredictable? You might as well say it's rational to believe in the meaninglessness of life; but why is a belief in mean-ing*less*ness more rational than a belief in meaning*ful*ness? It seems to you that Perry's perspective and yours are equally emotion-based and irrational.

"Stop saying stupid things, you're not a stupid woman," Perry said to you last month when the two of you discussed this. "Just because the doctors haven't come up with a scientific explanation for your illness yet doesn't mean you're the plaything of some retributive, sadistic, petulant, primeval god. Like something in a black and red mask at a Mardi Gras festival, punishing you for finally, after all these years, believing you are as good as anyone else, and for having, and enjoying, a good and normal life."

But Perry is wrong. This is precisely what this illness is about. It strikes only when you forget who you truly are. When you have dared to think of yourself as a normal person and have been acting like one. Between your job, your volunteer work, your family, and your social obligations, you put in eighteen-hour days, one after another, neglecting your body and not caring for yourself. Lots of normal people do this. But you are not normal. "People like you don't drive cars, hold jobs, get married, or have children," your mother explained to you with cruel satisfaction when you were a teenager. And whenever you forget this or carry on in denial of your medical past: *Bam!* the Sickness God fells you like a tree. The punishment for your hubris is five to ten days of illness, lying helplessly in bed. That's what you get for taking for granted your magnificent and immeasurably precious normal life. You have a husband, two kids—both away at college—a house, a car, and a job (a career, even). No one would ever guess you are not normal, that until age eighteen you were a disabled person. An epileptic. That you had, from birth, a neurological disorder that you then—as sometimes happens with epilepsy—outgrew, and because of this you were granted the amazing gift of a normal existence—something that, earlier on, was often beyond your wildest dreams, a mere fantasy hopelessly out of reach. It was expected that you would always have to live with various limitations and restrictions; yet somehow, magically, this did not come to pass. For no reason you can think of, certainly not because of any special merit on your part, fate conferred on you a normal life. Something Normals never give a second thought to. They take for granted everything they have. And now, because you've become more normal over the years, so do you.

What you have is a miracle of miracles. But do you spend every day down on your knees thanking God for your good fortune? (Your "luck," if you will?) Do you live a life of gratitude, constantly counting your many blessings? Of course not. You take your body, your health, your normal life—the gods' astonishing gift to you—

the miracle you never thought you'd have or deserve—as something that's yours by right. Worse yet, you gripe from morning till night about trivia, about the inconsequential inconveniences of everyday life. You complain that you'll be without your car for a few days because it needs servicing, or that you can't find shoes of the right colour to match your new dress, as if you're a genuine Normal who doesn't know any better. But you're not and you should know better. And the God of Sickness visits you once a month to remind you of this, and to get you to appreciate the incredible gift that is your life.

⌐ You run away from these reflections into the arms of Netflix and find a stupid comedy. Four thirty-somethings, two male, two female, looking for sex and romance, but in all the wrong places. They'll have to rely on luck (Perry's version of God or destiny), and at the rate they're going, they'll have to be exceptionally lucky to find happiness, or even an average, nothing-special mate. In order to keep watching, you fight the weights on your eyes that are trying to force them shut. You crave distraction, some lightness after your dark and heavy thoughts, and you are also mildly curious as to which of the four characters, if any, will be blessed with good fortune. Maybe luck is a good enough explanatory theory for the few happy people in this universe, or for the sunny moments that occasionally shine through the clouds onto each person at some point. Even you sometimes think "Luck is on my side" when things are going well for you—meaning, mainly, when you're not sick. But when you are—and maybe this sounds strange—you'd rather believe that these bad times are not totally random and devoid of meaning; instead, that a living, breathing being is responsible for your illness and suffering. That way, as indifferent or cruel as this god seems to be, you at least have someone to argue with—someone with whom to plead, beg, negotiate. If you can negotiate and try to influence, there is something you can do about your sickness, and there is hope.

Now you understand—which you never did before—why the Greeks had so many different gods: one for war, another for love, a third for agriculture, and so on. Because you want a specialist in your field, someone who can deal with your specific problem. When you stop receiving your daily mail, you want the address of the postmaster general, not the guy in charge of restaurants. In your current situation, you want the Sickness God, the one who can eliminate sicknesses like yours.

The fever is back and the weights on your eyes are winning against your best effort to keep them open. You don't really care what happens to these silly, horny young people. You pull the blanket over your head and sleep.

⁓ For supper Perry brings up soup and chicken, but after two slurps of the soup, you push it away. Perry feels the back of your neck and hands you two aspirins with a glass of water. You hesitate—you hate pills of any kind, even aspirins—but Perry urges you to swallow them, and you do. He lays a damp compress across your forehead. It feels lovely and cool. You should have been using compresses and aspirins all day, but you forgot about these fever-ameliorating strategies. When you're feverish, your problem-solving ability and your capacity to care for yourself fly out the window. You don't think in a sensible, practical way. But also the compresses and aspirins did not occur to you because you always react to illness as something to merely endure, passively if not patiently, the way you endured your childhood neurological illness, and your childhood itself. As if sickness were an omnipotent god before which you are a helpless child. It slips your mind that you can, at least, ease the most uncomfortable symptoms of the illness. You forget that you're an adult now and there are things that you can do.

Already the compress is warm, almost hot, the same temperature as your forehead. Perry exchanges it for a second, cooler one. He lies next to you on the bed—he's not afraid of catching whatever you have; you both know, after three years of this, that it's not contagious. Holding hands, you watch an old episode of *Everybody Loves Raymond* until your eyes start to close. Perry turns off the TV and kisses you on the forehead.

"What kind of a kiss is that? I'm not a child," you say, sounding like a child.

"No, you're not," he says soothingly, and kisses you lightly on the mouth.

"Am I okay?" you ask (a question you ask only when you're ill).

"You're sick, but you'll get better."

"How can you be sure?"

"Because you always do. Eventually."

He's smiling at you. You want to thank him and tell him you love him, but from the sea below you, hands are pulling you downward and you're already asleep.

Sunday

DAY TWO OF the illness. Lunch with Perry is over and there are six hours ahead of you until he returns with supper. Today, on top of fever and exhaustion, there is vertigo and nausea. If you make even the slightest movement, the room spins around and you feel like throwing up, so you lie in your bed rigidly immobile, like a dead person, while the time passes. You're here, but you're not really here. You're in some in-between place—in limbo, or maybe purgatory. Drifting, floating.

You'll never be well again—you know this now. It's true, as Perry is so eager to point out, that you've always recovered in the past, but so what? There's a first time for everything. This, how you are right now, might be exactly how you'll be spending the rest of your life. Not literally dead, but also not actually alive. You see no reason for hope anymore. The seven specialists you've seen have all thrown up (not vomited; just thrown up) their hands. All these pairs of hands except for one belonged to men, and you can't help thinking that if you were not a woman, and a middle-aged one at that (soon turning forty-six), these men would not have been so quick to conclude that this illness is all in your head. Most of them implied it is psychosomatic, which is just another way of saying that this sickness is your own creation and therefore your own fault. These male gods of medicine, despite their disdain for anything unscientific, are ultimately in agreement with the Sickness God, who is also male. All these males perceive your sickness as a product of your own failings, whether these are (in the worldview of the doctors) psychological, or (in the worldview of the Sickness God) moral. In fact, it seems that these two worldviews aren't as different as some people think.

You did consult once with a female physician, on the urging of a friend who encouraged you to "avoid the male-dominated medical system which is damaging to women" and "take control of your body and your health." The female doctor you saw last year, unlike the previous five doctors, took you seriously, did not blame you for being sick, and was respectful, even kind. But she had no more answers for you than anyone else.

A few months ago, you tried one last doctor, number seven. He reviewed your lab results, all of which had come back negative, and asked you the same dozen questions all the others had. Such as:

Is there any obvious trigger for these bouts of illness? (No.)

Did you eat any foods you are allergic to? (No.)

Have you been exposed to asbestos or any other toxic material at home or at work? (No.)

Have you been in proximity to anyone with pneumonia, the flu, bronchitis, or a tropical illness? (No.)

With each negative reply, this doctor (bald with gold-rimmed glasses) regarded you more and more skeptically. He seemed disappointed in you, even annoyed, as if you were playing some game with him and wasting his precious time. You understand him, in a way. No one likes to feel a failure, and no doctor can diagnose an illness without some positive lab results, which you did not provide him with. From his point of view, you had not done your part. He said to you coldly, "Next time you feel sick"—note: *feel* sick, not *are* sick—"drop into our clinic and we"—the royal we, as though he were a king—"will look at you then."

You stared at him, astonished. At the start of this interview, you'd described your sickness in great detail, but apparently he hadn't understood you at all. When you are in the talons of this illness, you can't get from your bed to the bathroom without clutching the wall inch by inch. You could no more haul yourself to a clinic than leap tall buildings in a single bound. Of course, this doctor (or any other doctor) would never dream of coming to see you at your home—home visits by doctors ended when you were a toddler—so no doctor in the past three years has ever seen you while you were sick. As a result, by the time you are seated across from a doctor in his or her office, you've already recovered, and feel and look fine. There is nothing for a doctor to observe then—no discernible evidence. *Evidence.* As though this were a court of law, and you, your physical and mental health, and even your validity as a human being, were all on trial. And found wanting. Not just an *in*valid, but in*va*lid.

You did try once to get the data that he, and all these doctors, so badly wanted. It was soon after the fifth doctor ordered you to call an ambulance the next time this illness struck, and have a hospital's emergency room personnel do a full battery of lab tests on you: blood, urine, the whole shebang. Somehow, with Perry's help, you got an ambulance to take you to the emergency room at the nearest hospital, only to discover that you'd have a four-hour wait because being "tired and weak" counted for nothing compared to a heart attack, stroke, car accident, or shooting. Perry left you seated on a chair in the waiting room to go get you a coffee, and by the time he returned, you, too weak to sit upright, had slid down almost to the floor, and were white-faced, shivering, and bathed in sweat. He took you home, you were sick for nine days (the longest you'd ever been sick till then), and you never tried this again.

Now you explained this to the seventh doctor and tried to provide him with some additional data. You elaborated on what you'd already told him, describing in carefully chosen, precise words what this illness is like, and what your experience of living with it has been for the past three years. But what are words (so pale and paltry) worth, when weighed against the objective truth of lab reports? This doctor, this bald eagle with beady eyes, gave a quick shrug, shrugging off your offering. "Well, you're fine right now," he said, "that's the main thing. You should be grateful for that." And he hustled you out of his office as fast as decently possible.

The "main thing," actually, that you've learned from the seven experts you've seen is that when doctors are unable to diagnose your medical problem, this means, to them, there *is* no medical problem. Having gone through this seven times now, each time more discouraging than the one before, there is obviously no point in continuing to consult additional doctors. No one will be able to help you; you'll always get the same result. So all you can do is lie here for the rest of your life like someone who's already dead.

"Ime parsaa!" you scream. (Suck an asparagus!) (Finnish)

"Ualach sé chapall de chré na h-úire ort!" (Six horseloads of graveyard clay upon you!) (Irish)

The phone is ringing, interrupting you in the middle of your cursing. You're not sure you want to talk to anyone but, careful not to move your head because that could trigger more vertigo, you pick up your phone.

"Hi! How are you?" Fern asks.

"Not bad," you say, lying. Fern is one of your closest friends, but you don't want to complain or bore her with this illness of yours, which you and she have already discussed numerous times. "What's new with *you*?" you ask, hoping that if you ask quickly enough how *she* is, and sound sufficiently interested in her reply, she won't probe for details about your "not-bad"ness. Even though you do feel bad. Physically, morally, and in every other possible way.

Your trick works, and Fern replies at length, prattling on about her daughter's upcoming wedding. Your pajamas are cold and clammy. You really should change them, but that would necessitate getting out of bed, finding a fresh pair, removing the old ones and putting on the new, and all that is way too much work for you. Your temperature must be a hundred and fifty degrees, yet somehow you hold up your end of the conversation, occasionally commenting or asking a question. Eventually Fern asks what you meant by "not bad," and you casually say, "Oh, you know that thing I get sometimes. Same old. But I'm getting better."

Your second lie. You're not getting better. For all you know, you'll never get better. At this point you are only on Day Two of being sick, and stretching out ahead of you are at least three more days of illness, and maybe triple that, or even the rest of your life.

Fern knows, of course, that periodically you have to spend a few days in bed because of an illness that has no name. But, like the rest of your friends, she has no real understanding of what it's like to live with. How every month, for a week or longer, you are in purgatory. "Feel better soon," she says to you now. "Drink lots of tea," and signs off. She is meeting her daughter in half an hour to go for a run. You couldn't go for a run if your life depended on it. In fact, this ten-minute phone call has totally knocked you out. Drained and depleted, you drift into a foggy, feverish sleep. As you're sliding under, it occurs to you that the doctors are right. You do lie about your illness. Only not in the way they think. You never exaggerate how sick you are; the lie is in the opposite direction. With everyone but Perry or doctors, you minimize your sickness. While intensely nauseated, burning with fever, and too weak to sit up in bed, you'll say on the phone or in an email, "I'm a little under the weather today"—implying that your illness is the normal sort of illness that Normals experience from time to time (a cold, the flu, fatigue from overwork), and that it's nothing more than a minor nuisance. You pretend that your illness is normal and so are you.

But you are not lying at all when the latest bout of it is over, and you speak about it only lightly, saying, "I was a bit sick last week but now I'm fine." One of the many weird aspects of this illness is that once you're well again, what you've recently been through doesn't feel the least bit real. It's a distant dream. It's as if there are two of you: the healthy normal you, and the sick abnormal you, and never the twain shall meet. They can never be in a room at the same time. Like an actor playing two different characters in a play: whenever one of them appears on the stage, by necessity the other is absent. They cannot co-exist. More than this, whenever you are sick, you cannot understand, or even recall, what the healthy you felt like, or thought, or wanted—and vice-versa. You watch the other like observing a complete stranger. This wall between your two yous is a kind of amnesia, the way the human body cannot feel the physical pain of a remembered injury. You resemble a young child who lives only in the present, and whoever they are at a given moment is all that they are, or ever were.

＊＊

You wake up two hours later feeling fine. Completely fine. You are not sweating or even hot. You move your head this way and that: no vertigo or nausea. You're not weak. You're not tired. You sit up in bed easily; your body's obeyed your command with no objection. I'm okay, I'm healthy again! you think joyfully. Sure, you've been sick for only two days and usually this thing lasts at least five, but so what? Maybe this time it's a shorter cycle. There are exceptions to every rule. You walk to the bathroom in a normal way, moving at a regular pace and not once holding onto the wall. You pee, wash your hands and face, brush your teeth, and smile at yourself in the mirror. You strip off your damp, miserable, smelly pajamas, laugh as you hurl them into the hamper, and dress in real clothes, pretty clothes, for the first time since Friday morning. An exercise outfit splashed with orange, yellow, and green triangles, cute summer sandals, and even a string of beads. You descend the two flights of stairs effortlessly, with only one foot per stair, not two (the toddler style you revert to when you're ill and afraid of falling). In the kitchen, sunshine from the windows lights up the floor and counters, making all the silver appliances gleam. What a joy to be back in the world! To see something besides the four walls of your sickroom; your unwashed, crumpled bedsheets; the night table with its pills, glass of stale water, and used compresses; the residue, on the floor, of half-eaten snacks and drinks; and, facing you when in bed, the etching of biblical lovers (who they are exactly, you don't know) that you and Perry received as a wedding gift and that you have never liked. It was made specially for you and Perry by an artist friend of his in Amsterdam, and since Perry doesn't mind it, here it has stayed for the past twenty-two years. Maybe it's time to rethink this.

The bowl of shiny red apples on the counter looks appetizing. You bite into a tart one with a crunch, prepare yourself a snack of cheese and crackers, and munch away cheerfully at the round aqua glass kitchen table while reading the newspaper. Perry startles you, coming up from his office and crying out in astonishment tinged with anger, "What are you doing here? You should be in bed!"

"I'm okay," you tell him. "Really. I'm fine now."

"How can you be? It's only the second day. You're going to make yourself sicker. This is going to add on two, maybe three, more days—"

"I'm fine, I tell you. And if I say I'm fine, I'm fine. I know myself better than you do."

Perry frowns, deliberating for a moment. Then he shrugs. "I have a meeting in a few minutes, but I'll join you for a quick four o'clock tea."

"Four-fifteen, but who's counting?"

You watch Perry's back as he silently, morosely fills and turns on the kettle. After a while you ask, "How did your meetings go today?" This is the normal you enquiring. It's the first time since Friday morning you've asked Perry anything about himself, and this is typical of when you're sick: you become very self-centered, even though usually you are not at all narcissistic. Perry pours two cups of tea and brings them to the table while recounting the phone call he had this afternoon with one of his biggest clients. This account has run into unexpected difficulties but he is hopeful things will sort themselves out. You listen sympathetically. You remind him of a strategy he successfully used last year with a different client in a similar situation. He likes your idea, is appreciative, and returns to his office nodding.

A minute later you hear a burst of laughter. It's him guffawing with Charlene. It doesn't matter, you tell yourself—he's married to you, not her; she's just a lonely single woman—but still, you put on music to drown them out. Soon you're dancing and singing along to "I Heard It Through the Grapevine" and "Stop in the Name of Love" (both about infidelity, you realize as you boogie), and then

"You Can't Hurry Love" and "Make Your Own Kind of Music." You've never been a good dancer, but you love dancing anyway (who says you have to be good at something to love it?). In ballet class in first grade, you were uncoordinated because of the epilepsy meds you were on, but when your ballet teacher instructed the whole class: "Be A Tree," you became a tree. Your arms/branches ended in fingers/leaves that twirled in the wind, your root/feet danced in the soft, fragrant earth, the sap/blood rose through your thighs/trunk to your mid-point and tingled all your skin/bark. You were a tree. And now you are a Motown woman and you're the music itself with its pounding rhythm. The wooden floor is dancing back at you, it is dancing with you, and maybe you're going to die someday, but that isn't yet, and perhaps all this dancing and joy will make you sicker, but you don't give a damn. The main thing is you're alive right now, you're alive and you're dancing, you're a tree and a woman and the earth and this music and you're dancing in the wind, and no one can take this away from you, ever.

⁓ To his credit, Perry doesn't say "I told you so" when he comes up from his office an hour and a quarter later and finds you lying on the living room carpet. When you danced to the first four songs, you were sweating normal, healthy, virile sweat, but then you started dancing to "All I Have To Do Is Dream," and it changed to sick sweat, accompanied by vertigo. You collapsed onto the forest-green carpet and lay there with your eyes closed, too dizzy and feeble to get up.

"I'm okay," you reassure Perry when you see his stricken face. "I'm just resting."

After supper, which you eat reclining on the living room couch, you watch TV with Perry and then he helps you, very slowly, climb the thirty steps to the bedroom. Your trip downstairs will cost you. The price will be an extra day of illness in bed, maybe even two or three, as Perry said, but it was worth it. If you hadn't gone downstairs, you'd have almost drowned in misery. Now you understand the crazy things people sometimes do for a teaspoon of pleasure, even at risk to their lives. Like during the Spanish flu pandemic, when socialites attended balls and parties and drank and danced all night. You climb the last stair, your elbow supported by Perry's strong, steady palm, and you wonder what is foolhardy and what is sensible, what is intelligent and what overly cautious, and what the name is of the wisdom that risks everything to seize the best, or even the only remaining, part of the day.

Monday

ON MONDAY, DAY Three, you wake up to the smell of your grandmother's cinnamon buns. Round pinwheels topped with sweet,
white, translucent icing. They're warm, and when you bite into
them, the icing, half-melted, runs into your mouth. Their aroma,
when you were a girl, hit you like a wild hug and maddened you
with hunger and desire as you entered the house after school. You,
Bruce, and Grandma would sit around the small square table in the
kitchen, feasting happily, one of you occasionally moaning with
pleasure. On cold winter days, there was sometimes hot chocolate,
too, to go with the buns, and Grandma would place one large
marshmallow in each cup, calling it a snowman. Its head would bob
on the cocoa waves, gradually dissolving like an iceberg in the
ocean. Right now, you'd love a cinnamon bun and hot chocolate for
breakfast. You'll have to tell Perry.

But you're too late. You notice the breakfast tray on the floor
near your bed, covered with a dishtowel, and on top of it a note.

> *Sorry, but today is crazy—I have meeting after meeting
> with no breaks in between. I'll try and pop up later but in
> case I can't, here's breakfast and lunch.*
>
> *Love, Perry*
>
> *PS) I thought of asking someone else to bring lunch later
> on, but I thought you might not like that.*

"Someone else"? There is no one in this house but Perry, you, and Charlene. And no, you would not like that floozy to come up here and see you in your dirty, grey pajamas, stinking in bed, an old invalid, while she prances in all peppy, sexy, and vigorous, with her thick vermilion lipstick and her skirt up to her ass. No, you would not want that at all.

You wonder what lies under the dishtowel. What did Perry leave you for breakfast and lunch? Or: *What did Perry leave you for* (breakfast and lunch)? He left you for Charlene. He probably doesn't really have "meeting after meeting" today, or anyway not with clients. He just wants to hang out in the basement with Charlene, laughing, joking around, sticking his hand down her blouse, between the ample breasts exploding from her too-tight top. He is busy "meeting after meeting" with her—with her boobs, her belly, and everything below.

You tell yourself to stop this—*you're being ridiculous*—and just eat your breakfast. But you can't. For the third day in a row, Perry has brought you the same boring breakfast (bagel and cream cheese) and lunch (a smelly tuna sandwich with one sliced apple and an oatmeal cookie). What lack of imagination. You'll have to explain to him the next time you see him—which probably won't be till suppertime (twelve hours from now!)—that a person cannot eat the same shit day after day after day. They'll go crazy. Or maybe Perry already knows this. Perhaps this is precisely what he's feeling at present: that a man gets bored and needs some variety in his diet. You wouldn't blame him if he felt this way. After all, look at yourself: you're dirty, and sick, with a malfunctioning body. Who would want to make love to that?

Even so, you *would* blame him. Of course you would. And you'd never forgive him. You'd divorce him immediately—or else you'd refuse to divorce him and continue living with him just so you could torment him day in, day out. Maybe, when he least expected it, you'd even murder him with a butcher knife. You never think such thoughts when you're healthy. Only when you're sick, and then they breed like rank weeds. It's all part of the illness—you know this. The physical and mental are connected. Still, what if there actually is some basis for your suspicions? Perhaps when you're healthy your senses are less acute, so you simply live in a state of blissful ignorance. Maybe you see things more clearly and accurately when you're sick. As your father used to joke: "Just because you're paranoid doesn't mean they aren't out to get you!" How can you ever know for sure what is true?

You make your way to the bathroom, baby step by baby step, supported by the wall. After peeing, washing your hands and face, and brushing your teeth, you inch your way back to bed, and then rest for twenty minutes from all this exertion. You eat half of the yucky tuna sandwich. This tires you and you rest again.

Now what? What are you supposed to do now? You've fulfilled all your morning obligations—bathroom and breakfast—and the rest of the day stretches out blankly before you. You reach for your phone. It contains dozens of apps; which one should you open? You want access to the world, but which world? Each app is a portal to a different one. Definitely don't open any of the news apps. There's no good news: they'll only make you feel worse. What you want is an app that will take you to a good world. A world that will comfort you, put its arms around you, love you.

There is no such app. There is no such world.

In desperation, you google your own name. The first item that pops up is a lecture you gave a year ago at an international conference. The second: an article you published in a journal of art education. The third: a newspaper interview with you on International Women's Day about your volunteer work at a women's shelter. You click on the first item, and there you are: smiling in a lavender pant suit with high heels and a silver-and-pearl necklace. A healthy, attractive woman. Someone professional, sophisticated, charming. You were a great hit at that conference. The American colleague who thanked you after your well-attended talk mentioned the graphic short story prize you'd recently won, and he referred to you as "a rising star."

You know this woman, but she isn't you. She's only who you used to be. And may, perhaps, be again sometime. But even if you emerge from this latest bout of illness and manage to teach your class this Wednesday, things will never be the way they once were. You're different now. You've been changed by this illness. Even during the periods when you're well now, the inevitable return of sickness lurks at the corners of everything, tainting it, shadowing its edges, like a picture frame leaking corrosive black ink into the bright colours of a painting.

Will you be able to teach this Wednesday? That's only two days away. You told Ned you'd be fine by then, but perhaps today or tomorrow you should warn him that you might have to cancel, after all. No, don't do that. There's still a chance you can come through. Statistically it's possible. You could wake up tomorrow or on Wednesday morning in perfect health. How disappointing that would be for Ned! That self-important, mediocre, squat little man— so Napoleonic in style it's surprising he doesn't walk around with his hand between the buttons of his jacket. He's the only colleague in the department you never took the trouble to get to know because his comments in meetings were always so banal. You were never rude or mean to him; you just ignored him—and he ignored you. And this was fine because he was irrelevant. Until suddenly he wasn't. Out of the blue he became the chair of the department (only because no one else wanted the job), and instantly started being an asshole to you. He's consistently given you the worst schedule of everyone, requiring you, over and over, to teach three of your four classes all on the same day; he's assigned you at least one new course every term; at faculty meetings he's congratulated all the other instructors on their accomplishments, but never you, not even when you won that big graphic short story prize; and he's stuck you on six committees every year, double the departmental average. It's well known that the non-tenured teachers at colleges always get exploited, but in this case it's obvious that Ned has it in for you in particular. You and he usually pass each other in the hallway silently, with barely a nod.

But two and a half weeks ago, as you were about to go home following your three Friday classes, he summoned you to his office and reprimanded you for giving two of your students C minuses on their mid-term assignments. These two students, best friends as it turned out, had come to him to complain, and he wanted you to raise both of their marks.

"But C minus is what they both deserved," you said. "I'll show you their assignments."

"It's a matter of keeping all the faculty in line," Ned said.

Most likely he meant it was a matter of maintaining consistent grading practices across all the teachers, but "keeping everyone in line" (especially you) was probably more exactly what he was really about, the authoritarian twit. He spoke to you sternly then, as if you were a recalcitrant teenager needing to be ordered to clean your room:

"These students told me they are in the B range in all their other courses, and I think they should get B's in your class, too."

"But how can I?" you asked. "Their work was terrible. I remember exactly what they handed in. There was no evidence at all that they'd read anything, or learned anything. They didn't attend even half of my classes. It was kind of me to give them C minuses instead of D's."

"I can't waste my time," Ned said testily, "arguing with every student over their grades."

With this, he sank even lower in your estimation than he'd been before. You understood now that not only was this man too lazy to deal with disgruntled students, even though that was an integral part of his job description; he was too weak to stand up for his colleagues. "I want their revised marks by tomorrow morning at the latest," he said.

This is where you made your first mistake in that meeting. You should never have said what you did; it was stupid. Just three little words: "And academic integrity?" you asked.

You might as well have slapped him across the face. Well, in effect you did. You impugned his integrity as an academic, as well as (by implication) on a personal level. An impressive accomplishment for just three words.

Little Napoleon flushed. "That is just one element in keeping a department running smoothly. You can't have the same student getting an A in one class and a C minus in another."

"What if they do better work in one class than another? Or what if one course is easier than all the rest?"

Your second mistake. Everyone in the department knows that Ned's classes are notoriously and ridiculously easy, and that students register for them in order to get an easy A. Ned, of course, interprets his large class sizes as evidence of his popularity.

"That is called academic freedom," he said huffily. Which it isn't. This isn't what academic freedom is at all. He then took—even though it's illegal to smoke in here—a puff from his pipe, an affectation he'd assumed only after becoming a chair. (You wish he'd become a literal chair instead, so you could sit on him and that way he'd at least be useful for something.) His pipe puffing and huffing reminded you of the wolf with the three little pigs: *I'll huff and I'll puff and I'll blow your house down.*

"In any case," he said, "many of our students plan to go on from here to do their Masters, and they can't get accepted anywhere unless they have good marks. Also"—another puff on his pipe as he glared at you—"our enrollment is down for next year, so we have to position ourselves as an attractive choice: a school that is sympathetic to students and supportive of their goals."

This infuriated you. "Well, then," you said, feigning innocence, "why not just give everyone an A in all their courses?"

"I am considering that option," he said.

You don't remember anything after that. Just that you despised this man as you stomped out of his office, and you still do. This was seventeen days ago and even now you seethe when you think about it. Perry's first response when you got home that night was, "Oh, what the hell, give them their lousy B's." You yelled at him, "Then what's the point of marking students at all? In fact, why even give them assignments? I could just hand them each an A when I meet them on the first day of school and save myself a whole lot of time and trouble." "Maybe you should," Perry said, not puffing on a pipe but looking almost as smug as Ned when he was.

All that evening you and Perry went back and forth. While preparing supper, eating it, cleaning up from it, watching TV, and getting ready for bed. Now, lying there together, you said for the tenth time that evening, "It's not fair. What about all those students who busted their asses to earn a B in my class?"

Perry laughed at you. "Fair? You're forty-five years old and you still think of the world as a place that should be fair?" But before you could get indignant, he added, as if to appease you, "He's an idiot," and your anger dipped a little. He went on: "We know that, and so does everyone in your department. Intellectually, creatively, Ned's got nothing, and that's why he's so envious of you. He's twelve years older, he'd been slogging away for over a decade in your department, without getting anywhere, when you came along, and in less than a year surpassed him, winning that prestigious prize. Plus, you're well-liked by your students and colleagues, which he isn't. All he's good for is administration, so he runs your little department like the petty tyrant he is, trying to make it into his empire. So of course he has to take you down a peg. Or two. Or twenty."

"Okay. True. But what do I do now? Do I really give B's to these lazy, crappy students?" You continued in this vein for a while, still agitated. Perry didn't tell you to calm down because he knew that would set you off like a firecracker. He just listened with his amused, green, clever eyes. And by the time you switched off your bedside lamp, you had grudgingly reached the conclusion that you would give these two young women their B's. But wow, it burned you up.

And there was nothing else to do with this fire but burn yourself up in sex.

⁓ Now you're feverish. Burning of a different kind. From your night table you grab two aspirins and swallow them with the glass of stale water. The compress from last night is dry; instead, you press an apple slice against your forehead. You roll it back and forth, from left to right, right to left, then use it to caress your cheeks, neck, and the back of your neck. The slice of apple is now warm and useless; you throw it back on the tray. Your ears are ringing so loudly you can't hear anything but this. You lie in bed alternating between shivering and boiling; you listen to what is a roaring, rushing ocean between your ears. Gradually the noise subsides. The world becomes quieter. You can think again. You seize your laptop (*seize the day; seize this moment*), and for forty uninterrupted minutes you are once more the woman in the lavender suit, reviewing your teaching notes for Wednesday. Your lesson plan is solid in content, but this class will be deadly dull in execution—as grey and joyless as an execution would be. Even in your reduced condition, you can recognize this. So you add in some fun, interactional exercises that you've used in other courses and that went over well. Satisfied, you close your laptop, proud of yourself. You still have your brain; you still are you. Your pajamas are damp, cold, and uncomfortable, and that ringing in your ears is starting again (though as yet at a fairly low decibel), but you could probably do a bit more work before you crash. There's a brief tug of war between the Don't Push Yourself Too Hard team and the Do As Much As You Can one, and the Do As Muchers win. You answer three emails and text your kids, Ronnie and Sarah: *Hi, how are you, I miss you, I love you*, ending in a smiley face. A text that implicitly lies because it doesn't mention the state you're in, and have been for the past three days; a text that is truthful in telling Ronnie and Sarah you love them, because you do. Even if at present they feel so far away as to be almost irrelevant to you. Actually, when you're sick, everyone feels so far away they are almost irrelevant, except for Perry because he takes care of you. But irrelevance is irrelevant when it comes to Ronnie and Sarah. You love them with a love that is more than mere emotion; it is a matter of principle—a bedrock premise, and the bedrock promise, of your life. It doesn't matter that you don't feel love right now for anyone, not even for yourself—or maybe especially not yourself. (How could you, when your body constantly vacillates between flaming and freezing, you want to vomit half the time, your vision comes and goes, and the clanging in your ears is rising again in volume, soon to reach a deafening pitch?) Even so, you remember lovingly Ronnie and Sarah's tiny fists as babies, their plump toddler arms and legs, their slobbering hugs and kisses and their infinite love. That was nearly twenty years ago, but that's what you think of as you gaze affection-

ately at the texts you've just written to them: *I miss you, I love you.*
There it is, your love laid out in black and blue, like a bruise: black
lettering on a glowing evening-dusk blue screen. Glowing as if from
your love.

⁓ A man is walking in front of his house—it has a white façade, a
white picket fence, and red and yellow tulips out front—and he is
just from the waist down. You see his khaki shorts, hairy legs, white
socks, and beige summer shoes. Everything is perfectly normal except that he's been sliced in half horizontally and the very top of him
is his waist. You wake up. You draw what you dreamt. You go back
to sleep.

⁓ When you awaken again, you eat the other half of the tuna sandwich. Perry cut it horizontally, and what you're eating now is the
bottom half. You change into a clean, dry nightgown, return to bed,
and lie there as the minutes creep by. *Time is creepy. A climbing
creeper. Time's a deceptive vine.* The clock says eight-twenty a.m., but
this can't be. So much has happened since you woke up this morning. You've eaten breakfast, washed, presented at a conference,
quarrelled with the head of your department, finalized your class for
Wednesday, replied to three emails, written love notes to your children, changed your clothing, and eaten your lunch. If you've eaten
your lunch, it must be lunchtime, mustn't it? It feels like you've been
awake for three or four hours. How could only eighty minutes have
passed? And even more urgently: How are you going to get through
all the remaining minutes in this day? The hours are what worried
Virginia Woolf, but you worry about the minutes. When you're well,
there are never enough of them, but now there are too many. There
remain fourteen and two-thirds hours till your bedtime. You quickly do the math on the calculator on your phone—that's eight hundred and eighty minutes. Far too many. You'll have to kill some of
them. Not spend them like precious gold coins, but waste them:
flush them down the toilet like human waste. But how? You don't
dare dance or even go downstairs again; yesterday this made you

sicker. On your phone you find a DIY fix-up-your-house show. Ten minutes in, your eyes are so blurry you can hardly see. You close them, rest them a minute, and open them again, but still you're half-blind. All that's visible on your phone are the colours of the apps. You can't do anything now except lie here like a mummy, your body wrapped into itself, with you trapped inside.

"May an long dai cham mui!" (You eat pubic hair with salt dip!) (Vietnamese)

"Fuck!" you bellow. "Cao ni zu zong shi ba dai!" (Fuck the eighteen generations of your ancestors!) (Mandarin)

"Perhot' podzalupnaya!" (Ass dandruff!) (Russian)

You curse, you holler: "Eat the pubic hair of your ancestors with ass dandruff!"

You howl like a wolf at the moon.

⁓ Somehow the remaining minutes in this long day have passed. You've been dazed for many of them, in and out of fever and sleep, and for part of the afternoon, extremely nauseated. At one point Perry ran into your room, holding out a banana, then ran downstairs again, like the rabbit in *Alice in Wonderland* fleeing down his rabbit hole. It was a hallucination, you were sure, but later you discovered a banana on your night table and ate it, and it was real. You had supper with Perry (again something real; not a hallucination), and you sobbed and screamed at him, "I'm sick and tired of being sick and tired! I'm sick and tired of my shitty life!" and then you watched TV together. When he tried to kiss you good night, you turned aside because you didn't know for sure where he'd been all day, and what if he was cheating on you?

Your night is fretful, your sleep fitful, broken repeatedly by dreams of animals chasing you, buildings exploding, tsunamis drowning whole cities. You're not getting better. You never will.

Tuesday

THIS MORNING, DAY Four, there is no ringing in your ears. There is no fever. Your eyes open easily and all the way. And you are cheered by the sight of the attractive breakfast Perry has left for you. Apparently, he couldn't find a cinnamon bun as you requested, but he clearly registered your need for some variety in your diet. On the tray he has placed a bagel with peanut butter (instead of the usual cream cheese), a banana (instead of the usual apple), a chocolate bar, and a kind of herbal tea (pomegranate) that you've never tried before. Everything looks interesting and appetizing, but you're not yet hungry. You'll eat later.

Perry, since it's a workday, must be downstairs in his office with Charlene. But today, for some reason, she seems to you like nothing more than a secretary, a hired employee, and certainly no kind of threat. You know Perry loves you and would not be unfaithful. The problem with Perry, though, is that he doesn't really know you. And he can't because he doesn't understand about the epilepsy. He's aware, of course, that you had some neurological problems as a child, for which you were sometimes on medication; but as he sees it, you then outgrew these difficulties, and anyway they're no big deal since that was all long ago. To him, your epilepsy is a simple fact no different than the fact—as he recently witnessed in an old photo album—that you wore your hair, when you were four, in two short braids. It has no more significance than that.

It's not his fault. You've never discussed it with him in any serious way. All he knows is the version of your past—the story—you chose to tell him: You had childhood epilepsy and then you outgrew it; been there, done that. But as a result of this truncated narrative, you always feel he doesn't really know you. Perhaps when you first met, and even during the early years of your marriage, you wanted it this way. But do you still? You're not sure. You've always told yourself, and you tell yourself again now: *What he doesn't know won't hurt him.* But maybe more to the point: what he doesn't know won't hurt *you.* Perhaps if he knows who you truly are, he won't love you anymore.

That four-year-old girl with her hair in short braids often wore a dazed expression. You know this girl inside out. You love her. She repulses you. You're afraid of her. You want to hug her. She is you— as much as the woman in the lavender suit.

* * *

The girl hated being four. When she was three, she had been herself: just Lily. But soon after turning four, she became a drugged robot. Her body wasn't hers anymore. Something had taken it over and now she was trapped inside a suit of armour that was glued to her skin, and in it she lumbered around stiffly, awkwardly, like a machine or a monster. She didn't look like herself, either, in the mirror: her face was swollen, and her eyes had a glazed look, as if she didn't know where she was, or even who she was. Which much of the time she didn't.

Somehow she guessed that all this was related to the bitter-tasting baby peaches they'd started making her eat four times a day. She'd observed her mother breaking open plastic capsules and spilling their foul-smelling white powder into the smooth orange purée. So one day when her parents held out to her an innocent-looking jar of baby peaches (previously one of her favourite foods), she tried not to eat it. "I don't want to," she said. "Do I have to?" Yes, she had to, Daddy said. She was sick, and this medicine would make her better.

Better. Better meant more good. These pills would make her a better, gooder little girl. Because she wasn't good. She was bad. Daddy had told her her sickness was called "petit mal," which in French meant a little bit of badness. She was lucky because there was another kind of sickness that was worse, "grand mal," which meant a lot of badness. She didn't have that. She wasn't very bad, just a little bit. But because of this bit of badness in her, she had to eat these disgusting-tasting baby peaches at every meal and once in-between. It was her punishment for being bad.

The bad thing about her was something in her brain, Daddy explained. Her brain had extra electricity in it, more than other people's, so sometimes it got overheated and went staticky like a radio. This made sense to her because sometimes their old radio did that, and you had to wait a few seconds, or even a minute, until the crackling sound stopped, and the voice or music came back. Daddy loved that radio, and when it went on the fritz, he'd wait patiently till it sorted itself out. Mom would hit it, though, and call it a worthless piece of garbage that should've been thrown on the junk heap years before. Daddy replied that they didn't have enough money for a new one, and he'd try to hush and shush her.

Her parents found out what was wrong with her brain after her mother took her, a few days before her fourth birthday, to a cold white room where an unsmiling woman in a white lab coat dribbled a frigid liquid glue called collodion into her hair, and then stuck long, green, snake-like wires into this collodion. Lily had to sit perfectly still, not moving at all and hardly breathing, until the cold wet stuff hardened. When it did, she had to once again stay totally still while a machine with a metal hand, making a scratchy sound, scrawled a drawing like mountains and valleys on a moving roll of paper that unrolled and unrolled and seemed like it would unroll forever. Afterwards, the unsmiling woman in the white lab coat rubbed away at the spots of hardened collodion with cotton balls and something that smelled vile and made Lily's eyes smart, and then she tore the snake-wires out of Lily's head. Despite all the rubbing, numerous pieces of collodion stayed stuck on Lily's scalp and in her hair, and at home Mom scrubbed her head hard to try and get it all out, which hurt and made Lily cry. And still it took two more washings till every trace of collodion was gone.

Daddy said that the drawing the machine had made was a picture of her brain. She didn't know what a brain looked like; all she'd seen on the paper were drawings of mountains and valleys, but these managed to convince everyone that her brain was bad. And now, because of that machine, she had to eat yucky-tasting baby peaches laced with drugs that made her groggy, stupid, clumsy, and uncoordinated. This machine, with its inhuman hand, had given her an inhuman hand, as well. Because, thanks to those peaches, her hand no longer worked properly. She couldn't draw anymore, or even hold a crayon the normal way. She could only clutch it as a monkey clutches the branch of a tree.

⌒ Before all this, when she was three, she was light and nimble. She ran around, indoors and out, playing with her sister and brothers and the kids from the neighbourhood, and never gave any thought to her body. If, in a game of tag, she wanted to tap someone's shoulder, her hand simply did this; it obeyed her command. And if she was playing by herself for a while, or drawing, no one hovered anxiously nearby and interrupted her every few minutes to check if she was all right. She'd often lie on her stomach on the living room carpet and draw detailed, colourful pictures. She loved colour so mainly used crayons, but occasionally she'd make a picture in black and white with the set of charcoals that Grandma gave her for her birthday (a gift that infuriated Mom: "She'll make a mess and get them all over everything!").

The day after the machine drew Lily's brain, she was drawing as usual, her hand moving as continuously as the machine's had. In her picture, a red girl and a green boy were throwing a ball back and forth, and in between them, a yellow boy, the monkey in the middle, was leaping into the air. Lily was in the process of adding a few raindrops to the story—sleet-like lines of a pale, diamond blue—

when something jumped in front of her, one inch from her eyes: *Snap! Snap! Snap!* Her mother was snapping her fingers close to Lily's eyelashes, startling, scaring her, meanwhile shrieking, "Lily! *Lily!* Can you hear me? Answer!"

Dazed, stunned, Lily blinked. Her mother's eyes were small and brown, peering at her.

"What?" Lily said, groaning.

"You had an attack," Mom said.

"No, I didn't." She didn't know what an attack was, but she knew what she'd been doing. She'd been drawing.

"Look," Mom said, pointing to her picture. A long, pale blue line that Lily hadn't drawn ran down the right side of the page at a weird angle, starting in the center and ending at the bottom. And lying nearby on the carpet, close to her mother's foot, was the light blue crayon she had been drawing with. It had been in her hand; why was it on the floor? She was confused. Now Daddy was in the room, too, and so were her sister and older brother—they'd all come running in when Mom screamed—and everyone was staring at her, asking questions she couldn't answer, expecting something from her she couldn't give. She understood, though, that she'd done something wrong. She wasn't sure what exactly, but she'd been bad again. She burst into tears. Daddy put his arm around her and tenderly said, "There there." Then he said to Mom, "You shouldn't shout at the child. You frighten her."

"I wasn't shouting at her. I was checking if she'd had an attack."

"And don't say 'attack'. Call it an 'absence' or a 'dream'." He stroked Lily's hair. "You were just having a dream, sweetheart. That's all. Everything is fine."

But it wasn't. Something was still wrong. They were all frowning at her or at each other. Speaking not in words, but with their eyes. She felt their frowns as disapproval: they were disappointed in her. She'd done that bad thing again. Even if she didn't know what it was.

⁓ "Dream" was Daddy's favourite word for the wrong thing that happened in her brain. Dreaming, she understood, was a bad thing.

She was not allowed to dream—not at night, but especially not during the day. Day dreaming, even for a few seconds, was dangerous. If you let your mind wander, it could wander off and never find its way back. It must, at all times, be kept on a tight leash. A few months before, their neighbour's Scottish terrier, Poochy, had run into the street and got run over by a truck. "That's what happens," someone said, "when you let go of the leash." If you don't hold on tight to your brain, it could run off and get killed. And you can't live without a brain. Daddy said so.

Her older brother Tim said he had lots of dreams. He dreamt of being an astronaut when he grew up, or a rock star, or a famous hockey player. Or all three. But her only dream was to not have any dreams. Ever.

* * *

You're an adult now, and a parent, so you can see how your father, in his kindness, didn't want his little girl to worry or be frightened, and this is why he picked a word for your seizures that he thought of as normal and everyday. A normal name for an abnormal phenomenon. He imagined that, through language, he could gently extract from your experience of epilepsy the twin poisons of fear and stigma, in the same way that, in one of your beloved picture books back then, a poisoned thorn was extracted from a lion's paw. All he accomplished, though, was to inadvertently inject this poison into the word "dream". He charged this normal word with extra electricity, electrifying it with abnormality and shame.

〜 Your mother used a different word than your father. Hers was "attack." An attack wasn't only what happened inside your brain; it came from the outside as well. For instance, when Mom yelled at you, "Answer! Answer!" and snapped her fingers in front of your eyes, and then shook you as she sometimes did. Her violence, her anxiety and panic, these were the attack—as much as (maybe more than) the seizure itself.

To this day, whenever you walk into a room—say, the teachers' lounge at work—if your mind is somewhere else and not fully focused, if you are not one hundred percent attentive to your surroundings, and "on," you half-expect to be attacked for this. It's always a pleasant surprise and a relief when this does not happen. In fact, your colleagues, with the exception of Ned, are usually glad to see you, and greet you with a friendly wave or hello. No one expects, or demands, your total attention, concentration, and presence in the here-and-now. You have to keep re-learning this lesson. That just because your mind has wandered a bit, you are not going to get screamed at, snapped at, or shaken till your teeth rattle.

You also, to this day—unless you're alone with Perry—dislike eating with other people.

* * *

Starting when the girl was four, it was a regular feature of family suppertimes that she would be closely observed throughout the meal. If she grew quiet or gazed off into the distance, she would get yelled at or snapped at by her mother, while her father and brothers and sister all stared at her from around the table. Whenever that happened, she'd realize she must have been dreaming again. She'd lower her eyes, trying not to cry.

"Don't worry, honey," Daddy would say. "You were dreaming, that's all. Now eat your supper."

She tried but couldn't. She was as exhausted as if she'd run a race. The conversation around the table was strained. Daddy was doing his best to make things seem normal, asking Tim in a false, cheery voice about his day. How was hockey practice after school? How was his science project coming along? Tim replied, and everything on the surface seemed normal. But it wasn't.

"Can I be excused?" she asked.

"Not until you've finished your supper," Mom said.

Again, she tried to eat. She took a bite of chicken and, with everyone watching, she chewed and chewed, and chewed and chewed, and chewed and chewed. The chicken was very tough, and it was tiring for her jaws to have to work so hard and for so long just to swallow one mouthful of it. Finally, she did.

"Now another one," Mom said.

The girl started to cry. "I can't."

"Let her go," Daddy said softly to Mom.

"She wins again," Mom said.

"She's sick," Daddy said, his voice impatient, rising to anger. "It's not her fault."

"Can I lie down in my room?" the girl asked.

"Yes. Would you like Mom to go with you?"

She shook her head, ignoring the look on her mother's face. She didn't want anyone with her; she wished to be alone. But she especially did not want Mom, who would sit on the chair near the desk, staring at her without blinking, and obviously longing to be anywhere else in the world. Up the fifteen stairs to her room the girl trudged heavily, dragging her burden of a body and her burden of a brain, until collapsing, relieved, onto her bumpy coral-coloured bedspread, and clutching to her chest her soft grey bunny rabbit with the floppy pink ears.

***

You never think about this sort of thing. You haven't thought about it in years—your epilepsy and all that. It's been buried, like some dark fairy tale from long ago and far away. You have no idea why you're visiting this place now. None. But this is where you are. In the enchanted land of remembering.

***

It started when she was four and continued for three full years. At ages four, five, and six, she was a drugged robot. She stumbled, dropped things, spilled her milk, and got yelled at or slapped for spilling her milk. *(Who says you shouldn't cry over spilt milk?)* And because her seizures—or "dreams", or "absences", or "attacks", whatever you choose to call them—occurred approximately once every minute, with each seizure lasting twenty seconds, she was usually disoriented and confused. When you're absent a third of the time, and are constantly leaving and re-entering "the real world," you miss out on a lot of information. Life to her was a jigsaw puzzle missing a third of its pieces.

Here's what she would have heard back then if listening to the above paragraph:

> *It started when she was four and continued for three full*
> *years. At ages slapped for spilling her milk (Who says you*
> *shouldn't cry over spilt milk?), and because her seizures—or*
> *"dreams," or "absences," or "attacks," whatever you seconds,*
> *she was usually disoriented and confused. When you're*
> *absent a third of the time, and are constantly leaving and*
> *re-entering "the real world," you of its pieces.*

Here she is, in first grade at recess, standing in the schoolyard, listening to a conversation between two girls. She has been following their dialogue but now they are making no sense. She frowns, trying hard to decipher what they're saying, when suddenly they've disappeared and she is alone in an empty schoolyard. *Where is everyone?* She's bewildered, panicky. She runs into the long school building through the nearest door, finds herself in a narrow, murky corridor, and glimpses the tail end of a line of children curving around a corner. She runs to catch up. She is always running to catch up. But this is not her class. It's older kids, big kids who tower over her and whom she does not know. They vanish around the corner and, alone in the hallway, she has no idea where to go. She tries to be brave but starts to cry. Eventually, along comes a grizzled, scowling man in overalls, bearing a bucket and mop. "What are you doing here?" he asks her roughly. "I don't know where they went!" she wails. He leads her to her classroom, depositing her in the open doorway, where she awaits permission to enter. Everyone else is already in their seats and the teacher, Miss Garret, is in the middle of instructing them. When she notices Lily, she looks displeased and asks testily, "Why didn't you come with the rest of the class?"

The girl stays silent. Telling the truth, that she didn't hear the bell ring, seems like the wrong answer, and Miss Garret is already annoyed with her so it's best to say nothing. "Sit down," Miss Garret says irritably, and Lily, with burning cheeks, walks to her seat, ashamed to once again be messing up and sticking out. Sitting in her seat, half of a two-desk unit she shares with a girl with a runny nose, Lily doesn't understand why everyone else always knows more than her. All the other kids seem to grasp easily what's going on around them—what is expected of them, and where they're supposed to be at any given moment. Only she does not. From this she deduces that she is not exactly stupid; just a little stupider than everyone else.

⌇ At recess one week later, the same thing happens again. She is eavesdropping on a conversation—this time about Barbie dolls—when suddenly she is one of only three children in a silent schoolyard, even though seconds ago it was noisy and full. Yet unlike last week, this time someone is pulling on her arm. It is a girl from her class saying, "Come on! The bell!" This is Ida, who will be her first friend.

⌇ There are always good things in life, even when you are a drugged robot. It's true that she was out of it one-third of the time, but she was also *in* it for the remaining two-thirds. She laughed with Ida, played games, sang songs, and learned to read. And on Wednesday afternoons in the school gym she took ballet. She was terrible at it, and the teacher often criticized her, saying her arms or legs were wrong and repositioning them. But Ida was no good at ballet either, and they'd walk home together, snow crunching beneath their boots, the snowbanks on either side of them as high as their waists, and they'd make fun of Mademoiselle, imitate her wrinkled nose when she was dissatisfied, twirl pirouettes, and show each other First Position, Second Position, Third, Fourth, Fifth. (Twelve years later, at eighteen, when Lily was learning sex and, as with ballet, was not very good at it, she thought of sexual positions in ballet terms: First Position, Second Position, Third, Fourth, Fifth; and was full of wonder that there were so many more than five.) Walking home with Ida, Lily sometimes stopped mid-position or mid-pirouette for a few seconds, stared into space, and then returned to what she'd been doing with no apparent awareness she'd been gone. But this was no big deal to Ida. She just waited till Lily came back and then they continued dancing.

Lily's younger brother, Bruce, was also like that. When the two of them were alone together and she blanked out for a while, he didn't freak out, yell, or hysterically call her name, like her mother or other siblings. He bided his time, unperturbed, until her return. She could sometimes tell, though, that she'd been gone because of the expression on his face when she resurfaced: a specific mix of watchfulness and sweet patience.

Bruce's favourite game was Blockhead, which their mother told them was another word for a stupid person. Bruce did not regard Lily as stupid, or even—because of her absences—weird. In Blockhead, you take turns adding an irregularly shaped, painted wooden block on top of all the others that you and your opponent have already piled up. It was now her turn. Bruce waited quietly until she stopped blankly staring and observed her as she selected a purple block with a carved-out orange archway on the bottom. Gingerly she balanced it atop the precarious tower, holding her breath, hoping she wouldn't bring everything toppling down. He watched her with wide brown eyes. She was his older sister. She was his guide, his friend. She was his archway, and he was hers.

Another good thing during those difficult years was that now and then on a Saturday, Daddy would take her, Bruce, and one or both of the older kids on an outing, "to give Mom a break." In the spring and summer this meant drives to the country, picnics next to lakes and waterfalls, and a stop on the way home for ice cream in exotic flavours, like pistachio. On one such outing they were picnicking in what seemed to be a public field when a farmer rushed at them out of nowhere brandishing a shotgun and shouted at them to get off his property right this minute or else. Lily was terrified but Daddy stayed serene, and on the drive home they all laughed about their adventure. In the fall and winter, when it was too cold for picnics, Daddy took them to the natural history museum to see the dinosaurs, or to the library or an occasional movie. At home her brother Tim and sister Heather squabbled incessantly, but on these outings, this was extremely rare. It was as if, at these happy times, they all inhabited a different world.

* * *

Two-thirds of the way through first grade, a few days after March break, Miss Garret gave the class a special test. There were two columns of pictures and you had to draw a line between the picture on the left and the one on the right that corresponded to it; for instance, you'd connect the apple with the banana. It wasn't hard. She could see quite easily what went with what, except for the dustpan with the broom because her mother didn't use a dustpan—only a piece of cardboard—so she'd never seen one before and had no idea what it was. This test was almost as much fun as a game, apart from her struggle, as usual, with holding the pencil. She held it like a sword pointing downward, closing her whole fist around it and dragging it toward her to draw a line, and when she pressed too hard to join the dog and the cat, she ripped a hole in the page, causing a crumpled scar like a miniature accordion. The teacher had said that when they were done, they were allowed to go outside, so Lily found Ida in the schoolyard and played with her until they were summoned back indoors.

A few days later, Lily's parents got a call from the principal, Mr. Barth—who everyone nicknamed (behind his back, of course) Mr. Barf—asking them to come in for a meeting. It took place the following day, and that evening, they returned home ashen-faced and quiet.

Lily was mentally retarded.

They'd sat, in shock, obediently, with their hands folded in their laps like first grade pupils, while Mr. Barf explained that Lily's IQ was very low, right on the border between Imbecile and Moron. He wasn't sure in which category to place her, even though—as he told them proudly—he had expertise in this area, having taken a half-day course. There was a big difference between an imbecile and a moron. An imbecile's IQ was between 26 and 50, and a moron's between 51 and 70. Imbeciles couldn't do anything much: they couldn't work and had to live in an institution, where they would more or less get babysat all day while they watched TV or blankly stared. Morons, on the other hand, if properly trained—and this was the operative phrase, he said: *if properly trained*—might be able to sort differently coloured plastic buttons in a sheltered workshop, or assemble boxes in a factory, the kind with internal grids that pharmaceutical companies use to package a dozen pills at a time. The difference between imbecile and moron was the difference between being (though he didn't use this exact term) a worthless nothing, and being (he did use this term exactly) a "contributing member of society."

Lily's mother, when relating all this over the phone to her sister, didn't bother to whisper in front of Lily or send her out of the room because obviously she wasn't going to be able to understand what any of it meant. But Lily understood enough. Enough to know that she wanted to be a moron: she longed, hoped, yearned—and yes, dreamed—to be a moron, and therefore a "contributing member of society." She didn't know what that phrase meant precisely but she could tell from her mother's voice that it meant not being a completely worthless defective (a favourite word of her mother's), not being just a useless piece of trash, good for nothing but the junk heap. If you were a moron, even if it meant you had to fold boxes day in day out for the rest of your life, you'd at least still be a person, someone another person could love.

Mr. Barf did not show her parents her actual test with its torn first page and the blank second one which had gotten tangled up with, and stuck to, the accordion-like wound. If her mother, with her sharp eye, had seen those pages, she might have identified the telltale pencil scrawl trailing off the edge of the page, demonstrating that Lily had been absent, seizuring, during one-third of this test, which would have also explained why Lily had failed to notice its second page. Perhaps then the principal would have taken these details into account and, instead of inadvertently penalizing her for her epilepsy, recalculated her score. If they'd redone the math, crediting her for the missing one-third of answers at the same rate she'd correctly answered the other two-thirds, her IQ score on page one would have been 75 (five points above Moron). And if they had generalized this to the missing second page, her IQ would have been 150, in the range of Genius.

Lily's parents did explain to the principal that their daughter had epilepsy, but this was of no consequence to Mr. Barf. He'd been rattling on, singing the praises of a special school for children like Lily, and when her mother reminded him about her petit mal, he said, "That's fine, this new school can accommodate kids with that, too." Apparently, his half-day course on mental retardation had not covered epilepsy; he seemed to think: Epilepsy, mental retardation, what's the difference? This girl is defective, something's wrong with her brain. Just throw all the loonies together, they'll get along.

Her father was hesitant about this new school. It would be a big change for Lily, he said. It was not located in their current catchment area, so she wouldn't be able to walk to school anymore with her friend Ida; she'd have to be bussed. And it was so far away she couldn't come home for lunch to take her midday pill, or continue her after-school ballet lessons, which she seemed to enjoy. Mr. Barf assured him, though, that this would be the best place for Lily because here she could get more attention than a regular school could provide, and it would help her thrive.

Both her parents were well-meaning and no fools, but they were not educated and were easily intimidated by this man in his suit and tie and starched white shirt, with a college diploma hanging on the wall behind his head. Within half an hour they had deferred to Mr. Barf's greater wisdom and signed a form agreeing to send Lily to a different school, a place for "children like her."

A few days after this meeting, they explained it all to Lily. She'd finish up first grade where she was and, starting in September, attend a new school, a "special" one, on the other side of town. She understood. She had done something a bit bad—petit mal—and her school didn't want her anymore.

* * *

Then there was a miracle and her life got saved. In the last week of June in first grade, her father was informed that in September he'd be transferred to a different branch of the company, one quite far away, at the northern tip of the city; so in July her family moved up there. Soon afterward, her mother, being conscientious, phoned Mr. Barf to notify him of their new address. She reached his voicemail and left a message, but got no reply. She tried again the following week, with the same result. It turns out, though she had no way of knowing this, that Mr. Barf, like her husband, had been transferred. (Or perhaps fired. What happened to him was never made clear.) In any case, a couple of weeks later she called once more and this time the school secretary answered the phone and took down the family's new contact information. It was a hot, sticky July, most of the school staff was already on summer vacation, and this secretary, Myrna Popper, was not well organized. "A bit vague" was how everyone described her, even during the school year when she was working under the watchful supervision of Mr. Barf. So all the details regarding the special school Lily was supposed to attend, including its name and location, were never mailed to her parents at their new address.

Lily's mother called the old school twice more, her final attempt being on the last day of August. Still no one answered the phone, so on the first day of classes, she took Lily by the hand and enrolled her at the local school, one block from their new home. Then, that same day after school, she drove Lily to her biannual checkup with her neurologist, as she did every fall and spring. Lily's latest EEG result was excellent, even in that part of the test where they'd flashed lights into her eyes to try and provoke a seizure (a stimulus that had had this effect in the past). The doctor was so pleased that he decided to take her off her medication for a trial six months. Within days, her coordination and fine motor skills had significantly improved, and she was no longer a drugged robot.

By the time (five weeks later) that her new school received the records from the previous one—records that labelled her unambiguously as mentally retarded—it was mid-October, and Lily was happily ensconced in her second grade class. She had made friends, attained an acceptable first report card, and overall adapted remarkably well to her new environment. Her teacher there, Miss Ball, whose face was as round as one, was lazy and in love. Engaged to be married at the end of the school year, the contents of her brain were as fluffy, sweet, and insubstantial as cotton candy, swirling pinkly with wedding fantasies and images of bridal gowns and bouquets. She had no interest in exerting herself on extra reading, such as the daunting file on Lily that had landed on her desk. Anyway, why *should* she read it? She already knew Lily, she'd been teaching her for five weeks. Lily, with her sweet smile, was one of three new pupils, and what Miss Ball had noticed about her so far was that she was quiet and well-behaved and that she performed averagely in most subjects but was talented in art. Also, Lily tended to daydream; but Miss Ball herself was pretty daydreamy these days, usually dreaming about her dreamy fiancé, so Lily didn't strike her as strange.

Miss Ball had spent the first two weeks of second grade reviewing the material covered in first grade. This was very helpful to Lily. Off her meds, the gauze drape between her and the world had lifted like a stage curtain, and now everything that Miss Ball taught seemed easy and obvious. Even arithmetic, which she'd had difficulty with in first grade. She was still shy and a little afraid of getting things wrong, but Miss Ball seemed to like her and didn't mind mistakes, so twice already Lily had raised her hand in class to answer a question. And now that her body was working properly again, in the schoolyard she played skipping rope and hopscotch with the other girls, learned with facility their clapping games, and got invited to their birthday parties. Also, to her great delight, as soon as she'd been able to hold, in the normal way, a pencil or crayon—a regular, slender crayon, not the superfat kind she'd clumsily clutched onto when drugged—she could once again draw. She produced detailed, vivid, colourful pictures. Two of these Miss Ball had displayed on the chalk shelf in front of the blackboard where, held in place behind a string, she showcased the best class work on any given assignment. Lily began to regularly receive stickers and stars on her artwork. She drew strange cartoons—people who were missing a mouth or eyes, or had enormous, misshapen hands; she drew black suns and cars without steering wheels—but her cartoons were always pretty and bright, with their horror hidden or contained. She garnered praise for her drawings from Miss Ball and the other kids, and even from the principal, who dropped in one day and selected Lily's picture, out of all the ones on the chalk shelf, for commendation. She asked Miss Ball who had drawn that picture and Miss Ball pointed to Lily, who was seated in the G row, the middle row of five.

Back then there were five rows in every classroom: E, VG, G, F, and U, which stood for Excellent, Very Good, Good, Fair, and Unsatisfactory. In first grade Lily had been in the F row. At this school, on the first day of second grade, she'd been assigned a seat in row G, Miss Ball assuming (till she had information to the contrary) that Lily was average. Lily was pleasantly surprised. She'd been promoted one category upward for no apparent reason, and since G stood for Good, now she was Good, not Bad. Not the least bit "mal." The day after the principal's visit, Miss Ball advised the class that Larry Looper was at home, sick, and would be absent from school for a while. Then she told Lily to move into his empty seat. Lily did not immediately comply. Larry's seat, exactly to the right of hers, was in the VG row. The Very Good row, where the smart kids sat, and she was not smart. Did Miss Ball know what she was saying? Was this some sort of joke?

"Hurry up," Miss Ball said, so Lily moved over. Moved over and moved up in the world. She could hardly believe it. Even the G row had been beyond her, undreamt of, until she came to this school, and now she was sitting in VG. The whole thing was confusing. She'd moved to a new neighbourhood and school, and now she wasn't mentally retarded anymore. She wasn't going to be an imbecile or a moron. She was going to be normal, like everybody else. And maybe—who knows?—even smart.

* * *

Smart. Hmm. You get out of bed, pee, and wash your hands and face. Under the covers again, sitting up, you eat half of the bagel with peanut butter that Perry left you for breakfast. It's tasty. You reach for the banana, but it almost collapses in your hand it's so mushy; you dump it back on the tray. You enjoy a large bite of the chocolate bar, then a sip of the pomegranate tea with its lively, intriguing new flavour. You were lucky with Miss Ball; she was a kind person. The first teacher you weren't afraid of. The first who didn't think you were a moron.

You lie down in bed and gaze into the distance. Yes, that was a very good year.

* * *

All through second grade she sat in the VG row, and she stayed there in third and fourth grade, as well. She was a Very Good student, bringing home report cards full of VG's with only a couple of G's, and always an A in art. Her G's in fourth grade were in the subjects she found most boring: geography (where they had to memorize the five main industries of France and England and the names of the three different types of rocks); and history (memorizing the date of the first successful expedition through the Northwest Passage and the years of all the previous, failed attempts). Learning nothing in history and geography except lists of facts was boring to the point of painful. Even remembering this now as an adult, thirty-six years later, is enough to make you woozy with misery. But in fourth grade, getting a couple of G's amid a sea of VG's was no cause for concern.

It was normal to be bored by some of your subjects and was even something to commiserate about with your friends.

The fourth-grade teacher, Miss Hillrod, was stern and forbidding. In the second and third grade, Lily had been unafraid to raise her hand and speak, but now she was very quiet and hardly ever contributed to class discussions. Miss Hillrod took this as an indication of intellectual dullness. In late November, just as she was deliberating whether or not to demote Lily to the G row, she asked the class why they thought President Kennedy had been assassinated on that exact day one year earlier. There were only two responses, both lacklustre. Then Lily said: "They killed him because he was a great man. He did brave things, so he was a threat. If he'd been like everyone else, they wouldn't have had to kill him." Miss Hillrod's eyes popped open with surprise. Staring at Lily, imagining she was merely parroting her parents, she asked her where she'd got that idea. Lily, perplexed by the question, said, "From my brain." Then she thought, but did not say, *My little bit bad brain.* After that, Miss Hillrod left her in the VG row, and a week later sent her down the hall for "a special test for gifted pupils." Lily didn't know what "gifted" meant but she didn't like the sound of "special". And she was wary of being placed alone in a room with a stranger who was going to ask her questions, perhaps like the ones on the test in first grade about the dog and cat, and the apple and banana, that had got her into trouble. But the administrator of this test was young, friendly, and cheerful, a psychology intern who told Lily her name was Karen and quickly put her at ease. Or as much at ease as Lily could be in this situation. Karen, who had shoulder-length brown hair and a green-and-blue sweater that Lily liked, said she'd be asking her twenty questions ("like the game!" she said). The first seventeen were straightforward. Then, for number eighteen, Karen asked Lily, "What kind of animal gives milk?"

"A cow," Lily replied unhesitatingly. This was the obvious answer, and clearly the correct one, since this is what they'd been taught in school as a fact: Milk comes from a cow.

Karen wrote this down. "Anything else?" she asked with assumed casualness.

Lily thought a bit. "A goat?" she offered timidly.

Karen, nodding, added this to the answer sheet. Then: "Can you think of any other animals that give milk?"

Lily considered this, then blushed. She was picturing a woman's naked breast. She knew that breasts give milk because she'd seen her mother feed Bruce from her breast when he was a baby. She didn't dare say this, though. First of all, she wasn't sure a person could be an animal; but even more importantly, it would sound weird to say "a woman's breast." Karen would probably think she was nuts—and bad, too, because *breast* was a dirty word.

While she struggled, Karen observed her intently. "You have another idea. I can tell you do. Come on," she said, "what is it?"

Lily liked Karen. And her eyes, as she waited expectantly for Lily's reply, were encouraging and kind. She seemed to be on her side, and Lily could tell that Karen liked her. Still, it wasn't worth the risk. She wasn't going to let anyone trick her the way they did in first grade and turn her again into an imbecile or moron. She knew what would happen if she said, "a woman's breast." She'd get removed from this school where she was smart and had friends, and transferred to a place for kids who were stupid or crazy. She shook her head. No way. She wasn't going to help them do this to her.

Karen was certain Lily had another answer up her sleeve, and tried twice more to pry it out of her. Her supervisor had instructed her to be on the lookout for test responses that demonstrated originality and a broader than usual outlook, and Karen had a feeling that Lily was holding out on one such response. But Lily's resolve was fierce, and eventually Karen sighed and gave up. And that was that. Lily did not get moved from her regular class to the special one for gifted children. And she was relieved. She didn't want to be special in any sense. Not gifted-special or retarded-special. She just wanted to blend in with everyone else.

⁓ It was not only on this test that Lily knew more than she let on, but in real life, as well. For instance, she never disclosed it to anyone, not even her siblings, that she knew her parents didn't love each other. There was a bit of love between them, but not much. Mainly what she discerned was irritation and frustration, and sometimes even hate. She knew this because of a game she'd invented: When people were speaking, she'd pretend to be deaf. This way, she didn't hear their words, only what they were saying with their eyes, facial expressions, and hand and body movements. It was easy, in this silence, to whiz like an arrow past people's words, all the way to what they truly felt. And she trusted this silent language more than the treacherous one of words.

One day she mentioned this game to a friend from school, but this girl had no idea what she was talking about. So Lily concluded that this thing she did was not normal, and after that she didn't share it with anyone else. Still, this incident caused her to ponder whether her differentness, her abnormality, was entirely a bad thing. Maybe, in a way, she had a superpower that other people lacked. She could see past words. She saw right through them as if she had X-ray vision, like Superman. Perhaps she was a sort of Supergirl thanks to the extra electricity in her brain. She could feel it glow and burn inside her. And someday, fueled by its crazy magic, she was going to take off like a rocket flying into space. She'd show them all. And she'd make Daddy, and everyone who loved her, proud.

⁓ Each night before going to sleep, tucked cozily into her bed, Lily would evaluate the day that was about to end. She did not reflect on how happy or sad she'd been, whether she'd had fun with her friends or learned something interesting at school. Her yardstick was how connected she had been to the world. How vivid were the pictures, colours, sounds, smells, events, and experiences of the day? For how many minutes in her waking hours had she been actively engaged with her surroundings, living in "the real world," as opposed to inside her own head? She knew that being present, and "in reality," was good, whereas being absent (for instance, by daydreaming) was bad. And in case this ever slipped her mind, she was reminded of it every day at school by a popular game called "Absent, Present." Two girls turned a skipping rope while all the others chanted over and over, to the same steady rhythm as the rope smacking the ground, "*Ab*sent, *Pre*sent." On each word you had to skip twice without stepping on the rope. And this was her life: she was absent, then present, then absent again, and present again. Always trying—as she transitioned back and forth between absence (her inner life) and presence (her outer one)—not to trip on reality's noose-shaped rope.

In flannel pajamas in her bed, gazing through her window at the half-moon, she considered her totally normal older sister. Heather was always present—connected to the real world—and living in the present tense. At the dinner table, all her attention was focused on the food she was eating and the family conversation around her. When playing dodgeball with friends in the street, she concentrated solely on the game and on trying to win. Unlike Lily, she never paused mid-game, stood off to one side, and stared for a while. Never. Lily had watched her all her life, so she knew. Heather was friendly and well-liked and was always with people. If, for some reason on a weekend, she had to pop into her room during the day, she didn't seize the opportunity to plop down on her bed and daydream for a while. No. Within three minutes she'd be on the phone to a friend, searching for something to do. Lily, on the other hand, rarely felt the need to "do" anything, nor did she crave constant company. Which proved there was something wrong with her. If you're normal, you are incessantly active and sociable. You never require solitude. But she did. She needed to think. She liked to think. One day she asked Heather what she thought about, and Heather replied, "What do I think about *what?*" It was shocking to realize that other people were not, all the time, thinking, as she was, but were only doing exactly what it looked like they were doing: kicking a dodgeball, dressing a Barbie doll, positioning a triangle atop a Blockhead tower. There was no inner life running in parallel to the observable one, like an underwater fishing line trailing invisibly alongside a boat in a lake. The ceaseless activity in her brain, all that extra electricity, set her apart from others. "Anti-socialness," her mother called it, but it wasn't that. She needed time to think about everything and try to understand.

Meanwhile at school, in fourth grade, she passed as normal. Her seizures, along with the horrible pills she had taken to treat them, were behind her now, and everyone at school assumed she was a normal person, and that she always had been. No one thought to ask her: "At your old school, were you mentally retarded?" Or: "Were you a drugged robot who couldn't hold a pencil properly and stumbled and dropped things all the time?" There had been no such questions; but still she half-expected, filled with dread, that she'd be found out. She knew she was only presenting a fake front, like the phony, painted stage sets made from thin cardboard that they used in their school plays.

Last week, she was in the grocery store with her mother when she spied a girl with Down's syndrome on the other side of the aisle. Their mothers were busy loading up their shopping carts on opposite sides of this aisle, while Lily and this girl gazed into each other's eyes. The Down girl's eyes were brown and deep and Lily felt herself sinking into them like quicksand. *I know you,* she told her silently. *I am you and you are me.* They continued to gaze, and then smile, at each other, until Lily's mother yanked her away.

* * *

It was an old couple—"Old"! They were probably fifty, only five years older than you are now!—who scraped the girl up off the street. First the old man tried alone and failed. So he took the arms and his wife took the legs, and they carried the girl out of the middle of the road where she'd been lying, and where, less than three minutes later, a big red truck rounding the corner would have run over her soft child's body, flattening it like a pancake. The old woman had been looking out of her living room window and seen something sprawled in the street. Initially thinking it was a dog, she called her husband over and pointed at it. "No, it's a little girl!" he cried and they rushed out of the house. The girl appeared to be sleeping so they tried to wake her with shouts and shakes but that didn't work. She was breathing but unconscious, and her unconsciousness made her heavy, which is why it required two adults, groaning, to carry a nine-year-old child from the street to the sidewalk, up their four front stairs, and into their modest living room. They laid her on the faded brown couch. "She probably lives nearby and was walking home from school," the man said, and the woman ran back into the middle of the road to retrieve the girl's schoolbag. Sitting next to the unconscious girl, she rummaged through her schoolbag until she found, on the flyleaf of the geography textbook, the girl's full name. Her husband fetched the little phone directory for their almost rural neighbourhood, dialed the first number on the list with Lily's last name, and got the girl's uncle. "I'll tell her mother," the uncle said, and showed up ten minutes later with a harried, anxious, pretty young woman. "Lily!" she screamed and ran over to the child lying on the couch, who looked dazed. "She woke up a few minutes ago," the old woman explained, "but I told her to relax until you arrived."

Lily, in fact, was not relaxing or relaxed. Mortified to find herself in a strange place, lying on an unfamiliar couch and being stared at by two strangers, she felt like Snow White awakening in an unknown cottage surrounded by seven white-bearded dwarfs. Here there were only two old, small people, but she was as shocked as if there were seven. So when the woman told her to close her eyes and relax, Lily, embarrassed by the whole situation, closed them and kept them closed for the next ten minutes, pretending to doze off. Till now she had spoken only three words. When first coming to, she'd asked, "Where am I?", which sounded like someone in a movie, and she'd thought that maybe she actually was in a movie, acting a role. "You fell down in the street and we found you," the woman said. "Close your eyes and relax. Your mother will be here soon."

Lily did not remember falling down in the street. All she recalled was walking home from school, her schoolbag unusually heavy because Miss Hillrod had given them both history and geography homework for the next day, and these were her two fattest textbooks. She'd been eating an apple, and now she was hungry. "Where's my apple?" she almost asked the two dwarfs, but realized she couldn't because she was feigning sleep. Her chin hurt, she didn't know why, and her head hummed softly like their old fridge before it broke down. She felt awkward and self-conscious in this strange place, being watched over by people she didn't know. And what was she supposed to do now—just lie here on their couch minute after minute, even hour after hour, while they stared at her? They seemed nice, but maybe they weren't. There were bad people in the world who hurt children, which is why she was not supposed to talk to strangers. So from now on she would not speak to these strangers. Not one single word.

What seemed a long time later, she heard, to her relief, her mother's voice in the hallway. Lily opened her eyes and her mother flew in, looking worried, and also angry, and right behind her was Uncle Harvey's kind, smiling face. "How are you, kidlet?" he asked, rumpling her hair. Her mother spoke quietly to the old couple while Uncle Harvey helped Lily sit up and then stand. She was a little wobbly on her feet but managed all right with Uncle Harvey's steadying hand on her elbow. As they approached the front door, her mother said, "Say thank you." So Lily obediently turned back and said "thank you" to the old couple, although she wasn't sure what she was thanking them for. They hadn't given her even a cookie, her usual after-school snack. She, Uncle Harvey, and her mother left the little brown house, and on the short drive home, with Lily alone in the back seat, her mother said without turning around, "They saved your life, you know." Lily did not reply; she merely gazed out the window at the street rolling by because her mother's words made no sense.

* * *

You still have in your photo album the picture your mother took two days later. In this blurry, black-and-white photo, you are standing in front of your home with Bruce (still shorter than you, though not for long), and slightly smiling. You remember how much it hurt to smile then, to move your face at all, but your mother told you to smile, so you did. The photo shows clearly the wound on your chin, which would morph into the scar that you have to this day. You fell because of a seizure, and were therefore unconscious when you fell, so your hands did not extend to break the fall and your chin crashed against the hard pavement. It still hurt when this picture was taken, and it hurts even now to look at it. There is a vestigial ache in your chin, in that precise spot, not only because of the fall itself, but because of what it meant and led to.

Fall—what a word. The primeval Fall. The fall from grace. For the three years before your fall, you'd been graceful, but after the fall they put you back on meds and you were once again clumsy and graceless.

Falling is also what soldiers do in war. Your father sometimes called you a soldier. "Be a brave soldier," he'd say when you were getting a shot at the doctor's. Getting a shot; not getting shot—which is what happens to real soldiers. "Falling in battle" means to die. Fall is the season of death: the time of year when the leaves on the trees die.

Falling that day in the street was the death of the normal life you'd been living, your brief season of being normal. That fall was your first grand mal seizure, and it changed everything.

* * *

Daddy tried, feebly, to call what had happened a "dream," like all her other seizures up to that point, but this did not feel accurate even to him. "Dreams" were petit mal events, which contained only a little bit of badness, but a grand mal seizure contained a lot. So now she was no longer only a bit bad, but very bad. Not VG, very good, but VB, and to punish her, they put her back on meds. They said, of course, that these were to help her—to make her "better," meaning more good—but they always claimed this when they gave her meds, and she knew it wasn't true. In early March, when the pills resumed, she returned to being a drugged robot. This time, though, she was in fourth grade, and not, like the first time they drugged her, four years old (*maybe four was a bad number?*), so now she knew what to expect from medication. And she watched herself, as if watching a horror movie, transform hour by hour, day by day, into a kind of Frankenstein. Once again she stared vacantly with glazed eyes, tripped over her own feet, constantly dropped and spilled things, and had no friends at school. Her only playmate was Frances who lived across the street, was a grade behind her in school, and was more like family than friend since their mothers had known each other since childhood. Toward the end of fourth grade, Grandma told her that hardships could be good things because they were opportunities to practice being brave and to demonstrate you had good character. So Lily, drugged and exhausted, trudging up the hill on her way home from school, would picture herself as a brave soldier, proving her mettle under harsh conditions. And when she'd made it to the top of the hill, panting and proud of her perseverance, she'd resolve to show she had good character by not even bragging about her accomplishment when she got home.

**

After falling in the street, there were three years of medication, or, as you think of them now, three more dead years. Years of which you have almost no memory. It's as though you didn't really live them. Well, you didn't; you were never fully alive when on those drugs. Fifth, sixth, and seventh grade are a blur. Those fucking meds, you think, lying in your bed, I hate them all. You recite, like a litany, the names of every epilepsy medication you can remember, the way a wronged person swearing vengeance commits to memory the names of their enemies:

"Phenobarb.

"Tridione.

"Dilantin.

"Zarontin.

"Tegretol."

Tegretol was the last one you were on. It was one of the worst, and you detested it. Out of curiosity, you google Tegretol, squinting at the screen of your laptop.

Carbamazepine, sold under the trade name Tegretol among others, is an anticonvulsant medication used in the treatment of epilepsy. It is also used in schizophrenia and bipolar disorder.

Schizophrenia? Bipolar disorder? What the hell … What were these doctors thinking, giving you this drug? Your friend Charlene, a physician, said last month (probably in defense of her own profession) about the pills her sick brother received in childhood: "The meds they gave people back then were the best they had at the time." But you don't care. You're appalled by what you've just read. And it sickens you to picture a child, like a baby bird, tilting its head back and opening its mouth-beak so that its mother-bird, father-bird, and doctor-birds can pour down its little throat thousands and thousands of pills, filling up its small body from its toes to its eyeballs. That's how full of drugs you were from age four to eighteen, with two breaks in between. They filled you up like filling an empty bottle, and once it was full, they screwed on the cap. You got screwed.

"Chupe mantequilla de mi culo!" you yell. (Suck butter from my ass!) (Spanish)

"Sanjam da prdnem na tebe!" (I dream about farting on you!) (Bosnian)

"Sana girsin keman yayi!" (May the bow of a violin enter your anus!) (Turkish)

From your breakfast tray you grab the mushy banana and fling it across the room.

***

It wasn't just having to go back on meds, after falling, that changed her life. Everything became different. Even the meds she had to take were unrecognizable. Instead of baby peaches with crushed pill powder stirred in, now she was given horse pills so gigantic she couldn't even swallow them. Daddy had to teach her: tip your head back, fling the pill to the deepest part of your mouth (right near the throat), and quickly chase it down with water. Daddy, using pretend pills for himself, made this into a game, a competition of who could swallow their pill the fastest. Usually, she won. Her pills arrived in a brown, four-sided glass bottle and were kept in the closet to the left of the kitchen sink. They had to be taken every four hours, which worked out to four times a day: at eight, noon, four, and eight. The four o'clock pill meant that she needed to come straight home after school and not linger or walk home with the other kids, because her pills were more important than friends. Her pill, she was given to understand, was her best friend—even if it made her face swollen and fat-looking, which bothered her now that she was ten and two-thirds and starting to care about her appearance.

In addition, there was now a whole new list of restrictions imposed upon her. These she experienced as not just punishments—or even as not-just (unjust) punishments—but as personal insults since it felt as though she was being treated like someone half her age. Her parents at this point limited her independence even more than Bruce's, and he was two years younger. Unlike her, he didn't have to ask their mother to come to the living room window and watch him cross the street every time he left the house. Each morning Lily fretted in case one of the neighbourhood kids, on their way to school, glimpsed her mother in the window and deduced from this that, although Lily was almost eleven years old, she still needed to be supervised when crossing a street. She'd never live it down.

Another major indignity had to do with baths. To this day, as a result of the way your—and only your—baths were managed back then, you hate baths with a passion. Last year on holiday in Paris, the *pension* where you and Perry stayed had no showers, only tubs; so during the twelve days of your vacation you stood every evening in the tub, refusing to even sit down in it, much less bathe, and would use only the hand attachment to spray-wash yourself. Perry could not understand your vehemence on this point, or the reason for your aversion to baths. He'd thought it would be romantic to bathe together in Paris.

⁓ The girl slid underwater, feeling the warm wetness cover her lips and nose, and she floated slightly as her bum drifted up from the cool floor of the bathtub. Her parents had explained that the thing that was wrong with her brain had caused her to pass out in the middle of a street and the same thing could happen in a bathtub, and then she'd slide under the water and drown. So even though, for the previous two years—starting at age eight, same as her sister and brothers—she'd been bathing all by herself, now whenever she took a bath, she had to call out to her parents every five minutes, "reporting" to them, so they'd know she hadn't drowned. One or both of her parents were always seated downstairs in the living room within easy hearing distance of the bathroom, reading—or pretending to read—magazines, and on the bathroom sink they had placed a travel clock to help Lily keep track of the time. Every five minutes she had to holler: "Repooooorting!" and they would shout back: "Okay!"

It's not a terrible thing to have to call out one word every five minutes, but it's not as easy as you might think. Five minutes often pass more quickly than expected, so Lily had to always keep her eye on the clock and not let her mind wander at all. She could not muse, for instance, on what kind of birthday party she wished to have when she turned eleven because, while considering all the options, she might fail to notice the big hand on the clock moving to the next number, and if she neglected to holler "Reporting!", her parents would worry. Generally she was diligent, and only once so far had she missed the five-minute mark. Her mother had had to yell upstairs, "Lily, are you all right?" Lily had yelled back, "I'm okay!" "You have to report!" her mother shouted. "It's been almost six minutes!" Whenever her mother was scared, she became angry; so after that, Lily was careful at bathtime to be vigilant and on guard. (*O Canada, we stand on guard for thee.*)

A few months later, she was in the bath picturing the Christmas decorations that had recently appeared along the hallways of her school, as well as in her classroom between the top edge of the blackboard and the bottom of the cursive alphabet. Bored in class, she had gaped at the adornments made from cardboard or Styrofoam and then painted: the red Santas and holly berries, and the white angels, cherubs, snowmen, and snow-covered Christmas trees. She was pondering now how to combine all these items into one—perhaps she could make a red-and-white snowman-Santa-cherub-angel with a garland of holly berries on its head, holding in its left hand a snowy fir tree. Suddenly her parents were in the bathroom with her, Daddy almost in tears: "Why didn't you answer? We called and there was no answer!" Mom chimed in: "We thought you drowned!" They were standing over her, staring at her naked body in the bath. She grabbed the floating white washcloth and covered her genitals, feeling humiliated and ashamed. She wasn't sure which was worse: her father seeing her naked (someone who loved her, but was a man) or her mother (someone who seemed to despise her, but was a woman). Lily's face was as red as holly berries while they lectured her on the importance of reporting, repeated how frightened they'd been, and warned her that if she couldn't be relied on to report every five minutes, from now on Mom would have to stay with her in the bathroom during her baths. Lily, appalled by this suggestion, promised to be more attentive in future. Finally, they left. Lily covered her face with her hands and whispered to her snowman-Santa-cherub-angel: "Save me from drowning." Then: "Save me from my parents."

They don't hate me, she reminded herself; they do this out of love. And even though it hadn't yet been five minutes, or even two, she screamed downstairs to the living room as loud as she possibly could: "I didn't drown! I'm not dead! I'm alive! I'm alive!"

* * *

In ninth grade she turned fourteen, and even though in the number fourteen there is a four (a number that to her seemed unlucky, even bad), on this birthday she was perfectly normal again. Her doctor had taken her off meds the year before, gushing over her progress—no seizures (petit mal or grand mal) for three years, and a good EEG—as though this was a personal achievement on her part like learning to high jump, and she now merited a reward. In any case, she was thrilled with the reward she received: an end to the horse pills, which had made her feel as monstrously big and ungainly as a horse. It took a couple of weeks to transition back to normal; and as this was occurring, she was acutely aware of the two different lives (drugged / abnormal and undrugged / normal) that she lived, the two realities she inhabited, and the two versions of herself, the two Lilys, that existed. She didn't know back then that Tegretol, the pill she'd just been taken off of, was being prescribed also for schizophrenia, but she did feel that her life was schizophrenic. Joseph in the Bible—known as "Joseph the Dreamer" (*if he "dreamed" so much, perhaps he, too, had epilepsy?*)—had interpreted Pharaoh's dream as meaning seven good years would be followed by seven bad ones. In her life she'd had three good years, followed by three bad ones, then four good ones, then four more bad ones. And three and four added up to seven, just like the years in Joseph's prophecy.

Now at age fourteen (two times seven), it was a relief and a joy to be Normal Lily again. Her own face looked back at her in the mirror, not the weird one swollen by medication. The awful fatigue and heaviness were gone, her body was coordinated, and at school she was friendly with her classmates and perceived as smart. In English they'd been reading *Flowers for Algernon*, a novel about an intellectually disabled man named Charlie who undergoes experimental surgery and briefly becomes a genius before the effects wear off and he returns to his original state. Lily (not that she thought she was a genius) identified deeply with Charlie's transformation from moron to genius and back, even though in her case (the opposite of Charlie's), the drugs made her stupider, not smarter. She produced a book report of such quality it surprised her English teacher, and also, when it got an A, her classmates, who knew she rarely invested effort in homework assignments. When someone asked her about this one, she replied cryptically, "Charlie's life is a metaphor," and turned away. Like Charlie, who'd observed his own transformation from stupid to smart and back to stupid, she was sometimes filled with dread at the likelihood, or even inevitability, that at some point— probably in four or five years, when some other incident happened and they put her back on drugs—she too would revert to moron-hood. Her lifelong vacillation between on-pills and off-pills, stupid and smart, was like the flicking of a light switch on and off, and ensuing periods of light and darkness. Sometimes she wasn't certain who, or what, she really was: dumb or smart, good or bad, beautiful or ugly. Maybe she was all these things.

⁓ In ninth grade she drew almost constantly, and on any scrap of paper she could find. She drew all over her class notes, her teachers' handouts, and the napkins in the cafeteria. In all her notebooks, one for each subject, there was not an inch on any page, even in the margins, that wasn't covered with cartoons. Every notebook contained hundreds of small figures and scenes—unlike the notebooks of other kids, which had nothing on their pages but neat lines of handwritten words. She was embarrassed by this need of hers to draw because it was something she could not control, like a toddler that can't help shitting its pants. Her cartoons, as the observable product of this need, seemed lovable to her but also vaguely dirty and shameful, like the armpit hair she had recently acquired. A relative who visited her parents, though, told her there was nothing wrong with armpit hair; where she lived in Europe, it was actually considered sexy. Lily was mulling this over the next day in art history class while doodling on the cover of her notebook, when the brand new art teacher noticed what she was drawing. Blushing, Lily quickly covered it with her hand and sheepishly began to apologize, but Miss Mellon interrupted her and warmly praised her cartoons. She told Lily to keep on drawing, and suggested she check out the school's art club.

That afternoon Lily, hesitantly and shyly, stopped by the art club; by the end of that week she was an integral part of its tight little group. She, Melanie, Jane, and Stephan hung around together between all their classes, shared a lunch table every day in the cafeteria, and after school and on weekends visited art museums, galleries, and—indulging Lily's love of cartoons and graphic novels—her favourite comic book store. To her mind, the four of them were very different from the other kids at school, whom she thought of as the normal ones. They all dressed the same and talked the same, cared only about sex and the latest fashions in clothes or music, and demonstrated zero originality or imagination. She knew she could never fit in with them, even if she'd wanted to—which made her feel, oddly, both inferior and superior to them. She fit in fine, though, with her art club friends. They, like her, weren't interested in clothes, conformity, or parties. What interested them was art. We're normal, too, she decided; just a different kind of normal. And it was in this kind of normal where she belonged. After high school she would study art. She'd be an artist when she grew up, and perhaps an art teacher, too—like Miss Mellon, with her frizzy hair and cheerful, encouraging demeanour. Though Miss Mellon at times could also be spacey. Lily had occasionally caught her standing and staring with her mouth slightly open. Lily's mother hated that: "Close your mouth," she'd say to Lily and her brothers, "you look like a fish." But Miss Mellon's spaciness didn't bother Lily. It was endearing in a way, sort of a normal take on a petit mal "dream". Altogether Miss Mellon had a different way of being in the world than any other adult Lily had met. She could tell she had a huge inner life. Miss Mellon painted when she wasn't teaching, and the paintings growing inside her like embryos seemed to be continually flickering behind her eyes. Her mouth was relaxed and ready to smile—a wide open smile that seemed to invite everything inside it, like a school of golden minnows swimming into a grotto. Totally unlike Lily's mother, who, unless she was speaking, always kept her mouth firmly closed. Her lips were often pursed with disappointment or disapproval; at other times with the effort to keep them from trembling for even an instant. As if—terrified of losing control—sealing her mouth could keep her safe.

* * *

Tenth and eleventh grade were a continuation of the ninth, with Lily spending all her free time with her art club friends. But at the start of twelfth grade, when she was seventeen, everything changed. During the summer, Jane's father, a historian, had received a job offer from the States, and in September the whole family moved to Chicago. Soon after this, Melanie got in with a trio of popular girls, all with long, straight, blond hair who were boy-crazy and fashion-obsessed. That left only Lily and Stephan in the art club group, which now no longer felt like a club or group at all, just strange. Jane and Melanie were like phantom limbs, vividly present with their absence, and it was awkward to suddenly be alone with Stephan. They met twice for club purposes; the third time, he came on to her. Startling her—she'd never viewed him that way—and she swung her mouth away from his. After that, though she tried to stay friends, they never regained a comfortable footing, and by the end of October their group was no more. It had dissolved like sugar into water.

Now she was alone, and lonely. And not only at school, where she had no one to eat lunch with or hang out with between classes (not to mention after school and on weekends); but also at home. Heather and Tim were away at college—Heather in second year; Tim in third—and Bruce had recently turned into a jock, perpetually busy with his sports teams and equipment. He was all but unrecognizable in a body augmented by shoulder pads, knee pads, and a face guard, and as part of a gang of smelly, burly, athletic fifteen-year-olds who told crude jokes slyly directed at her. As for her parents, her father, following a promotion, was working much harder than before, leaving the house early each morning and returning late at night, so she hardly ever saw him. Her mother was home most of the time, but usually bitter, dissatisfied with her life, and angry, so she was no pleasure to be around at the end of a tiring, lonely day. Sporadically Mom would be cordial or in a good mood, but even that could turn on a dime. For instance, on the cold afternoon in November of twelfth grade when they were in the car together, coming home after Lily's fall checkup with her neurologist. For the previous hour and a half, things had been quite amicable between them. Even though her mother had told the doctor that a couple of times since the previous checkup she'd caught Lily staring blankly, and maybe these were petit mal episodes. Lily had retorted that she'd merely been deep in thought while doing homework. The doctor was undecided. "Let's wait and see," he finally said. "Overall, Lily seems to be doing very well."

On the chilly drive home, she felt lonely. She missed her friends from the art club, and she missed having friends altogether. She also missed her brothers and sister. Lately, sometimes, her loneliness was almost unbearable. Noticing her mother's gloved hands on the steering wheel, she remembered that she'd planned to take driving lessons before leaving for college in nine months. She'd applied to a few schools and was waiting to hear back; at this exact stage in twelfth grade, both Heather and Tim had begun learning to drive. "I'll need to start my driving lessons soon," she said to her mother.

Her mother glanced at her sharply. "Epileptics don't drive," she said.

Epileptics? Lily had never heard this word before. *Epilepsy*, of course, but not *epileptics*. Was that what she was: "an epileptic"? Was the defining characteristic of who she was the seizures she used to have? Twenty years in the future, the terminology for people with disabilities would change, and instead of calling someone "an epileptic", "a diabetic", or "a schizophrenic", you'd have to say "a person with epilepsy," "a person with diabetes," "a person with schizophrenia." At that point, the word *epileptic* would be permitted solely as an adjective (for instance, an epileptic seizure), not as a noun (to describe a person). But on that day in the car in twelfth grade, according to the language of the time—and evidently also in the view of her mother—Lily was not a whole person; she was nothing but her epilepsy. Shocked into pained silence, she stared out the window.

"I'm only telling you the truth," her mother said. "Someone has to tell you the truth, even if it hurts. There's no point sugar-coating things, or coddling you, as your father likes to do. You're defective. You were born that way and there's nothing to be done about it. You'll never lead a normal life. You can't take driving lessons because epileptics aren't allowed to drive—it's against the law. And most epileptics also don't hold jobs, get married, or have children. It's entirely possible you'll never have a family, Lily. You need to be realistic and adjust your expectations."

No family? No husband or children? No work as an artist? Never to drive a car? Her mother's words were a kick to her stomach, and she felt wounded, internally hemorrhaging, while she gazed wordlessly at the road ahead. The physical road, but also the other road before her: a truncated life, a pathetic incomplete life devoid of love or independence. She desperately wanted for her mother to be wrong, yet she feared she was right. How *could* she have expected to lead a normal life? She wasn't normal and never had been. She'd been deluding herself.

"It's better to know the truth," her mother was saying. "That way you can prepare for reality."

The horizon, with its orange setting sun, dipped away from Lily, disappearing into the rolling asphalt. At home, she went mutely to her room. She did not speak to anyone for twenty-four hours. Then she phoned Margo and said yes.

⁓ Margo was part of a group at school that had never attracted Lily. It was comprised of kids in eleventh and twelfth grade who were not bright or interesting in any way; but some of them had been friendly to her, and Margo, who lived five doors away, had invited her to a couple of their pot parties. She had never gone. To her it seemed crazy that people would actually drug themselves on purpose, "for fun". She couldn't imagine anything in the world less fun than being drugged. And it was bizarre that they actually spent money to alter their states of consciousness as part of a journey of self-exploration. Her own brain took her on such journeys without her ever paying for them, or even wanting them; and for much of her life she'd been taking pills expressly to prevent these journeys and alterations of consciousness. So smoking dope felt ridiculous to her. Not to mention dangerous. Who knew how it could affect her brain? Perhaps it would cause a seizure. She'd heard that drug dealers sometimes laced pot with other substances in order to hook their customers on harder, more addictive, drugs. Occasionally even the dealers themselves didn't know what was in the drugs they sold; a joint could contain anything. A couple of kids in her class had acid-tripped without ever buying acid; they'd thought they were merely smoking pot but had ended up tripping, and they'd had bad trips at that. She could picture that happening to her. Getting tripped up and tripping her way into a seizure.

Even if that didn't occur, there were other, less obvious, perils with drugs. When people got stoned, they said, and did all sorts of things they never would normally. They revealed aspects of their inner, unconscious selves, and she could not allow that to happen. She had secrets to protect. Chief among them, the pills that she'd taken up until four years ago, kept in a dark corner of the kitchen closet—as well-hidden there as an in-the-closet person—along with the reason for this medication: the strangeness, the broken thing, in her brain. She would never risk revealing this.

This had been her firm position since ninth grade, when she was first offered drugs. Her consistent refusal to partake had closed off certain social possibilities for her in high school, but it hadn't really mattered because she'd had her own group of friends. But now her situation was different. She was friendless. And every opportunity available to her for social interaction—a formal dance at school, a game of bowling, or a casual get-together at someone's house—came with the implicit proviso that you'd smoke dope there along with the rest of the gang. Inevitably, at some point during the event, a joint would get passed around. She had experienced this twice already, and on both occasions, when the joint reached her, she'd mumbled something incoherent and handed it to the next person. Immediately this had set her apart. She'd never been invited again and had been marked as outside the social circle. Now, more than anything in the world, she wanted to be inside it. To not be lonely anymore; and to prove to herself and everyone else, including her mother, that she was normal. "Normal" meant having friends, and in high school that meant being part of a group. Any group; and Margo's would do. They were having a party this Friday night, at Margo's as it happened, and Margo had mentioned this to her two days earlier, near their lockers at school. Lily, as usual, had been non-committal. But now, twenty-four hours after her checkup at the doctor's, she phoned Margo and said she'd come.

⁓ This time when the joint reached Lily, who was sitting on the floor with everyone else, she didn't pass it on to the next person. She inhaled from it deeply, taking two big breaths, then pinched her lips shut, as she'd seen the others do. At first, she didn't feel anything unusual. Then a heaviness came over her, and after that, giddiness. Laughter began somewhere down in her belly, and once she started laughing, she couldn't stop. Everything seemed hysterically funny all of a sudden. People were smiling at her, enjoying her, especially a guy and girl right across from her, holding hands, and for the first time this year she felt like she belonged. After a while she was ravenous and stood up to get some chips and salsa from the snack table. The next thing she knew, she was lying on the hard floor, and the back of her head and her wrist hurt. Everyone was staring at her, looking frightened and appalled. What was going on? Why were they gawking at her? Her tongue felt dry and very thick in her mouth. A guy with greasy long hair kept knocking his head against the wall, saying, "Fuck fuck fuck," and moaning. Her parents appeared and her mother screamed, "You stupid girl!", which was mortifying in front of all these kids from school, even more than the fact that she was lying on the floor with her legs splayed wide open and her underwear probably showing. (*Why had she tonight, of all nights, chosen to wear a skirt?*) She closed her legs, which required a surprising amount of effort, and yanked down her skirt, but still everyone goggled at her like she was a freak. Someone was crying. She didn't think it was her but she wasn't sure. Whatever had happened, she'd ruined their party and they'd never invite her again.

⁓ The next day her doctor put her back on drugs. Not "fun" ones; the real kind. Powerful pills against grand mal seizures that transformed her again into a drugged robot: tired all the time, lethargic, clumsy. At school, a few days after the party, someone who had been there was standing near his locker, and when he noticed her coming down the hallway, he screwed up his face and, laughing, dramatically jerked his arms and legs around. Most of the kids, though, just avoided her now. I'll never be able to live this down, she thought. It's lucky this is my last year here. Next year I'll be in college and I'll never have to see any of these people again.

⁓ She left home for college without a driver's license, armed instead with a carry-on bag full of pills. She was loaded down, her head bowed like a burro's under its burdens, one of the heaviest of these being her parents' fears for her. They almost hadn't let her go away to college, so afraid had they been of what might happen to her far from home. But she'd fought back, and fought hard, and in the end they'd agreed. Mainly because they knew she'd have her pills with her. Her pills would keep her safe.

No one else in the dorm had both parents helping them settle in, and she was embarrassed by her mother and father's hovering, teariness, and anxiety. Impatient for them to leave as quickly as possible, she promised them, without argument or negotiation, everything they asked for. Yes, she'd call every Sunday; yes, she'd eat properly and get enough sleep; no, she wouldn't overdo things and get run down; yes, she would take her pills. She was relieved when finally they stood up to leave.

"You're an adult now," were Mom's parting words. "Act like one."

"I will," Lily said.

As her parents' backs receded down the long corridor, the first thing she did was unpack her blue carry-on bag, empty out all the pills, and flush them down the toilet. Her doctor had cautioned her never to stop taking her pills without consulting him first, and especially not to go cold turkey; it could be dangerous. She didn't remember the details of his warning—she hadn't really been listening. Perhaps her brain would explode? Or was it implode? She wasn't sure.

Wearily she sat on the narrow bed with its thin blue bedspread and waited for something to happen. Nothing did. Nothing at all.

The whole thing had been a sham. Like a small, foolish man posing as an omniscient Wizard of Oz.

Never again would she take another pill. From this day forth she'd be normal.

* * *

Normal—ha!

You sit up in bed, smirking. You've never been normal, not for one day in the past twenty-seven years since that afternoon in the dorm. Even before this unnamed illness struck, you weren't normal. You've only become, with time, better at hiding your strangenesses and abnormalities. Still, they're always there, lurking inside, and anyone who lived with you day in day out, like Perry, would know that. For instance, a couple of months ago you attended a play where, without warning the audience in advance, strobe lights were used. As soon as these started, Perry threw his jacket over your head—the same gesture as an executioner throwing a hood over the head of a condemned person—because flashing lights can trigger seizures. For the same reason, you refused to drive Perry and yourself to a concert ten days ago on a rainy evening, even though, with Perry's car in the repair shop, it was your car being driven. At night, the blinking, undulating headlights of the oncoming traffic discombobulate you; and it's even worse if it's raining: then the lights expand to monster size, flicker weirdly, and morph from one shape to another like spectres in a haunted house. You aren't sure if you actually "seizure" anymore, but flashing lights give you a feeling that you call "eppy". It's as if you're unravelling, literally coming apart—each molecule in your body dissolving—like when they "beam up" someone on *Star Trek*.

Ultimately, though, these sorts of eccentricities are no big deal in terms of your daily life. Perry doesn't mind covering your face at plays or concerts, or doing the driving—in fact, he enjoys being the driver (it's that male thing). He also welcomes the opportunity for gallantry, like the evening after the play, when he filled your glass with water (and then your goblet with wine) at the home of some friends. Obviously, you can pour your own drinks. But when you are either sleep-deprived or stressed—which unfortunately is quite a lot of the time—your coordination suffers. On these occasions, in order to pour a glass of water without spilling, you have to concentrate intensely, and you frown and hold your breath the way a six-year-old would if attempting this task. It requires your full and undivided attention, which means you must stop talking so you can focus on nothing else in the world except safely transferring the water from the pitcher into your glass. It always fills you with admiration when people do this sort of thing without a second thought. For example, your friend Shauna last week, chatting away volubly while pouring out two steaming cups of tea and serving you skillfully, quickly, and successfully a precariously wobbling wedge of chocolate mousse cake. You can serve a cup of tea if you must, along with a slice of cake—if it's normal cake, meaning relatively stable and untrembling—but certainly not at the same time as carrying on a conversation. No way. What's that expression people say to describe a very stupid person (an imbecile or a moron)? *They can't walk and chew gum at the same time.* Well, you can't talk and pour at the same time. You've never understood why socializing has to be combined with food. You're capable of conversing at a dinner party without spilling any food or drink on yourself, but it requires concentration and effort. And after an hour or two of this, you are fatigued.

All this is trivial, though. Your life, by any standard, is a normal one. You have a husband, two children, a home, a career, and you even (mainly in the daytime) drive a car. Your mother was wrong about all those things. You have achieved everything you dreamed of (*dreamed*—that tainted word!). Even so, you are not entirely normal. In your clumsiness and inability to tolerate flashing lights, there is still some residue from your epilepsy days. The ghost of the drugged robot lives on. And now there's also this bizarre sickness you get once a month. Perhaps the two things are related. Maybe what you have now is a consequence of all the pills you took? But then why did it wait till you turned forty-two to kick in? That makes no sense.

Also making no sense is Perry. Whatever is wrong with you—your present illness, your longstanding poor motor control—Perry takes it in stride. One of the things you love about him is that when you spill, drop, or break things, he doesn't get angry or ridicule you. You've been uncoordinated since the day you met and it's never bothered him. All he says as he's sweeping up the teacup shards from the floor is, "We'll have to buy another teacup" (or bowl, or plate, or vase). Then he sees your face and says kindly, "It's only a cup." He doesn't understand your mortification each time this kind of thing occurs. To him, your clumsiness carries no special meaning. Some people, in his view, are more coordinated than others, just as some people are better drawers than others. He can't draw; you can't serve mousse cake while chatting. So what?

To you, though, that shattered teacup (or picture frame, or blender, or cell phone) is a direct outgrowth of your epileptic past—growing from it like a polyp on the putrid, spongy flesh of a sick brain—and therefore proof of your defectiveness, and cause for the deepest shame. Perry's easygoing acceptance of your clumsiness is impossible for you to trust. It seems to you almost abnormal. You press him sometimes, demanding to know why your lack of coordination doesn't bother or anger him.

"I don't know," he says. "I guess to me it's just part of the package."

The last time you raised this, becoming quite insistent, he finally said with a sigh, "Do you *want* it to bother me? It doesn't. But if it matters so much to you, I can try."

Classic Perry. You smiled uncertainly. "Are you really sure it's okay?"

"I've only told you a hundred times."

You have similar conversations about your current illness. "Do you hate me when I'm sick?" you ask him. You hate yourself when you're sick, so it seems strange to you that he doesn't.

But he doesn't. He only wants you to get well.

You get out of bed, the carpet tickling your feet. In the bathroom the cold water splashed on your face is refreshing and makes you laugh. You feel fine. There is no fever, blurred vision, nausea, or buzzing in your ears. You're tired but it's not a drugged, confused sort of fatigue; only normal tiredness. Your mind is clear. You shower, washing off the smell and slime of sickness and these four awful days. You shampoo your hair, enjoying the luxuriant lather and rubbing it all over your body. There is a clash between its lavender scent and that of the body wash you now apply ("hot chili pepper"), but together they blend on your body into something new, at once soothing and stimulating, sweet and spicy. You dry off roughly with a towel and sit, naked, on the edge of your bed. You'll rest for a bit. Just In Case. But a couple of minutes pass and you are still all right, so you rise and start tidying your room. You toss all the stinky clothes into the hamper and clear away the dried compresses, pills, and used Kleenexes. From the far corner of the room you retrieve the banana you flung against the wall earlier this morning. You wipe off the banana mush from the spot that it splatted against and scoop up the strips of broken peel and dribbled pulp that have seeped into the carpet. You throw on some jeans and a sweatshirt and carry the tray with the remains of your breakfast down to the kitchen. The place looks like a cyclone hit it. Grimy dishes are piled high in the sink, nearly toppling; the table, counters, and stovetop are filthy; and something on the floor sticks to the bottom of your shoes as you walk, making a ripping sound with each step. You wipe the round aqua glass table, sit down, and rest. Your forehead is damp, you're sweating, but that's normal, isn't it, after all this exertion? The kitchen is silent. No laughter is trickling up through the floor from Perry's basement office. There's no sound at all. He could be doing his calculations, working on a spreadsheet for a client, with Charlene typing on her computer nearby. Charlene doing whatever Charlene does. Oh, who cares anyway? Never mind about that.

You're feeling fine. Could you really be okay now, and able to teach tomorrow? You've been sick for only four days; how can this bout of the illness already be over? Maybe you're not yet truly well. Perhaps this is a repeat of when you danced two days ago, and felt fine—in fact fantastic—but actually were not. You can no longer rely on your senses. You've learned to mistrust feeling well.

But you do feel well. It's not merely the absence of fatigue, pain, and your other symptoms; you feel energy, life, coursing through your veins. Outside the window a bird, perched on a snowy branch, sings a chirpy song. Imagine: February, and still there are birds singing! Apparently there is always cause for joy and celebration, even in the dead of winter. The windowsill is edged with frost in an irregular lacy pattern. It was a freezing February day like this one when you and Perry got married, surrounded by your families. Daddy's now dead. You slice some cucumbers. Chop chop chop, the sound strangely comforting in its even rhythm, the assertive, confident ring of the knife saying Yes. Yes. Yes. You're fine. You're fine. You're fine.

You dice a green pepper: a squishier, juicier sound, and the sharp green scent bites your nostrils. Green is the colour of spring; maybe in honour of spring, renewal, and health, you'll make yourself a snack of only green foods. Laughing, you throw onto a placemat a handful of pistachios; they rattle like dice as they fall, colliding into each other. You add a cucumber, a pickle, a pepper, and a scoop of mint chip ice cream. You devour it all in seconds, so fast that the cold of the ice cream hurts your teeth. Everything's delicious.

You push away the detritus in front of you on the kitchen table, including enough pistachio shells to have built a house or a tower with your kids when they were little. You phone Sarah. "Whazzup, Mom?" Sarah answers, and you laugh, high on the sugar from the ice cream or maybe just from feeling like yourself again, healthy and alive. Sarah's at work now, at her part-time job as a computer programmer, so she can only talk for a minute. A minute later you hang up laughing. Ronnie you'll call later; on Tuesdays he has classes all day. They're both coming over on Saturday for lunch. They don't know, and won't know, that you've been sick again. You won't tell them and, following your instructions, neither will Perry. Why should they be burdened with worry about you? It's not as if there was anything they could have done to help. And by Saturday you'll be perfectly fine. In fact, it seems to you—you can never be one hundred percent sure, but you believe—that you are perfectly fine right now.

You lean over and grab, from next to the house phone, a black gel pen and a pad of green, square, 4x4 inch Post-it notes. Seated at the kitchen table, you mildly, abstractedly begin to doodle. Soon you are drawing away happily, despite a vague sense of guilt. Instead of drawing, you could be reviewing your class notes for tomorrow or perusing the report for the meeting on fiscal governance you'll have to attend right before your class. (Such a boring committee!—your least favourite one of the six that Ned has stuck you on.) Alternatively, you could be answering at least some of the emails from the pile that has accumulated over the past four days; doing volunteer work (you sometimes make and deliver bag lunches to a homeless shelter); or "engaging with the world" through social media. But you have no desire to engage with the world. You want to be left alone to draw. There always seems to be something more important than your need to make art. When the kids were young, naturally their needs had to take precedence over yours. But now? Fuck it. You have a right to do what you want The universe can manage without you for a little while. What was that Pete Seeger song?

> *Well may the world go, the world go, the world go,*
> *Well may the world go, when I'm far away.*
> *Well may the skiers turn, the swimmers churn, the lovers burn,*
> *Peace may the generals learn, when I'm far away.*

Exactly. You wish no harm to anyone, and only the best for the world, but you're going to leave it for a spell. Your hand is continuing to draw, as if with a will of its own; it leads you forward, and you glide along with the joy of the moving pen. You feel a click inside you—familiar to you when you draw: the click of a door opening into dark, cold, hidden chambers in a stone castle. You wonder if this experience of yours when you're creative is, neurologically speaking, similar to an epileptic seizure—if, when you are drawing, your synapses fire lots of extra electrical impulses—because at these times you enter an altered state. You lose all conscious awareness of your surroundings, and even of your own body. So perhaps there is a relationship between art and epilepsy. Certainly there are many famous creative people who had epilepsy. You know by heart the list of names that you first discovered, and memorized, in college. It made you feel better about yourself and your epilepsy, and you were honoured to belong to this special, elite club—a far more impressive one than your Art Club in high school; this one spanned the entire globe and most of human history. Still drawing, you smile across the millennia at the other members of this club, your brothers and sisters in spirit: Leonardo da Vinci, Michelangelo, Van Gogh; Tchaikovsky, Beethoven, Gershwin; Dickens, Hemingway, Flaubert, Agatha Christie, Edgar Allan Poe, Lewis Carroll, and Dostoevsky (who wrote *The Idiot* about a man with epilepsy); Socrates; Newton; Caesar, Caligula, Alexander the Great, Napoleon, Lenin, Theodore Roosevelt, Harriet Tubman, and Joan of Arc. Joan of Arc they burnt as a witch. Over the centuries, epilepsy was believed to be associated with witchcraft or possession by the devil; its only cure: exorcism through death. As a child, you had a great cackle of a laugh, and Daddy used to say, "If you lived five hundred years ago, they'd have burned you at the stake." You've always felt an affinity with Joan of Arc.

Your hand has kept on moving during these ruminations and you've finished a drawing. You peel it off from the pad, put it aside, and start to fill in another Post-it with cartoons. You have always been afraid of the craziness in your mind but you aren't afraid of it when it comes to your art. Here it's okay. When Miss Mellon liked and accepted your artwork, it meant she also liked and accepted your mind; and since the days of Miss Mellon, quite a few other people have reacted the same way. In the land of comics it is safe to let your madness flap its vulture wings.

You draw and draw, and time passes, but you have no sense of it at all. You completely lose track of time when drawing. You're in a different time zone then: a zone of eternal time. Which is why you are so startled, jarred, even alarmed, by the loud, sudden **Brrrrring! Brrrrring!** of the phone. The sound is an attack on you: it is invading—breaking into, and breaking—your inner world. An echo of your mother shouting at you, trying to bring you back into "reality" from somewhere else. *Why are they always interrupting me? Why won't they leave me alone?* For just a moment, the lapse of one phone ring, you consider not answering the call. But you're not allowed to do that: to separate yourself, disengage from society. That's what seizures are, and they make people angry at you. But now you yourself are angry.

"Yes," you say into the phone with asperity. You know you sound cold, even hostile, but—regardless of who is on the other end of the line—you don't care. You hate being interrupted at any time, but especially when drawing, and all the more so now, when doing this for the first time in five days.

"Lily, it's Cheryl from school."

Ned's secretary. A total bitch. You can't stand her. She's Ned's little spy and reports back to him in minute detail about everyone. Probably even how many pee breaks each faculty member takes. It's Communist Russia in their department, thanks to Cheryl and Ned.

"What's up?" you ask. You almost said Sarah's "Whazzup," but caught yourself in time. You can imagine Cheryl reporting your *Whazzup* to Ned, telling him you sounded like a teenager instead of a professional instructor at a college.

"Ned wants to know if you're coming in tomorrow. If you'll be able to teach your Intro to Comics class."

"Of course I am. I told him I'd be coming."

"Well, he wanted to make sure."

He doesn't trust me. You restrain yourself from saying something you'll regret. "I'll be there."

"Great. I'll tell him."

You hang up. Asshole. He'd be over the moon if you'd had to cancel tomorrow's class; he could have got rid of you once and for all. Well, sorry to disappoint you, Ned. On a fresh Post-it you sketch a caricature of him, exaggerating his baldness, fat lips and huge ears, and placing his right hand inside the front buttons of his jacket. Then you crumple it and hurl it into the trash. You try to return to the drawing you were in the middle of when the phone rang, but you can't; the flow has been broken. That call fucked you up.

"Ned, you afatottari!" you cry. (Grandfather-fucker!) (Icelandic)

"Cagati in mano e prenditi a schiaffi!" (Shit in your hand and then slap yourself in the face!) (Italian)

"Kisama tama!" (Lord of donkey balls!) (Japanese)

Smiling, feeling better, you pick up your pen again. *Where was I? What was I doing?* Ah. Now it comes back to you. The second cartoon is close to being done—quickly you finish it. You rip it off the pad, set it aside, and fill a few more green Post-its with cartoons. Then you lean back and examine all your pictures. You're a little surprised; you're never sure what you're drawing until it's been completed. Slowly you nod, satisfied.

A door opens and Perry appears, as if on cue arriving to reward you for accomplishing this task. He reminds you of a university chancellor at a graduation ceremony about to place a mortarboard on your head. Or a king, a crown. You laugh. "I'm well," you say.

"I can tell." He is gazing at you with obvious pleasure. "You have colour in your face. You look like yourself again. And you're drawing."

A habit of a lifetime—you can't help yourself: you cover the drawings with your hand.

"Is it lunchtime?" you ask. "I'm starving."

Wedensday

STRIDING DOWN THE long corridor of the school, I feel strong and capable, my usual healthy self. The walls are brightly lit, my heels clickety-clack along the floor, and everything around me is cheerful and familiar. The colleagues I pass on my way greet me pleasantly, and so do the secretaries when I enter the main office of our department, even Cheryl with her phony smile. My mailbox is crammed to overflowing and I'm running late, rushing to make it on time to the college-wide meeting on fiscal governance. Returning to the hallway, I see my favourite student, Holly, sitting on the floor with another student, someone who twice has been belligerent toward me. It's startling to see them together—a sort-of-friend of mine in cahoots with a sort-of-enemy. Last Friday Holly was in my class when I got ill, ended the lesson early, and fled the room, staggering.

"Lily!" she calls out now. "How are you? Are you okay?"

"I'm fine, thanks, Holly. Never better. See you on Friday!"

I wave at her, ignoring her glowering friend, and hurry off. Fifty yards on, I get waylaid by two Guatemalan students holding hands —apparently they're a couple now—who inquire about my midterm assignment. I answer as briefly as I can, and by the time I arrive, panting, at the meeting, everyone else is seated and the proceedings are about to begin. I take the only empty chair, located between two burly men: one from my department and the other a stranger from elsewhere in the college. An acrid tang of cheap coffee hangs in the air, emanating from the paper cups dotting the table and mixing with the musty smell that reigns in all these old classrooms. The next fifteen minutes are as dull as I expected. I did, in the end, read the report that we're discussing, but even so I have nothing to contribute and just listen passively. Which is fine. All I'm required to do is attend the meetings of this committee, and I am doing that, thereby fulfilling my contractual obligation. Ned won't be able to find fault with me, at least in this respect. He is not here, of course, the lazy sod; he almost never shows up to committee meetings. But he does review all the minutes afterward, and as long as he sees my name among those listed as Present, as opposed to those listed as Absent, I am safe.

Absent, Present—those words again.

The voices drone on and on. I glance around the table at my colleagues, half of whom I hardly know. No one here has any idea that I've been sick for the past four days, not even the three people from my own department. How could they? Who's ever still at work at four-fifteen on a Friday afternoon, other than me, the sucker with the worst possible teaching schedule? And even if they knew I'd been absent, they'd probably have imagined—given that it is mid-February in Canada—that I had only a bad cold or flu. Everyone assumes I am normal, same as them. I scan all the faces: what a healthy-looking crowd! Not a sniffle or a cough in the bunch. Though who knows—perhaps some of them, like me, have a hidden, secret illness.

The discussion flows on and the room fills with dollar signs. We view financial charts on a screen and hear gloomy economic forecasts. Today we have to decide whether to continue with our traditional investments plan or try a new approach. It's not the first time we've discussed this, and ordinarily I consider this topic not only boring but inconsequential. Our college is in an excellent and enviably stable financial situation, thanks to two large endowments—it is not in dire straits or at risk of having to close down any departments or programs—so, for the foreseeable future anyway, it won't make any difference which strategy we pursue. Today, though, I gradually become interested in the conversation. It's a relief, after being sick, to focus on something that is outside myself and relatively

trivial. A debate has begun and some of the speakers are quite im-
passioned. Directly across from me, an obese economist is thumping
the table with his fist, and on his third thump he knocks over a
coffee cup and out spills a lazy dribble. For a fraction of an instant,
I'm alarmed for him: *Will he get in trouble for spilling his drink?* but
immediately that dissipates: *No, of course not.* He himself seems to
barely notice the coffee—which the blond woman next to him has
quickly thrown a couple of napkins over—as he angrily asserts the
desirability of investing in venture capital. I couldn't care less about
venture capital, but I gaze at this man in fascination. Such intensity
and ardour! How marvelous that someone can care so much about
a matter so trivial. This man seems like a classic example of health
and normalcy since, to me, the essence of a healthy, normal life is
the capacity to be enthusiastic about little things. This obese economist most likely would not consider venture capital "little," but that's
exactly the point. Normal, healthy humans experience the trivial
details of their lives as important. Whereas a sick person does not.
When you're sick, the illness boils down your life to its bare essen-
tials, steaming away everything else, and leaving you with nothing
but big existential questions that have stark, binary answers. Such as
(if you have Stage Four cancer): Will I live or will I die? Or, in my
case when sick: Will I, or will I not, be able to resume a normal life?
For sick people, nothing matters except the two potential outcomes
available to them—one good, one bad. It's very black and white. In
contrast, a healthy person has a huge multiplicity of potential outcomes, goals, interests, commitments, and entanglements, and because there are so many, sometimes even in the hundreds, each one
is quite small in size. Way smaller than either of the two halves of a
binary focus (such as Life vs. Death, or Sickness vs. Health)—so
sometimes sick people view healthy people as trivial. It is wrong,
though, to belittle the littleness of each of their many concerns.
Because each of these tiny particles, like the shards of broken coloured glass inside a kaleidoscope, comprise the building blocks of a
normal life. They are the cells in its body. And without them, we
would only be able to envision our world through a bi-chromatic,

black-and-white prism. Missing out on all the beautiful and diverse colours of life.

All around me people are arguing with each other, including the man on my left with the blond woman; meanwhile, the dribbled coffee (the sopping napkins notwithstanding) has almost reached my section of the table. I am happy. Having just concluded that the capacity for triviality is the litmus test of health and normalcy, I now know for sure that my latest bout of illness is behind me because on and off all morning, starting with the drive here, a most trivial thought has been swimming through my mind. I have been obsessed with maple syrup. More precisely, the lack thereof. My local supermarket and all the corner stores in my neighbourhood are completely out of it, and I must get some by tonight at the latest. Fern's husband Cliff's favourite dessert is maple syrup cake and I've promised to make one and bring it over tomorrow night to his birthday dinner. So it's crucial that I track down some maple syrup today. (*Crucial!* Am I actually using the word *crucial* in relation to maple syrup?) I also need (*Need?* Really?) to stop at the dry cleaner on the way home today because the outfit I want to wear tomorrow night has been waiting there since before I got sick. Such trivial thoughts. Such healthy, normal-person thoughts! I feel a surge of gratitude. I'm so thankful for my health, for this little bit of goodness—this petit bon, not petit mal—that tears sting my eyes. *Get a hold of yourself, you're in a meeting, for Christ's sake!* I blink them away.

The meeting adjourns and I saunter down the corridor toward my office to grab a quick lunch before heading to my class. I am strangely euphoric, even though there is nothing special about walking down a corridor; corridors are merely a route for getting from one place to another. Unless you want to wax all philosophical or poetic and say a corridor is a metaphor for our lives: the brief, lit passageway between two dark eternities (the one before our birth and the one after our death). But I am no philosopher or poet, and I don't care if a corridor is something big and symbolic or small and concrete (as this corridor, made of concrete, literally is). I am just glad to be here now. There is a bounce, almost a dance, in my step, as I continue down the hall, and I am grinning foolishly, even when I reach my office and sit at my desk. I eat the delightful avocado sandwich I brought from home, followed by a sweet and perfect clementine (*Oh my darling Clementine!*). And that's what I'm humming as I make my way to class.

* * *

I like my Wednesday class. The twelve young people in it are all hard workers, keen about cartooning, appreciative of my teaching, and on time with their assignments. My colleagues disdain, and dislike, teaching first-year foundation courses, but I like getting students first off the bat so I don't have to waste time helping them unlearn all the nonsense they were previously taught. Last time I taught a second-year course, it took weeks to unravel all their woolly misconceptions, and then several weeks more till they understood how to re-knit their ideas from scratch. With today's course on cartooning, I'm trying to lay down a foundation for them as solid as the cement foundation of a house, one on which they can securely stand and also build their own artwork and careers, so these don't topple, technically or artistically, like blocks in Blockhead. This afternoon I quickly get my students laughing and involved. The exercises I finessed two days ago work exactly as I hoped. We take a ten-minute break after the first half of the class; then, for the second half, two students present on their projects. I always tell my students they should draw from the heart—*draw* with the obvious meaning, but also *draw* as in "to haul up from a deep well." Your cartoons, I say, should contain blood—blood from cutting the pound of flesh closest to your heart. And in their proposals for a graphic novel, both of today's presenters have followed this advice. The first presentation is about a failed romance, and Leticia has tears in her eyes as she posts on the whiteboard her red, yellow, and green illustrations of a sleazy-looking guy cheating on his girlfriend. In the following frame, with Leticia using Reality Check Comic font, the tearful girlfriend asks the reader: "How much of your heart should you give to another? The more of yourself you expose, the more vulnerable you are. How much can you ever really trust someone?" I am fortunate to have Perry, someone who would never cheat on me. I know this with the hard certainty of bedrock. Our marital bed is not rocky. Notwithstanding my moments of "sickness paranoia," as I think of it: the insecurity and jealousy I feel only when I'm sick. Leticia's graphic novel is set in the 1950s and she has provided a soundtrack to accompany it. She has the girlfriend—while she's vacillating between self-delusion and facing the truth about her boyfriend—singing, "All I Have To Do Is Dream." One of my favourite songs, and one that I danced to three days ago. Leticia finishes presenting, and her classmates ask her questions and offer feedback on her proposal. Then I add comments of my own.

Now it is José's turn. His idea for a graphic novel is the hard-hitting, bitter story of his family's efforts to cross the border from Mexico into the United States, and their trials and tribulations in this process, including getting fined, imprisoned, and sent back to Mexico three times. José's two central images are a barbed wire fence and a blue-uniformed border official with cold brass buttons turning away a ragged family of five.

I know this border official. I can see him handing me back my passport. Sickness is a foreign country with its own rules and laws. When I arrive there every month, they take my passport away. Then they hang me for a while over the edge of an abyss, and pull me back again barely in time, right before I reach oblivion. A form of torture, a sort of waterboarding without the water. Each time that I return from the abyss and once again am well—which always feels like a miracle, Lazarus rising from the dead—I no longer belong in this country of illness, and the border official gives me back my passport. This happens only to me. Only I am allowed to leave. I'm the lucky one, the sole escapee from this sickness colony. Everyone else will be trapped here forever. As I depart, they all watch me from behind the Plexiglass wall at the airport with large, envious, beseeching, pleading, hopeless eyes. The eyes of the damned. I ascend the escalator like an angel ascending to heaven, and the hands of the people I've left behind in hell wave from below like electric eels reaching out to me.

I shake off this image, stand, and facilitate a class discussion about José's project. Then I proffer some feedback of my own and, to illustrate the point I'm making, I pivot to face the half of the whiteboard without José's sketches. I pick up the blue marker with the blueberry smell—*Who invented scented markers? They should be arrested*—and raise it toward the board. And with this exact hand motion, I recall—one second before the marker touches the whiteboard—how, last Friday, the marker became suddenly too heavy to hold and I found myself drenched in sweat. (Body memory, they call this: I didn't remember this hand motion from Friday, but evidently my body did.) What if the same thing happens again now? Will I get sick the instant this marker makes contact with the board? I touch the marker to the whiteboard. Nothing weird occurs. The marker begins to draw, and the cartoon it produces is as skillful and precise as ever. Using this cartoon, I teach for ten more minutes, then the class concludes. A few students linger to talk to me. After they disperse, I step out into the hall, and as I approach the elevator to exit the building, I see Ned walking toward me. His ears are sticking out even more prominently than usual. We nod at each other. When we're within hearing distance, he says, "You're here." His tone is regretful, as if he wishes I were still sick so he could fire me once and for all.

"Yes," I reply, feeling strange to be confirming that I am, actually, where he sees me. "I just finished my class."

He nods gravely and continues down the corridor. I follow him with my eyes. *Asshole.*

Driving home, I take the route where the highway skirts the lake in the shape of an archer's bow. I call Ronnie on speaker: he's about to enter a seminar so we chat only briefly. As I'm hanging up, I spot a mini-market off to the left, jump across two lanes, and screech to a halt in its parking lot. I'm in luck: they have maple syrup! I buy six mini-bottles, each in the shape of a maple leaf. Browsing the rack of mini-cakes (is everything in a mini-mart mini-sized?), I spy some ready-to-eat cinnamon pinwheels and devour one of the two in the packet before even reaching the cash. I hand the cashier the half-empty wrapper, along with a bag of multicoloured marshmallows (miniatures, of course) and a single sachet of cocoa. At home I will float some marshmallow mini-snowmen in a sea of hot chocolate.

⁓ I exit through the back door and come face to face with the lake. It is a deep indigo broken up with floating patches of ice, and the sky above it is a paler shade of blue with orange streaks near the horizon. To my left, some seagulls take flight, noisily flapping their wings, and they squawk as they slice through the pastel sky in a perfect V-formation like fighter planes in wartime. To my right, there's a cluster of denuded trees with their arms arched upward imploringly, and I hear the whoosh of traffic from the other side of the mini-market. Inhaling the bracing winter air, I catch a whiff of decaying kelp. The waves crash rhythmically against the rocks, and I sense, rather than see, the fish leaping below the surface. I know they are there—along with a magnificent underwater world. So much is hidden from view. I looked fine at school today; no one could have guessed how sick I was just two days ago. But I'm normal now. The illness is gone. Nothing's left of it but a faint shadow, like those lizards in Mexico that you see only a flash of once they've already skittered away.

The end of my long red scarf is getting whipped every which way by the wind. It hits me in the face; I grab it and wrap it a couple of times around my neck. How strange yesterday morning was, with all that reminiscing about my epilepsy. This almost never happens. I keep the heavy, creaking lid of that Pandora's box firmly closed. Or maybe that's not what epilepsy is. Perhaps it's a treasure chest like Aladdin's, its crown jewel being the gift of creativity, for me as it was for all the famous people on that list. No, I don't believe that. Still, I'm lucky I had epilepsy as a child. I was lucky to have epilepsy and not (as they called it then) mental retardation, because you can outgrow epilepsy, but you can't outgrow M.R. I had epilepsy, so for my first eighteen years I was abnormal, but then I outgrew it. The epilepsy, I mean. You can't ever really outgrow being abnormal. You don't wake up one morning the same as everyone else, talking and dressing the way all the other girls in seventh grade do, with their Cossack boots and tall white fur hats.

I notice this lake is bordered by a forest and remember that in there somewhere there's a zipline that Perry and the kids once rode on. It cuts through this forest, appearing as a single red thread in a lumpy, dark green sweater. There's a red thread running through my life, too: sickness. First the epilepsy; then this mysterious illness. Is there some connection between them? I don't know. I'm no doctor. Yet it seems doubtful since what I have now is not neurological, but viral. The two pieces of this jigsaw puzzle don't fit. I suppose I could force them together, if this were a C minus graphic novel, by making my current illness psychological. I could have the protagonist come to terms with the epilepsy in her past; then, magically, her present-day illness would vanish. What nonsense. I could never write anything so ridiculous and phony. The only link I can see between my two illnesses is that, because of them, I've never been able to take my health for granted, as most people do, so I've never been normal. And I don't imagine this will change.

I watch, and listen to, the waves. They roll in, frothing and crashing against the shore, then roll out again. Wave after wave after wave. Waving hello and waving goodbye. Their roar is so loud I barely hear my phone ringing. I let it go to voicemail. Between the phone and email, it seems I always have to be connected to somebody or something. At times I feel like part of a colony of ants (and aunts, and uncles), with no way to escape its collective mind. I might as well be in Orwell's *Nineteen Eighty-four*. I am not allowed to separate myself from the herd, to be alone with my thoughts, in my own private world, for longer than five minutes. If I ever do, someone will scream at me, snap their fingers in front of my eyes, shake me until my teeth rattle, or barge in on me in the bath. Of *course* someone had to interrupt me while I tried to stand quietly for a while by a beautiful lake.

I'm annoyed with the caller but curious, too, so I check my messages. It was Thea touching base about Saturday night, when Perry and I will be meeting her and Phil for dinner and a play. Twice in the course of this play there will be strobe lights, so ordinarily I'd avoid this show, but it's gotten such fabulous reviews I decided to make an exception. I'll have to make sure to get the aisle seat, and have Perry sitting next to me, with Phil on his other side. That way Thea, three seats down from me, won't see when Perry throws his coat over my head. Phil won't notice a thing like that—a mathematician, he has his head in the clouds, filled to the brim with numbers—but Thea would for sure. And it would puzzle her, and at the intermission she'd inquire about it. Probably I should prepare some story in case she notices anything. Maybe I'll say I always get cold in these drafty old theatres and Perry's coat keeps me warm. This wouldn't account, of course, for why Perry threw his coat over my face, rather than around my shoulders. Perhaps I can say that my face gets cold? No, that's absurd. I'll have to come up with something better by Saturday.

If you're hiding something, it means there is shame underneath it. Even if you think there isn't. I read this somewhere and have no idea if it's true. But what is true is that none of my friends know about my epilepsy—not even Thea, Fern, or Dierdre, my three closest. (Closest, closets—almost the same word.) The topic has never come up and I've seen no reason to raise it. If I chose to at some point, I'd have to confront the stereotypes they most likely have about people with epilepsy, thanks to our negative portrayal in movies and our image in the popular imagination. My friends almost certainly picture someone on the ground with their arms and legs jerking crazily, and perhaps they're also drooling or wetting themselves. I'd have to educate them and explain to them that—even if I once had a grand mal seizure—that out-of-control person has nothing to do with who I am now. Why would I do this, though? What possible benefit could result from going into all this with my friends? None that I can see.

Bang! Startled, I spin around: Behind me the door has slammed. From inside the warm, brightly lit mini-market, someone has emerged and is coming toward me, into the cold shadows. A man. A large man. And I am all alone.

Ah, it's only the cashier: the efficient, brown-skinned guy with the broken-looking nose. We nod at each other while he lights a cigarette. It must be his break time and he's stepped out here for a smoke.

"Nice sunset," he says.

"Sure is."

There's a companionable silence between us as he smokes. Then he grinds the butt under his heel, says, "Have a nice evening," and goes back inside. The sun is dropping behind the horizon, and I feel the biting chill emanating from the lake. I should get moving. I'm cold and I don't like driving home in the dark. Walking to the car, I unfurl the scarf from my neck and wind it, like wrapping a mummy, around my forehead, nose, and mouth. My breaths come back to me warm, smelling and tasting of wool. As I bend down to get into the car, my phone rings. It's Perry asking when I'll be home.

"I'm on my way," I tell him. "Twenty minutes max."

I hang up smiling. Such a sweet guy. He probably asked this because he's preparing supper for us and wants to time it right. I'm lucky to be married to him. And I'm proud to be married to someone normal with no disability of any kind. I'd wanted to marry a Normal, the way an immigrant to Canada might hope to marry someone they think of as a "real" Canadian—someone who was born in Canada—to help ease their way into the new country. I was a foreigner seeking citizenship in the country of Normals. But I also loved Perry. We loved each other.

Now, though, as I drive home, I wonder if love is enough. If it's possible for any normal person, however loving and well-intentioned, to truly understand, and accept, someone like me. How would Perry react if he knew—really knew—about my seizures, my meds, and all those years of being a drugged robot? It's unclear. Because when you love someone, you're not loving just who they are now; you're loving also who they were—or who you imagine they were—before you met. Like that red-haired guy I met in college who asked me if I'd been popular in high school. It was important to him to ascertain that not only was I, at that fraternity party, attractive and charming, but that I always had been, and was never a wallflower. Perry loves who I am now, as well as the cute little girl he's seen in photos. But he's unaware that this girl is not all that I was.

I love driving, and there is pleasure in the confident, competent grip of my handsome green leather gloves—a birthday gift from Perry—on the steering wheel as I turn off the highway. It's true that I do sometimes feel there's a hole in our relationship because Perry doesn't fully know my past. But who's to say that a good marriage requires full disclosure? When I was a graduate student, I read a research study where they asked married women in Japan and the United States if they agreed with the statement: *There are some things that are best not shared with your husband.* Only ten percent of the American wives agreed with this, but among the Japanese it was close to ninety. As a young woman back then, I felt sorry for the Japanese wives: I thought their marriages sounded incomplete and lonely. But now these women seem to me wise. Not everything has to be shared. Perry already knows plenty about me—including about my current illness, which he has accepted amazingly well. Even so, this illness is a cartload of horse dung dumped onto the flatbed of our marriage. Somehow our marriage bed has survived this. But why would I dump onto it another cartload of shit? Everyone has their limits. Every relationship, like a truck, has a maximum weight it can carry. I am not willing to jeopardize what I have with Perry by laying on him my whole epilepsy story. I not only love him; I need him and depend on him, especially when I'm sick. To lose him would be to tumble off a cliff. A sheer drop downward. Sheer terror as I fall.

I drive through silent, snow-covered city streets. There are almost no cars. Just snow: snow on the roads, on the sidewalks, on the front lawns, on the rooftops—all of it glistening under the evening street lamps, brilliantly luminous and transcendent. Leticia's protagonist: *The more you expose yourself, the more vulnerable you are. How much can you ever really trust anyone?* Poor Leticia with tears in her eyes. Her presentation was good, though, and it was creative of her to include a soundtrack. I sing:

When I want you in my arms
When I want you and all your charms
Whenever I want you, all I have to do is
Drea-ea-ea-ea-eam, dream dream dream
Drea-ea-ea-ea-eam, dream dream dream ...

Suddenly I stop. *Dream? Dream!* How have I never noticed this before? Never made the connection in all the hundreds of times I've listened to this song. I love this song and it's about "dreams". That lovingly poisoned word.

I'm entering our neighbourhood and it feels familiar and comforting. Only three or four minutes till I'm home. This evening I should take it easy, this being my first day back at work after five days of illness, but I probably won't. I'll make Cliff's maple syrup cake. That's what I always do. That's what I always do wrong. I push myself. Normal people can push themselves—they can do a full day's work and then come home and do another dozen things that need doing around the house—but I can't. If I do that, I get over-tired, and the next day I can't sit up in bed. The only way to prevent a relapse and to stay well is to always view myself as a sick, or at least a "vulnerable," person. But it's intolerable to see myself this way. So I push—I drive—myself. Not to be merely normal, but super-normal. I drive myself like a racing car, trying to override all my limits.

I pull into our driveway and sit for a moment. It's so paradoxical. When I'm well, I need to think of myself as sick, in order to stay well. But if I regard myself as well (or "normal"), I become sick (and "abnormal"). It's all too subtle for the likes of me.

* * *

The house is warm and fragrant. In the hallway, hanging up my coat, I call out to Perry: "Chicken, broccoli, potatoes!" It's a game we play.

"Three out of three!" he shouts back.

In the kitchen, supper is tasty and relaxed as we exchange our news of the day. He's got a new client, and I'm glad for him because business has been slow the past few months. He, in turn, is relieved that I'm still fine and he's pleased my class went well. We laugh about Ned and update each other on the kids. After supper, he starts cleaning up while I, standing in the pantry with my back to him, assemble the ingredients for the maple cake. I hear a long silence and feel a tap on my shoulder. I turn around; he's holding something out to me and asking, "What are these?"

At first, I can't see what's in his hand. Then I recognize the green Post-it notes from near the phone that I drew on yesterday morning. As soon as I finished drawing, we ate lunch, so I must have removed them from the kitchen table, put them on top of the dishwasher, and forgotten all about them. My heart begins to pound.

"Oh, those," I say. "They're nothing." And I reach out to take them from him.

But he ignores my outstretched hand, and turns aside, frowning and studying the drawings. "What do you mean 'they're nothing'? They're very strange and disturbing. Almost sci fi."

"They're just pictures," I say nervously.

He's viewing each of them slowly, like checking a potentially defective deck of cards. "They're different in style from anything else you've done," he says. "And you've never drawn kids before. Tell me what these are." He peers at me. His tone was curious and friendly, it seemed merely conversational, but underneath this I could hear an edge of insistence. He is demanding an explanation. I don't want to give him one. I shouldn't have to. These pictures are mine. But I recognize that now that I am normal again, our relationship, too, has returned to normal. When you're sick, it's strange: you have the illusion that if only you were healthy, everything would be perfect. But once you've regained your health, you see that all you have is everyday life, with all its imperfections and annoyances. Now that I'm not sick anymore, gone is the gentle Perry who tends me when I'm ill. My bunny-rabbit-soft friend; my loving, almost maternal, caretaker.

Here once more is the usual Perry, who sometimes gets angry or stubborn, and out of the blue can become controlling and dig in his heels.

"I don't wish to discuss this," I say. "Give them back. They're mine."

Instead, he spins around, stretches his arm upward, and with his back to me, starts smacking our kitchen cupboards. *Smack, smack, smack, smack, smack*—he has stuck my five pictures onto the skinny white cupboard doors, one on each. The Post-its are shocking green against the white, and as square and box-like as five transplanted hedges against a white sky. Probably he didn't mean to be cruel, and perhaps he doesn't even realize he has placed the drawings out of my reach, but I feel frantic. Heather and Tim (never Bruce) used to do this: they'd grab a drawing of mine and wave it above my head, and I'd go crazy trying to retrieve it, leaping over and over again as high as I could, a diminutive monkey in the middle. Only when I'd screamed and begged and was in tears would they relent. I won't give Perry the same satisfaction.

"These are so creepy," he says, pointing at the pictures he's displayed. "And violent, too." He is gaping at them, mesmerized.

You're creepy and violent, I think but don't say. I squint so that all I can see are the five green hedges, not the actual drawings. I don't want to look at them. I'm normal now, and have been since yesterday, and feel no desire to re-enter the world these pictures represent. Yet at the same time I am drawn to them. I am drawn to what I have drawn. So I tilt back my head and peek upward. There, exhibited on this home-made gallery:

A girl with a dazed expression and a mark on her chin.

A little girl with snakes growing out of her head.

A child face down in the street, a schoolbag next to her sprawled-out right hand.

A teenager on her back on the floor, surrounded by kids on cushions and curls of bittersweet smoke, while her arms and legs jerk wildly.

A child face down in a bathtub, its dead body floating on the surface of the water.

These pictures hurt. I avert my eyes. Perry is still gazing at them, entranced. I sit at the kitchen table and stare at the linoleum floor, which is surprisingly filthy after my five-day absence from housework. I'll have to mop it tomorrow. Maybe the other floors, too. This house needs a good cleaning.

"Why does she have snakes in her hair?" he asks. I glance up; he is gesturing toward the second green square. "Is this meant to be a young Medusa?"

I don't reply. He has mixed up my pictures and exhibited them in the wrong order. It perturbs me but I resist the impulse to re-arrange them. Not that I could even if I wanted to: he's posted them at a height of seven or eight feet.

"And this child in the tub—is he floating, or did he drown? These cartoons are disturbing as hell."

This reminds me of this afternoon, when José and Leticia displayed their work on the whiteboard. What Perry just asked is similar to how I sometimes query my students about their projects: I enquire about a detail or two, followed by an overall remark. Though I would never tell a student their work was "disturbing as hell." I feel like I'm the student here, with Perry the teacher, and very soon I am going to have to explain my work, and myself. What was my intent with these cartoons, what devices and strategies did I employ in their execution, and to what extent do I believe I have succeeded in accomplishing my goals? When I teach, after the student presents I get the whole class to weigh in. Who will weigh in now, in addition to me and Perry? The teapot? The dishtowel? The vase of flowers?

"I don't know," I say listlessly. "You decide for yourself."

He is still standing, his back to me, peering at the drawings. The kitchen is dirty and disorderly, with greasy plates, pots, pans, glasses, and cutlery dumped haphazardly into the sink or strewn across the counter. The smell of leftover chicken and broccoli lingers unpleasantly in the air. But none of this exists for Perry; only my pictures, which have been hung on the cupboards like condemned criminals on gallows.

He whirls around and says, "Tell me what these drawings are."

"Why do you care?" I ask. "They're only cartoons."

"Then why won't you talk to me about them?" He steps closer to me and there's a pleading tone in his voice. "You always do when you show me your work. I'm always the first to see anything new."

"I know, but this time I feel different."

"You're acting secretive. Almost like you're hiding something."

I turn away from his accusing face and toward the drawings, which I am beginning to feel alienated from, almost as though they were drawn by someone else. Or as if their exposure to the air of this kitchen, containing this tense conversation about them, has changed them. Chemically even, the way spies' messages in invisible ink turn visible when exposed to certain elements. Perry viewing my drawings has altered their chemistry. And my own chemistry is reacting: I feel I am no longer me.

"Don't be silly," I say. "I simply don't want to discuss them now. Why are you making a big deal out of this?"

"Why are *you*?" he asks, glowering at me.

I glance at my pictures on the cupboards. These drawings are mine, not his; why has he taken them from me? If I were a foot taller, I would leap up and, like swiping at a tree branch laden with oranges, swipe down my pictures, and run off with my fruits to a secret hiding place where he wouldn't be able to see or ask about them ever again. But I can't, so I decide to act cool. Perhaps if he thinks these drawings don't matter to me, he'll leave them alone.

"I'm not. I told you, these pictures aren't important."

His eyes glitter. "Really? Okay. If they're so unimportant, how about I throw them out?" He swivels, reaching upward toward the five green squares.

"No!" I scream. "Dooooon't!" I'm surprised by the volume and vehemence in my voice.

So is he. Shocked, he drops his hand. "Wow," he says, stupefied. A curl of grey hair falls over his ear. "Okay, Lily. You win. Whatever this is about, have it your way. I thought we had no secrets from each other but I guess I was wrong. You're keeping something from me, and all of a sudden I'm on the outside."

"It's not a secret, Perry."

"Then why won't you tell me?" He looks, and sounds, close to crying.

I feel miserable but don't know what to say. Even if I wanted to share with him that part of my past, I have no idea how to go about it.

"What did you do, Lily?" he asks, trying to lighten the mood. "Commit a murder? Drown some kid in a bathtub?"

I smile wanly and shake my head. He is still standing, the pictures like a backdrop behind him, and I'm still seated at the table, which increases the height difference between us. He towers over me and, feeling dwarfed, I counterattack. "You have secrets, too, Perry. You don't tell me every little thing."

"I don't have secrets from you."

"Oh, yeah?"

"Yeah."

"What about Charlene?"

"What about her?"

"I hear you laughing together."

"So? We joke around sometimes."

"You don't laugh that way with me."

"Oh, come on. You can't be serious. Do you actually think ...?" He seems so stunned by what I'm suggesting that I can't help but believe him.

"Not really." Embarrassed, I stare down at the glass table. It has a scratch. "But when I'm sick, I wonder ..."

"And when you're not sick?"

I smile in spite of myself. "I don't wonder."

"So there. This is nothing. It's only your sickness. And you know it."

"I do."

"So why even raise this?"

"I'm not sure. You were pressuring me.'"

He nods slowly. Then he frowns. "Wait—are *you* having an affair? Is this projection?"

"No." I am indignant. "Of course not."

"All right," he says, his hands in his pockets. "I don't understand what all this is about, and it's making me nervous. But if you want your precious drawings so much—here, take them." He tears off the Post-its from the cupboards with a ripping sound—*zzzap zzzap zzzap zzzap zzzap*—and there is also a kind of ripping inside me. He hands me back my drawings.

I lay them down, this time in the right order, on the round aqua glass table. It is as round, aqua, and glassy as a lake, and on it there are now five floating square lilies.

Perry slumps down near me at the table, his head in his hands. He looks deflated, all the air gone out of him, a ruined balloon. I see how hard this has been on him—not only this conversation, or this week of my illness, but these last three years since I got sick. He seems older, tireder, frailer than I realized. He's usually so steady-as-you-go and unemotional that it's easy to forget how sensitive he is. He's not just my helper and protector; he is Perry, with his own insecurities and fears. And when did his hair turn this grey? It's a jolt to recognize how self-centered I've been, and how much I've taken him for granted.

What his bullying couldn't accomplish, his vulnerability does. I caress his shoulder. "It's not a secret," I say. He's still staring glumly at the table. "I don't have secrets from you, Perry. These pictures are about my epilepsy."

He looks up at me, astounded. Bewildered. "Your epilepsy? How?"

My mouth feels full of cotton wool and I have to push my words past it to get them out. "I had epilepsy when I was a kid."

"I know that."

"No, you don't. You don't know anything about it. All you know are the facts."

"I only know what you've told me. How can I know things you haven't told me about?"

"Maybe you don't want to know them," I say.

"I do."

"No, you don't."

"Don't tell me what I do and don't want. I'm eager to hear what's on your mind and what you've been drawing." He is handsome in his brown sweater.

"Trust me, you'll be sorry. It'll change everything between us. You'll never see me the same way again."

"That's ridiculous. You talk as if I'm a stranger who doesn't know you. What difference can a few pictures make? I'll still love you no matter what. Nothing can change that."

He's so naïve. Of course something can change that. All sorts of things can change that. Love is not immutable; and love is not always kind. (Isn't that a poem from somewhere?) "There's a lot you don't know," I say.

He brings his face close to mine. "So tell me."

I want to, but I don't know how. So I lie. "I'm making a graphic novel about this. About growing up with epilepsy." As soon as these words are out of my mouth, they are no longer a lie. Speaking them has made them true.

"I see," he says softly. He points to the first picture. "Is this where it begins? With snakes? They're very primeval! Garden of Eden-y. Does it all start in a garden?"

His eyes are emerald green. Shrewd, watching, alert, like a tiger's. No one else has eyes like these.

"Not exactly."

"Then where?" he asks.

He is interested. He's listening. There is a cracking inside me, a glacier breaking open in a warm, thawing sea. I know now how to tell this story. I place my finger on the forehead of the first girl—where her brain is, her crazy, bad brain. Then I touch the largest, fattest, most central snake growing out of her head. It bites me. I feel the pain of it—as well as the pain in my scalp from all the needles they stuck into it. The stench of the collodion nauseates me and makes me dizzy and weak. I'm afraid of the electricity they're going to turn on soon and inject into my head, and I don't want to sit in the chair where they will do this, the electric chair. I remove my finger from the snake. I take a couple of deep breaths. *I'm not a child anymore. I'm an adult.*

"She hated being four," I explain to him. "When she was three, she'd been herself. But soon after turning four, she became a drugged robot. Her body wasn't hers anymore. Something had taken it over and now it was like she was trapped inside a suit of armour, and she lumbered around stiffly, awkwardly, like a machine or a monster."

I continue and tell him the whole story of the first picture. He listens closely, his eyes on me. When I'm done, he starts to speak, but with two fingers I cover his lips. He nods. We gaze at each other as though we're playing a game of chess, each of us studying the other, trying to guess their next move.

I touch the second girl on her sprawled-out hand. "It was an old couple," I say. "Old! They were probably only fifty, just five years older than we are now! They scraped the girl up off the street. First the old man tried alone and failed. So he took the arms, and his wife took the legs, and they carried the girl out of the middle of the road where she'd been lying, and where, less than three minutes later, a big red truck rounding the corner would have run over her soft child's body, flattening it like a pancake."

I relate the rest of this story, and then the remaining three, until he's heard all five picture-stories. All of them told in the third person, as if that distant, long-ago girl has nothing to do with me. At the end of the fifth story, he is holding my left hand. I have no idea how that came about or when he took it; I slide my hand out of his. Outside the window the night is pitch black; the inside of our house is totally silent. I'm anxious about how he'll respond, but I'm not sorry I told him all this. Maybe I wanted him to know. Conceivably, I left my pictures on top of the dishwasher half on purpose, cognizant that he's the one who always loads and unloads it and was bound to discover them. Leaving my drawings there was like Hansel and Gretel leaving breadcrumbs behind them, to find their way home.

"Wow," he says. "Lily. I'm so sorry what you went through."

"Well. Now you know everything."

He tries to embrace me, but I resist. "Do you see me differently now?" I ask.

"If you mean, do I still love you," he says, half-smiling, "of course I do."

"Okay, you love who I am now. But you don't love the girl I was. You couldn't. Not this one—" I point to the girl with the mark on her chin. It looks like the physical expression of a curse, a sort of mark of Cain. "Or this one, or this. Or this ..." I touch each girl in turn.

"Of course, I could. I do."

I shake my head. "No one could love that girl. She wasn't cute, or beautiful, or at all how you picture her. You don't know how I was back then. I was disgusting."

"You weren't disgusting. You were sick."

"I was disgusting. I was a monster."

"You were a sick child."

He seems to love those girls more than I do. Which means that he loves *me* more than I do. It's a strange feeling when someone loves you more than you love yourself. And it's confusing to argue with them about your lovability because you're arguing against your own interests.

He tries to convince me. "What if one of our kids got sick?" he asks, and these words, even though they're only words, flush me with fear. "If Sarah or Ronnie had a sickness, God forbid—diabetes, or CP, or something else ... I don't know, epilepsy—would you, because of that, not love them? Would you stop loving them if they were ill?"

"Of course not. What a stupid question." There's nothing about Sarah or Ronnie—nothing they could say, or do, or be—that would wipe away my love for them, like erasing chalk from a slate. It's impossible to imagine such a thing, even hypothetically.

"See?" he says. "That's what I mean."

I see his point. And it works with regard to my children, but not with regard to the girl I once was, to that drugged robot. Even my infinite love for Sarah and Ronnie, and Perry's deep love for me, cannot eradicate the shame and self-loathing that for years melted like warm liquid collodion into my bones, and hardened there, until they became part of me.

And yet ... his love has softened, and lifted, the top layer of that glue. I can feel it. At least for now.

He gazes at me, smiling. Then he bends his head down toward the table—What's he doing? It looks as if he's going to sniff it!—and kisses, without touching them, each of the girls in the pictures. One he kisses on her chin, one on her back, one on her sprawled-out right hand, one on her jerking leg, and one on her cheek. He sits up. Then, leaning forward, kisses me on the mouth.

I laugh. And laugh. Perry is pleased. "Let's put these pictures on the fridge," he says. "As we used to do with the kids' artwork. You can leave them there, Lily, as long as you want."

I've never displayed any of my cartoons at home. I've never wished to. "I'm not sure," I say. "But maybe they can stay here for a bit." Just for tonight I will leave them on this round aqua glass table, like all my past selves floating on a lake. Floating, not drowning.

I stand. "We have work to do," I say. "We have to make a maple cake."

We make maple cake.

Then we make love.

Acknowledgements

It is a pleasure to acknowledge and thank everyone who has helped to make this book a reality.

Firstly, I am deeply grateful to Guernica Editions for publishing these novellas. It is an honour to be associated with what I consider the finest literary publisher in Canada. Specifically, I thank Michael Mirolla, Co-publisher and Editor-in-chief, for his leadership at Guernica and his appreciation of my work; Anna van Valkenburg, Associate Publisher, for her helpful and pleasant collaboration; David Moratto for his marvellous book covers, and Sonia Di Placido for her editing.

A heartfelt thanks, as well, to my friends—in Canada and else-where—who help mitigate the isolation of the writing life with their affection, good humour, intellect, and openhearted conversation.

Last but not least, I thank my husband, Dr. David Weiss, for his support and love during the sometimes harrowing writing of this book. His thoughtfulness, playfulness, intelligence, and enthusi-asm brightened my days and helped to sustain me. To him, my deepest gratitude.

About the Author

DR. NORA GOLD is a prize-winning author. Her first book, *Marrow and Other Stories*, won a Vine Canadian Jewish Book Award and was praised by Alice Munro. Her second book, *Fields of Exile*, won the inaugural Canadian Jewish Literary Award for best novel, and was acclaimed by Ruth Wisse and Irwin Cotler. *The Dead Man* was honoured with a Canada Council translation grant and published in Hebrew. Her recent book, *18: Jewish Stories Translated from 18 Languages*, which was praised by Cynthia Ozick and Dara Horn, is an anthology of translated works that originally appeared in the prestigious literary journal that Gold founded and edits, *Jewish Fiction .net* (www.jewishfiction.net).

Gold has a PhD in social work and, while a tenured professor, she conducted research on illness/disability, sexism, and antisemitism. After leaving her academic position to write fiction fulltime, she spent six years as the Writer-in-Residence at the Centre for Women's Studies at OISE/University of Toronto, where she created and co-ordinated the Wonderful Women Writers reading series.

Gold also co-founded three progressive Canadian organizations, all devoted to strengthening democracy, civil rights, and social justice in Israel. She is active on social media, posting regularly on LinkedIn, where she has over 100,000 followers. For more about Nora, visit www.noragold.com.

Yom Kippur
in a Gym

Essential Prose Series 215

Canada Council for the Arts   **Conseil des Arts du Canada**

ONTARIO ARTS COUNCIL
CONSEIL DES ARTS DE L'ONTARIO
an Ontario government agency
un organisme du gouvernement de l'Ontario

Canadä

Guernica Editions Inc. acknowledges the support of the Canada Council
for the Arts and the Ontario Arts Council. The Ontario Arts Council
is an agency of the Government of Ontario.
We acknowledge the financial support of the Government of Canada.

Yom Kippur in a Gym

NORA GOLD

GUERNICA
EDITIONS
TORONTO · BUFFALO · LANCASTER (U.K.)
2024

Guernica Founder: Antonio D'Alfonso

Michael Mirolla, editor
David Moratto, interior and cover design
Guernica Editions Inc.
287 Templemead Drive, Hamilton, ON L8W 2W4
2250 Military Road, Tonawanda, N.Y. 14150-6000 U.S.A.
www.guernicaeditions.com

Distributors:
Independent Publishers Group (IPG)
600 North Pulaski Road, Chicago IL 60624
University of Toronto Press Distribution (UTP)
5201 Dufferin Street, Toronto (ON), Canada M3H 5T8

First edition.
Printed in Canada.

Legal Deposit—First Quarter
Library of Congress Catalog Card Number: 2023948158
Library and Archives Canada Cataloguing in Publication
Title: In sickness and in health ; Yom Kippur in a gym / Nora Gold.
Other titles: In sickness and in health (Compilation)
Names: Gold, Nora, author. | container of (work) Gold, Nora. In sickness
and in health | container of (work) Gold, Nora. Yom Kippur in a gym
Series: Essential prose series ; 215.
Description: Series statement: Essential prose series ; 215
Identifiers: Canadiana (print) 20230566294 |
Canadiana (ebook) 20230566340 | ISBN 9781771838658 (softcover) |
ISBN 9781771838665 (EPUB)
Subjects: LCGFT: Novels.
Classification: LCC PS8563.O524 I5 2024 | DDC C813/.54—dc23

In memory of my grandmother,
Leah Steinman Gold,
who loved to read, and who hosted
literary evenings in her home in support of
Montreal's Yiddish writers and poets.

PART ONE

THE GYM

THE GYM IS filling up with people in their finest, fanciest clothes. No, they have not come to work out in their suits, ties, and dresses. They're here for Yom Kippur. They seat themselves gingerly on uncomfortable folding chairs and glance up warily at the basketball hoops hanging over their heads like swords of Damocles on this Day of Judgment. Higher yet, at the space just below the ceiling (where the Women's Section might be in one of those old shuls), a running track silently encircles the room. Down on the floor, there are the squares, circles, and parabolas of a basketball court, markings that define the parameters of players' movements, the way Jewish law does for Jewish lives.

Most people here look chastened, weary, and pale—some faces are as dead white as the concrete walls of this gym—since they've been fasting for twenty-four hours. Others betray themselves as nonfasters by their rosy cheeks, bouncy gait, and the absence of any visible exhaustion or strain. But faster or non-faster (or faster or slower), all the individuals in this stifling room—eight hundred souls packed like sardines, a random catch of the Jewish people—are together in the same boat. According to tradition, shortly after sundown tonight, in just one and a half hours, the gates of heaven will close for another year and the fates of everyone here will be sealed. Some will live, some will die. Some will prosper, some will fail. There will be successes and there will be suffering. And all you can do to try and tip the balance in your own favour is pray, admit your

mistakes and commit to do better, and donate to the needy. The rest is out of your hands.

A serious business, to be sure. But still you have to admit there is something incongruous, even comical, about holding a Yom Kippur service in a gym. It's a situation that invites jokes, injecting levity into what would otherwise be an unrelievedly sober, somber day. When the rabbi here (who is not actually a rabbi; only a third-year rabbinical student) told his classmates about the High Holyday gig he'd got for himself, they—rabbis being no crueler than anyone else, but also no kinder—couldn't restrain their laughter. High Holydays in a *gym?* They'd been invited to lead, or anyway assist at, services in dignified, pompous shuls with plush seats; this skinny, mousy classmate of theirs was going to officiate in a basketball court! Jokes —told mostly, but not all, behind his back—were perhaps inevitable. For instance: How is what you do in a gym similar to what you do at a High Holyday service?

Answers: In both cases—

> The exercise feels like a marathon, an endurance test.
> It's hard, demanding work but worth the effort.
> Sometimes you're operating alone; other times you're
>   part of a team/collectivity.
> Your performance is evaluated by a judge or referee
>   (either in this world or the one above).
> And so on.

None of these parallels, however, occurred to the people who organized the High Holyday services in this gym. They were just being practical. As members of a modest, downtown shul, short on cash but long on passion for social action, they wanted to offer High Holyday services to all the unaffiliated, lost, and lonely Jews in downtown Toronto. These three adjectives merged in their minds: they assumed that if you were not affiliated with a shul, you must be lost and lonely. So one of the board members persuaded his sister-in-law, who worked at the downtown Jewish Community Centre, to let the shul use its

gym free of charge for these services. Then the board collected a little money to hire a rabbinical student and, hoping to recoup at least part of this cost, decided to charge all attendees "pay-what-you-can."

The rabbinical student—whom almost everyone present assumes is a real, ordained rabbi—is winding up Mincha, the afternoon service. The only sound you can hear, other than a baby's intermittent crying, is the rabbi singing the prayers. The congregants, now on their third and last day with this rabbi, find him satisfactory. Young, friendly, nervous, and eager to please, he is the sort of young man whose thin cheeks more than one maternal older woman in the congregation has the impulse to pinch or fatten up. He is dressed in traditional garb, of course: the white robe symbolizing a shroud, reminding everyone present of the fleeting nature of their lives and the inevitability of their deaths. His voice as he sings is reedy, thin, and strained. He has done okay so far, leading the services last night and almost all of today, but he knows that Neila, the closing service of Yom Kippur, which starts soon, will be his real test. His strength is ebbing and he wonders if he will be able to make it to the end without losing his voice altogether. Yom Kippur finishes tonight at 7:57, and now it's 6:30, so there is almost an hour and a half to go. Already some people are gazing up longingly at the big, old-fashioned clock on the wall, as if willing the stern black hands to turn more quickly, so Yom Kippur will be over and they can go home and eat.

The rabbi (we'll call him that here because this is how almost everyone at this service perceives him, and we are, at least in part, what others perceive us to be, isn't that so?) concludes Mincha, using for the final prayer, the Kaddish, a lively, rousing tune that he learned from a British friend. At the very end of this prayer, the congregation—which, throughout Rosh Hashana and Yom Kippur, has been joining in at every appropriate moment—enthusiastically shouts out the final word, the Hebrew for *Amen*: "Ah-*meyn!*" There is joy and camaraderie in the room, the euphoric esprit de corps that unites a sports team when it's doing well.

Smiling, the rabbi says, "Soon we'll be starting Neila. So now take a few minutes for yourself, for some private, personal reflection.

5

If you wish, you can read some of the piyutim, the liturgical poems, in your machzor, 'El Nora Alila' for example, or look at the readings in the booklet, 'Thoughts for Yom Kippur.' Alternatively, you can just be with yourself, with your own thoughts and meditations. This is some quiet time for you to be alone with your soul and reflect on the past year and the coming one. In five minutes we'll begin Neila."

Some quiet time for them, he thinks, gratefully collapsing into his seat on the makeshift stage, but also some quiet time for me. Now he'll have a few minutes to catch his breath, collect himself, and muster his strength, like an athlete preparing for the last and hardest stretch to the finish line.

A dome of silence descends over the room. Earlier today, the congregation leapt at any opportunity to chatter among themselves; now it looks like they are entering the deep work of self-examination, of facing—or trying to face—the real truth about themselves and their lives. Or maybe they are simply too tired after a day in shul for even desultory chitchat. In any case, the silence here gets deeper and thicker, metamorphosing like a pea soup as it simmers. Meanwhile a few people notice a little girl no more than three years old, wearing a red dress and with dark curly hair, standing alone in the middle of the gym—smack in the center of the main aisle connecting the rabbi's seat at one end, and the ark (which is actually an equipment locker) at the other. The girl stretches her arms out wide and begins to spin around. Slowly at first, then faster, and faster, twirling at top speed wildly, ecstatically, until she suddenly collapses in a laughing heap on the floor. People watch, mesmerized. Then her baby voice cuts through the silence, ringing out loud and clear, reaching up to the highest rafter, and maybe even the heavens: "Ah-*meyn!*"

People smile and laugh. Her mother, in a forest green dress, rushes over and scoops her up.

TOM

ENTERING THE ROOM as the rabbi is completing Mincha, Tom nods at him perfunctorily, and the rabbi, nervously smiling, nods back, struggling to pray, nod, and smile all at the same time. He knows that Tom is the shul's representative to these services and a member of the committee that hired him; he hopes that if he does well this year, Tom will recommend hiring him again a year from now. Tom doesn't think much of this rabbinical student, though. It's true that some of the congregants like him, especially the older women. The children and teens relate well to him, too, with his shy smile, high-fives, and lack of pomposity, unlike so many other rabbis. But this young man strikes him as scrawny, uncharismatic, and terrified of his own shadow. Maybe if they do this service again next year, Tom will suggest trying a woman rabbi. That's the latest thing.

He is pale and tired from fasting, but as he makes his way to a seat in the front row, he smiles at people and stops a few times to shake someone's hand or lean down to kiss a cheek. Once seated, he nods at the congregants across the aisle. An active member of Toronto's Jewish community, he is known, respected, and generally liked. A few minutes ago, out in the hallway when returning to the gym from the bathroom, he ran into someone who recognized him from his community work, and they chatted for a while. Now he listens to the rabbi squeaking his way through the end of Mincha and assigning everyone five minutes of soul-searching. Tom doesn't go in for that sort of thing. He doesn't like being criticized, not by

others, and not even by himself. He knows, though, that Neila, The Closing of the Gates, will be his last chance this year to forgive and to be forgiven. To make his peace with people and with God.

All around him the room is silent. It looks like all the adults are obeying the rabbi and engaging in "personal reflection". Or maybe they've just withdrawn into themselves out of lassitude. To the apparent frustration of a young boy and girl repeatedly pulling on their mother's skirt and their father's pant leg, wanting to be played with, read to, or fed. Kids don't like it, Tom thinks, when their parents mentally abandon them.

He looks up at the high windows. Outside, the sky is a deepening blue—that specific shade it gets when it's no longer daytime but is not yet evening. This is the time, that liminal moment between day and night, when as a child he always cried. His crying jag at this time every day was such a fact of life, such a predictable occurrence in his family, that they nicknamed it "Tom's Nightfall Cry." Whenever the sky turned this colour, he'd cling to his mother and sob as if the setting sun would never rise again. But then of course it always did.

He glances at the clock: Only another hour and a half, thank God, till all this is over and he can go home. Home to Carolyn, in bed with a migraine.

"Yes, there's only another hour and a half," the walls say to him. "So come on, Tom. Take this a little more seriously. Do some personal reflection. Contemplate your life. Try to be a better man."

No, he replies. There's no point in even trying. This year I've flunked Yom Kippur. The holiest day in the Jewish calendar, the day for pondering only the most sacred and elevated subjects, and all I can think about is how much I hate my father.

It started at noon today. He was okay last night during the service, and this morning, as well. But then at midday it came time to say Yizkor, the prayer for close relatives who have died. For the past nine years he's been saying Yizkor for Mom, so there was nothing unusual about the actual recitation of this prayer. But now he had to say Yizkor, for the first time, for Dad, and all he felt was rage. And

it hasn't subsided six and a half hours later—he's still fuming like a volcano. Why should he recite a loving memorial prayer for a father who was violent and abusive—an uneducated ignoramus who beat him every chance he could, on any pretext, and often without any pretext at all? A father who told him daily that he was a worthless piece of shit and that he wished Tom had never been born. Why should he pray for a peaceful afterlife in heaven (in "the world to come") for an asshole who made his son's life in *this* world hell on earth? And why should he refer to Dad in the Yizkor prayer as one of "the righteous" in the Garden of Eden, and ask God to kindly remember his soul? He couldn't ask God for that. He didn't ask God for that. The only prayer he has for his father is that he should burn in hell.

* * *

There is a snorting horsey sound on his left. It's the woman sitting next to him, someone he doesn't know. She's laughing, and for a fraction of a second he thinks she's laughing at him. But no, that's impossible. She can't have read his thoughts. But then what *is* she laughing about? There's no reason for mirth on Yom Kippur. Maybe she's a crazy person. This service is open to anyone who wants it; it probably brings in all sorts of people off the street.

She is snort-laughing so hard now that she has tears in her eyes, and he considers moving away from her to another seat. But that would be very conspicuous in this still, silent room, and it could insult her. He is not a great believer, but he's also not about to insult somebody one and a half hours before the Closing of the Gates. So he remains in his chair, just sliding it surreptitiously an inch or two away from her. And she is laughing-crying so hard she doesn't seem to notice.

LUCY

SHE WIPES THE tears from her eyes and keeps on laughing. Last night she and Larry laughed as they hadn't done in over a month, not since he got diagnosed with Parkinson's. Or rather, misdiagnosed. Larry is only forty-two and Parkinson's is something that old people get. Those stupid doctors don't know what they're talking about.

Their laughing fit started indirectly because, when it was almost time to go to shul last night for Kol Nidre, Larry looked so exhausted she suggested they skip it just this once. With relief he agreed. They were sitting at the dining room table, still strewn with dirty dishes from their elaborate pre-fast meal (not that Larry was supposed to fast, but he'd said he wanted to try to anyway). She was just beginning to wonder how they could pass the time this evening—they couldn't watch TV as usual since it was almost Yom Kippur already—when her eye fell on the envelope. It was still in the exact same spot on the telephone table where she'd dumped it five weeks before. That day, the nurse at the hospital had given them a bunch of forms to fill out at home, among them one called "Your Advanced Care Directives." This nurse, perhaps thinking she was being tactful, told Larry when she handed him this form: "You don't want Lucy to have to guess what you will or won't want when the time comes." The "will or won't" pissed Lucy off. The nurse should have said "what you would or wouldn't want," not "what you will or won't." "Would or wouldn't" means if you should ever, at some distant time, get close to dying. "Will or won't" means you're going to be

there soon, honey. In just a year, or a few months, or even a week, before you turn around, you're going to croak. Why, thought Lucy, don't they teach these nurses some grammar?

"There's that stupid form," she said last night to Larry. "The one from that idiot nurse." She brought it over to him, saying, "Let's have some fun with it. Let's tear it to shreds."

"Sure, why not?" he said, smiling. "A nice light way to kick off Yom Kippur."

Smiling too, she sat down and, with their elbows touching, opened the envelope. The "Your Advanced Care Directives" form was ten pages long, fastened with a pink paper clip.

"Consider these medical situations," she read aloud from the first page.

"Question One A. You are seriously ill with cancer but your mind is still very sharp. Physicians recommend chemotherapy. They explain that this treatment often has severe side effects such as pain, vomiting, and weakness. Are you willing to endure these side effects if the chances of regaining your current health are less than twenty-five percent?

"1. Yes.

"2. Yes, on a trial basis.

"3. No.

"4. I am uncertain."

Larry was frowning. "I don't know," he said. "I have no idea."

"Me neither. 'I am uncertain.'"

"Twenty-five percent doesn't sound like much."

"No. Seventy-five percent maybe. Or even fifty. But twenty-five ..." She grimaced. "You read the next one, Lar."

"Question One B. You are seriously ill with terminal cancer but your mind is still very sharp. Physicians offer chemotherapy to buy time, giving you an eighty percent chance of an additional six months. Do you want this treatment even though it may have severe side effects?

"1. Yes.

"2. Yes, on a trial basis.

"3. No.

"4. I am uncertain.

"I am uncertain. It's just six months, after all," Larry said.

"I know."

But then she pictured him being about to die. Being one or two days away from death. And at that point she'd want him to keep on living, and for as long as possible. Even one more day, or a week, would be an enormous gift. Six months, something to treasure. "Then again," she said, "it's still six months."

Larry did not reply, just stared out the window. She continued:

"Question Two. You have advanced Alzheimer's disease which has progressed to the point where you can no longer feed or toilet yourself." She laughed. "You can't even feed or toilet yourself? Oy!" Larry did not laugh, or even smile. She resumed. "You no longer recognize your family either, but you are not in pain. Do you want to be fed (by either spoon or tube)?

"1. Yes.

"2. Yes, but spoon-fed only.

"3. No.

"4. I am uncertain.

"Spoon-fed? Tube-fed? Oh my God!" She stretched her hand out in front of Larry's mouth and, miming holding an imaginary spoon, pretended to feed him. "Eat up, sweetie-pie," she said, repeating what she used to say to Jessica and Darren when they were toddlers. "Open wide. Here comes an airplane!"

He lightly swatted her hand, laughing. "Get away from me."

She was laughing, too. "How many more of these are there?" She flipped to the end of the form. "Twenty in all. Okay. Let's do just one more." She scanned a few pages. "What do you prefer? Diabetes, gangrene, kidney infection, congestive heart failure, or more Alzheimer's?"

"None of the above."

She was still flipping pages, reading. "Wow, get a load of this one! Question Seven. You are in a permanent coma and your body is kept alive by artificial means such as mechanical breathing and tube feeding. Physicians say you will never recover because your brain has

been severely damaged, but there are a few documented cases where people have recovered from a persistent vegetative state. Do you want to be kept alive in this way just in case you someday recover?

"What do you think, Lar? They can freeze us! Like on *Star Trek* —remember that episode?"

"Yeah, right. I have the option to wake up two hundred or two thousand years from now and not recognize anything in the world around me. Rip van Winkle II. No, thanks."

She nodded vaguely, still scanning the form.

"I don't want to do any more," he said. "I've had enough."

"Just one more. Last one:

"Question Ten. You have advanced Alzheimer's disease and no longer recognize your family. You've been hospitalized twice in the past year for pneumonia, which was cured by massive doses of antibiotics. Now you've developed pneumonia once more. Do you want aggressive treatment in hospital again, or do you prefer to be kept comfortable at home until death occurs naturally?

"1. I want aggressive treatment, including antibiotics, to keep me alive.

"2. I do not want treatment to keep me alive. I want comfort care at home.

"3. I am uncertain."

He shifted in his chair and now their arms no longer touched. "No treatment. Pull the plug."

"Really?"

"Yeah."

"You'd actually want to die if you got Alzheimer's?"

"Absolutely. Once my mind is gone, I don't see any point in living."

Spoken like a true intellectual. To him, the academic, the mind is everything. Take that away and nothing's left. She was surprised last night by her sudden, fierce anger. As if he was giving up, copping out, in some way devaluing not just his life, but hers as well— maybe even their whole life together. She said primly, tightly, "There is more to life than the mind. There is more to *me* than my mind."

"Like what?" he said, sneering. "Your *soul?*"

It always takes her aback how quickly he can turn against her. But last night, instead of caving in as she so often does, she rallied, not only for herself but for him.

"We're not just brains," she said. "If I can still enjoy sitting in a park in the sunshine, eating my favourite cranberry cookies, why shouldn't I be allowed to do that? Why should I be killed off just because I don't remember some people's names? Memory isn't everything."

He snickered. "That's fine for you, Lucy. When you're a babbling idiot who can't even recognize the people you love, I'll make sure you get every possible treatment to keep you alive. But when I'm like that, like I said, I want you to pull the plug."

She didn't like this. She stood up, went to the kitchen sink which was filled with soapy water and soaking dishes, and immersing her arm up to the elbow, extracted the little black plug. "There," she said. "I've pulled the plug." She brought it back to Larry, swinging it, slightly dripping, on its metal chain. She swung it back and forth like a pendulum in front of his face. "You are getting sleeepy," she said in a deep, hypnotizing voice. "You are getting verrrry, verrrry sleeeeepy."

He reached out and grabbed her around the waist. "And you are getting sexy," he said. "Verry, verrry sexy." He pulled her downwards onto the kitchen floor, just like when they were younger, when they were first in love. She started to laugh and kept on laughing. As he reached out to stroke her face and her breast, she noticed his hand was shaking. It was funny how his hand shook—he didn't, he couldn't, have Parkinson's, she was sure of that: he was too young; those doctors were all wrong—but it was so funny that she laughed until tears filled her eyes. Larry looked confused, not understanding her laughter, her unexpected happiness, but anyway he laughed along, too.

Now in shul, remembering this, she's laughing and laughing and laughing, not seeing or hearing anything around her.

TOM / IRA

THERE ARE STIRRINGS now around Tom in the gym. People are getting restless. The five minutes for Personal Reflection must be over. He glances up at the clock: it's been seven minutes. Seven minutes and ten seconds. Eleven. Twelve ...

The rabbi approaches the podium. "Before we start Neila," he announces, "a few brief comments."

Oh no, Tom thinks. Not another speech. Why don't you just get on with Neila so we can all go home?

"This is the final hour and twenty minutes of Yom Kippur," the rabbi says. "Your last chance, for a whole year, to obtain God's forgiveness. So don't squander this opportunity. Don't think to yourself, 'I am a pretty good person overall, my sins are relatively minor. I'm not a murderer or a rapist, so I don't need to do teshuva.' No! A thousand times no! Everyone has to do teshuva! Everyone! Even the greatest, holiest people the world has ever known—even they had to do teshuva!"

His face is turning red and he is more emotional now than he has ever been before throughout these three days of high holidays. He seems almost like a different person from the one this congregation has come to know. Tom watches him with interest and even some admiration: this milquetoast has some passion in him after all. Then he sees, at the edge of the rabbi's profile, on the other side of the aisle, a white-faced young man. He has the same delicate, fragile

look as his sister Polly had at that age and he is listening to the rabbi with an expression of fear. Tom wonders why.

"None of us is exempt!" the rabbi cries, pounding the podium. "None of us! Not me! Not you! No one!" He scans the room, looking intently from face to face, and Tom has the eerie feeling that this rabbi has penetrated his veneer and seen who he really is. He knows that's ridiculous. Still, a vague feeling of dread comes over him.

"Even the High Priest in ancient times did teshuva on Yom Kippur! Even *he* did teshuva! And his went much further than everyone else's. He'd stand in front of the entire community and publicly confess all his sins. Then he'd list the sins of everyone in his household. He confessed everything. He held nothing back."

Really? Tom thinks. He held *nothing* back? He really told them *every*thing? Every filthy fantasy? Every embarrassing blunder? He can't imagine exposing himself like that in public. He has spent most of his life and a huge amount of his emotional energy concealing from the outside world the truth about himself and his family of origin. This afternoon the Torah reading said: "Do not uncover your father's nakedness," and he hasn't—he has never uncovered his father's nakedness. For fifty years he has been a good son and a good Jew and he has covered up for Dad. He has done this by lying: lying in the things he's said and in the things he hasn't ("sins of commission" and "sins of omission"). Why? he wonders now, glancing around the shul. Did he do this to protect Mom? Or perhaps to protect himself—to hide his shame at having been his family's whipping boy? Whatever the reason, he has always been loyal and kept silent. But now Dad is dead. Now both of them are dead. So who is he being silent for, and why?

To keep up appearances, maybe. He's glad, after all, that he passes for normal in the world, that he looks okay on the outside. Nobody he works with or meets through everyday contact would ever guess that he was abused as a child, or how vulnerable he still sometimes feels. He is grateful for this hiddenness. It provides him with some safety and dignity.

There is another reason, too, for guarding his family's secret and protecting Dad's good name. Dad was very successful in his business, Mishivitz Demolition and Construction. He demolished Tom, and Tom has therefore had to construct, and reconstruct, himself. But Dad came across to everyone else like a really nice guy, especially after he won the contract to renovate Toronto's biggest, wealthiest, and most prestigious shul, which made him rich and also something of a philanthropist. He donated generously to hospitals, universities, and various Jewish causes, and for this he was honoured a half-dozen times and also made Treasurer of that big, wealthy, prestigious shul. Over two hundred people, most of whom Tom didn't know, turned up at his funeral three months ago. So thanks to Dad being so respected in the community, Tom has always gotten a lot of referrals to his medical practice. "Go to Tommy, Bill's boy," people said. "His dad is a good man; you can trust a Mishivitz." Tom's medical practice has done very well for years and now it's booming. So much so that he just bought a gorgeous old house in Yorkville with four of his associates, which the five of them will work out of when the renovations are complete. He is also in the process of adding an extension onto his home to accommodate Carolyn's mother and her wheelchair. What would happen to all that—to his success, his credibility, and his place in the world—if he exposed the truth now about his father?

Carolyn's right. Nobody likes a victim, and nobody likes being shown the clay feet of someone they've admired. And anyway, what is there to be gained by outing Dad now, after all these years? Uncovering his nakedness, and all of theirs? Nothing. Nothing at all.

So for the thousandth time he decides to keep silent.

* * *

The white-faced young man across the aisle, Ira, is studying Tom. His face, his clothing, his posture, everything he can see. Tom, he concludes, is one of the world's Normals. Well-fed, middle class,

satisfied with his life, at peace with himself, smug in his expensive jacket. He's a guy who has it all: wife, family, financial security, a house in the burbs, friends, and a successful career. When this guy entered the gym a little while ago, Ira noticed that he got a smile and a nod from the rabbi. He must be someone important. A big shot. Someone with standing in the world. Unlike me, Ira thinks. I have none. I have only sitting in this world. No, not even that. I have nothing. I am nothing.

"In the minutes remaining to you tonight," the rabbi is saying, "find the courage to tell the truth about yourself to God. Don't hold anything back. Don't hide anything. (What's the point, anyway? God knows everything.) Look at yourself in the mirror, take a good hard look without turning away or making excuses for your faults. And if you truly face yourself now, then God will forgive you. I am sure of it. Because our God is not only a God of justice, but also a God of mercy and compassion. As it says in Psalm 145: 'Gracious and compassionate is the Lord; patient and abounding in love.' Our God is not just a king who judges us. God is also our tender, loving father, near to us at all times and waiting for us to return to him."

A kind, loving, compassionate father—the idea moves Tom, despite his cynicism. Imagine what that would be like, what that would have been like when he was a boy, having a warm, tender-hearted father. Someone who cared about you, understood you, forgave you your little human mistakes. Instead of whipping you for them.

The rabbi pauses. He scans his notes and continues. "Many people misunderstand the concept of teshuva. It is not about beating yourself up. True, ten times during Yom Kippur we recite the Ashamnu, confessing all our sins, and soon we'll be doing this again for the tenth and last time. Ashamnu, bagadnu, gazalnu—We have been guilty, we have betrayed, we have stolen. This admission of our failings, individually and collectively, is essential to doing teshuva.

"But an honest, balanced accounting of ourselves, a fair balance sheet, so to speak, also includes the good things we've done, or tried to do, during the past year. We are not just our defects and failings, thank God. The great Rav Kook said, 'Just as there is great value to

the confession of sins, there is also great value to the confession of our positive deeds, which gladdens the heart and strengthens the holy paths of life.' He even wrote an alternative Ashamnu. Like the traditional one, this is an acrostic following the order of the Hebrew alphabet: aleph, bet, gimel, etc. But instead of Ashamnu, Bagadnu, he wrote Ahavnu, Berachnu. We have loved, we have blessed, and so on.

"So, as we complete our teshuva for this Yom Kippur, let's remember to acknowledge our good qualities, too. Otherwise we could become discouraged or despairing, God forbid. We could fall into the trap of thinking, 'Why bother trying to improve at all? Why work on becoming a better person? It's a hopeless task. I'm basically no good.'"

Ira starts in his seat and stares at the rabbi, shocked and wide-eyed. Tom can't help noticing because this white, Polly-like face is at the edge of the rabbi's profile.

"This is wrong," the rabbi says. "In Judaism we do not ascribe to original sin. We don't believe that human beings are fundamentally evil. Flawed? Yes. Imperfect? Yes. We are only human, after all. But basically bad or evil? No. Every one of us, every single one of us here today, was created in the image of God."

Tom watches the face of the young man fill with longing and hope.

"Some people think that teshuva means repentance, but this is incorrect. Teshuva means Return. Return to your soul, return to your true nature. Return to who you really are."

Sure, Ira thinks. Return to your true nature, to who you really are. But what if you don't know who you are? What if you don't know your true nature? Then what do you do? Where do you return to then?

The rabbi looks at him. He knows, Ira thinks. I don't know how he knows, but he does. And automatically, unconsciously, he pulls down the sleeves of his shirt to cover the scars on his wrists.

The rabbi, finished with his speech, stands quietly for a moment, chalk-faced, exhausted.

Quickly he does the Ashrei prayer and then says, "Please rise." The whole congregation rises—Ira, Tom, and Lucy among them.

RACHEL / IRA

RACHEL RISES, TOO. Standing on Ira's right, she rocks from side to side to the tune of the Hatzi Kaddish. The shul's cook and baker, she is the one who prepares the shul's post-services kiddush on Shabbat and holidays, and right now she's hungry. This is not because of the partial—very partial—fast she's been doing since last night. She is always hungry. There is a disease called Prader-Willi syndrome where the sick person is always hungry; Rachel does not have this disease but she is always hungry and thinking about food. From the moment she wakes up in the morning until the instant she falls asleep at night, food is on her mind. The pleasure of making it. The delight of sharing it. The shameful ecstasy of gobbling it up all by herself. Without batting an eyelash she can devour half a chocolate cake in a sitting. She eats enormous amounts of food and still rarely feels full.

She is not obese. She isn't "a house," a square shape, or shapeless. She's just "pleasingly plump," as her mother used to say (and she herself fit that description). In any case, Rachel thinks it would be suspicious, and even bad for business, for a cook to be skinny. You'd be kind of a negative advertisement for your own work.

Now, one hour before the Closing of the Gates, at this crucial existential moment, she is worrying about honey cake. Yesterday afternoon she baked ten pans of honey cake for the people here to break their fast with tonight. The vice-president of the shul, Gary, had told her to prepare the usual amount for the members of the

shul ten blocks away, and only half of that for the people here "in the gym." He'd said "in the gym" in a derogatory tone; he hadn't favoured the idea of this "extra service at the Jewish Community Centre" but had been forced to go along with it. Well, he'd been totally wrong. She could see with her own eyes as soon as she walked in here today that there were as many people here as at the shul, in fact way more. She was shocked. How would ten pans of honey cake suffice for all these congregants? The cardinal sin for her, the sin of all sins (never mind all those little sins in the Ashamnu), would be to serve a group of people an inadequate amount of food. Whenever she invites six people for dinner, she always prepares enough for ten or twelve. What if they want seconds? What sort of a hostess doesn't make extra?

And now this. On Yom Kippur of all days. To not have enough food for people breaking the fast.

Maybe, she thinks hopefully, not everyone, an hour and a quarter from now, will want honey cake. Some people don't like honey cake. In fact, some people don't like cake at all. Then again there are those who do like cake, perhaps even love it, but won't eat it. Women, for example, who are watching their weight. If this group here is typical, at least a third of the women will forgo the honey cake, in spite of being famished after fasting for twenty-five hours. These foolish slim women will opt for a handful of grapes or a couple of low-fat crackers brought from home in a baggie, rather than her luscious cake. Morons. But just this once she hopes this happens. That way, her mistake (Gary's mistake actually, but she's the one who will be blamed) will be less visible to all.

Never mind, she tells herself. Think sweet thoughts—her mother's advice to her whenever she feels blue. So now she contemplates the delicious opera cake that she will make tomorrow for her friend Carla's wedding. Her mouth waters picturing it. But mixed in with the sweet jam-and-raspberry topping is the subtle tang of lemon juice: Will she forever be only the caterer at these weddings? Will she never be the bride? She's thirty-five now. The clock is ticking. The Gate is Closing.

She blows the lemon juice out of the recipe, smiles, and savours the rich flavour of the beautiful cake. Without even realizing it, she is lightly smacking her lips.

* * *

Ira gives Rachel a dirty look. People are disgusting. On his right he has this lip-smacker and on his left some kind of celebrity. Ever since she arrived an hour ago, people have been coming over to fawn over this woman whose name sounds something like Charmer, and she's lapped it up like a queen accepting homage as her total due. It makes him sick. He wishes he could get away from these two women. But what did Sartre say in *No Exit?* "Hell is other people." So it doesn't much matter who he sits beside. He's like Sartre in *Nausea*; anyone would nauseate him.

He frowns at the rabbi doing the Hatzi Kaddish. This rabbi said that since we're all created in the image of God, we should love ourselves and include in our self-assessments today an appreciation of our positive attributes. Sure, Ira thinks. That would be a great idea if I could think of any. But I can't. In fact, if I did what we are really supposed to do on Yom Kippur—judge ourselves honestly, not with that mushy mix of "justice plus mercy" that is popular now— then my conclusion would be that I don't deserve to live.

He thought things would be different when he came to Toronto. In the big city there would be new people, boundless choices and opportunities, and exciting experiences. A fresh start after the oppressive over-familiarity of the small Manitoba town where he grew up. In a place that size, there's no escaping your past. You poop your pants in kindergarten and everyone's still remembering this at your funeral. He was hopeful when he arrived here three and a half months ago, and he was happy at first. He enjoyed his classes in philosophy at U of T and on his tenth day here, he met Ken. The next two months were euphoric. His days felt full and worth living, even when Ken and he argued, and for the first time in years he could picture a sunny future for himself.

But then Ken left. He never explained why. Just stopped returning Ira's calls. Ken never loved him—he understands this now.
To Ken, he'd been nothing more than a fling, just another young
gay guy from the sticks in love for the first time. Probably Ken was
flattered to be his first lover, as well as his mentor on the Toronto
gay scene and life in general in the big city. Eventually, though, the
charm of that wore off and he'd started boring Ken, and then an-
noying him with his cloying dependency and demands. And as soon
as he started using the word *love*, it was over in a puff of smoke.
Within days, the magic that had transformed Ira into someone
beautiful, glowing, and lovable evaporated, and he was back to his
old self again: plain, uninteresting, and ugly; Cinderella returned to
her rags.

He glances down at his machzor, fallen open to a random page.
Glory, glory, glory is our God. The whole world is full of His glory.
What bullshit. The god who is running the world now, the one whose
"glory" is filling it, is a psychopath living in the White House. An
American president who hates gays, Blacks, Hispanics, Muslims,
and Jews—in fact, everybody except rich, white, Christian bigots
like himself. Ira can feel this man's evil presence looming like a
darkening, ever-expanding cloud over not just America but the entire planet.

It's all so hopeless. Everything is going under, and no one's lifting a finger to save it. Certainly not that well-fed guy across the
aisle, or the woman next to him with the strawberry blond hair
(probably his wife). They look so normal—so stupid and smug. They
don't know, or care, about what's happening in the world, and they
could never in a million years understand someone like him.
Someone who's planning to kill himself. That rabbi was funny with
his U'n'taneh Tokef prayer a few hours ago: "On Rosh Hashanah it
will be inscribed in the Book of Life, and on Yom Kippur it will be
sealed: who shall live and who shall die; who by water and who by
fire, who by sword and who by beast, who by famine and who by
thirst, who by earthquake and who by plague, who by strangling
and who by stoning." This innocent rabbi could never have guessed

that for people like him, this prayer wasn't a warning; it was a menu, a list of options for how to commit suicide. There are so many ways to kill yourself. By water, by fire. By sword or by beast. This time he's going to use pills; the other methods are too messy and uncertain. Enough already with razor blades in bathtubs! That didn't go very well last time. He can decide about what exact kind of pills tonight when he gets back to the dorm. One thing he knows for sure, though: there's no point in living. Because there's no way to escape loneliness. He's been lonely his whole life and he doesn't want to be lonely anymore.

Why did he even come here today? He can't remember. Maybe he thought he'd find something in this service to convince him that life has some value or meaning. That it isn't just a total waste of time. Perhaps he was giving the world one last chance, a kind of test: *Prove yourself to me.* His mother used to say to him, sadly, worryingly: "You're always testing people." A test she consistently failed. And now so has the whole world.

Yes, tonight will be the night. And this time he'll succeed.

All around him people are singing a long, extended, multi-note "Amen." Amen, the end of the Hatzi Kaddish. Yes, he thinks. The end. *The end.* And smiling ghoulishly, he joins in the singing for the first time today.

* * *

Rachel is not singing. She's thinking about how to make an opera cake. It is not a simple operation. There are five different components to it, which you have to first make separately and then painstakingly assemble.

For the syrup, you need caster sugar and kirsch. Remember to use caster sugar. You can use granulated sugar but it's not as good because granulated sugar takes longer to melt with the water.

For the joconde sponge, you use egg whites, more caster sugar, ground almonds, icing sugar, sifted flour, and butter.

The chocolate ganache is made with double cream and dark chocolate. Don't use chocolate with seventy percent cocoa for the ganache because it separates; use thirty or forty percent instead. Also, remember to break the chocolate into pieces first so it melts faster, and don't forget to remove the chocolate from the heat before adding the butter. That's better for the chocolate, and the butter will melt perfectly well off the heat.

For the crème au beurre, use three egg yolks, butter, vanilla paste, and once again caster sugar.

Decorate with seedless raspberry jam, sieved, and forty small raspberries.

Mmmm. Mmmmmm. Rachel smiles and smacks her lips again.

TOM

THE WEIRD WOMAN on his left—still laughing intermittently, even now while she's praying—has a freckled face and the same strawberry blond hair as his older sister Edna. His younger sister Polly, on the other hand, has dark hair like him. But both sisters treat him like crap. Last week at Edna's son's wedding, when he and Carolyn first walked in, Polly and her husband Arthur—not ten yards away—saw them arrive, but didn't smile at them, wave, or even nod; they just turned away and continued talking to whoever they'd been talking to. Later, when Arthur was working the room and ended up near Tom and Carolyn's table (where Tom was sitting alone; Carolyn had just gone to the bathroom), he blanked over his eyes and walked past Tom like he wasn't even there. He did the same thing twice more that evening, ignoring Tom in a gathering of three or four people as if he were invisible. Edna and Jim were only slightly better. They nodded at him and Carolyn coldly from across the room when they entered, but did not come over to greet them. After these slights, Tom, laughing to himself about his sisters and their husbands, but also chagrined and determined to be acknowledged, went up to each of them individually, forcing himself on them by saying hello. They replied either in monosyllables or not at all, just turning away, giving him their shoulders or backs.

What has he done to deserve this? he wonders in the silent gym. He has no idea. He's always treated the four of them courteously and has never done anything intentionally to hurt them. Still, they

hate him. So he's afraid of them now and wishes they weren't in his life. He'd like to never have to see any of them again, but he has no choice: there's another wedding coming up in three weeks—this time Polly's daughter's—and you can't miss your niece's wedding. Besides, he loves this niece, as he does all his nieces and nephews.

His stomach lurches, though, at the thought of all the events he'll have to attend during this wedding weekend: a Friday night dinner, a Saturday night party, the wedding itself on Sunday, and then a Monday morning brunch. All this will kill him. His sisters and their husbands will snub him over and over again—they'll hurt him as they've always hurt him—yet he can't not go. He's trapped.

The whole thing is a nightmare emotionally speaking, but at least intellectually he can see the situation with some objectivity and clarity. Thanks to a book on dysfunctional families that Carolyn brought home from the library a couple of years ago, he knows that in his family of origin he was, and still is, the family scapegoat; and that although this role contains a certain power (the power, for instance, to explode a family's myths and lies), it makes the individual in this role extremely vulnerable. He also recognizes that his sisters are, to a large extent, operating unconsciously. They are constantly re-enacting, like an old play, all the roles, rules, and practices they inherited from the Mishivitz family structure they grew up with. A wobbly, sick structure built on a wobbly, sick marriage. His sisters at this point are no different than antiquated streetcars sliding along automatically, unthinkingly, on electric tracks laid down for them fifty years before.

In a sense, he thinks, you could say they are just following a family tradition. But family traditions, according to that book, have deep, unconscious roots, and therefore are tyrannically resistant to challenge or change. Which is probably why his efforts all these years to alter the old patterns and improve these relationships have never succeeded.

Understanding this is reassuring. It provides him with some lucidity he can clutch onto when away from his sisters. But it disappears in an instant, along with his sense of safety and boundaries,

whenever they are physically nearby. It's their bodies that are the problem: the smell of his sisters, each with her own particular scent, when he tries to hug or kiss them. In the face of this immediacy, his sisters' undeniable realness, his defenses fall. His defenses fail.

He knows both of their bodies intimately. Until he was five and Polly was four, they bathed together every night. On one such night, he reached toward her in the warm bathwater, gingerly, wonderingly, touching her vulva: *Is this like me? I thought she was like me, but in this way she is different.* Then she reached out and touched his penis. *Our bodies are different. We are not the same.*

With Edna, who was four years older, he never bathed, but he knows how she tastes. He can still feel the touch of her lips on his, and her tongue deep in his mouth. They lay together on a plastic chaise longue in California on a family sun holiday—he was seven, she eleven. The night before, they'd seen French kissing in a movie on TV, and Edna wanted to practice this now so she'd know how to do it with boys when the time came. (That time came soon, in fact; just six months later.) The two of them had been swimming in the ocean so her lips tasted of salt and sea, but the inside of her mouth was sweet and pulpy. After what felt like a long time, he pulled away, laughing. This sort of kissing seemed stupid; why did grownups like it so much? As he withdrew, Edna's red-blond hair swished like corn silk across his face and she whispered, "Don't tell anyone." For once they were allies, partners in crime, instead of adversaries, competitors for their parents' love. (He had Mom's, she had Dad's; they each wanted what the other had.)

In the following months, Edna began to smell different. She gave off a sharp, biting smell as she entered adolescence, especially when sweaty after jogging or on the day after a party. Throughout her teenage years they'd line up for the bathroom every morning and often he'd breathe in her post-sex, or drunk (or druggy), smell. He knew all her smells. And he knew exactly what she'd been up to without ever having to be told.

Polly, on the other hand, had an innocent, baby powder smell. Not only as a child, but even at twelve or thirteen. Then at fourteen

she started adding a splash of Jean Naté to her morning ablutions. After that she'd brush her bushy, dark mane with a Jean Pierre hairbrush (Jean this, Jean that, was all the rage then), tearing briskly, impatiently through the thick tangles, sometimes ripping out clumps of hair. "My rat's nests," she called them. He watched her with fascination. *So this is what girls do.* He'd never brushed his hair except on important occasions like his bar mitzvah. Other than that, his hair just fell messily wherever it wanted.

So even now, after everything that's happened, he can't help loving his sisters, because of who they were back then. Edna, when she wasn't being contemptuous, could be generous, even sweet. One day, walking him home from school—she in grade five and he in grade one—a boy with a crush on her gave her a chocolate bar. Immediately she split it in two and gave Tom half. And occasionally she'd look at him admiringly, like when he said something clever in front of company, or won that science prize in grade six. He was always surprised and gratified by that expression on her face, of almost proprietary pride, as if he were her child.

Another thing about Edna: she had the most gleeful, contagious laugh you've ever heard. When she found something funny, her arms drooped, her whole body jiggled, and she cackled like a hyena, sometimes laughing so hard she wet her pants. She hasn't laughed this way in years—with total abandon, out of control. He hasn't seen her out of control since they were teenagers. She's so reserved now, always buttoned-up and buttoned-down. Except when in a rage. She's become, in this respect, more and more like Dad over time.

As for Polly, all those years ago she was ineffably soft and tenderhearted. At night she'd climb into his bed and cuddle up to him, snuggling close, with her thumb in her mouth and a blanket stroking one cheek. "Don't go away, Tom," she'd say. He'd reply, "I'll never leave you." She nestled against him at every opportunity, not just at night but in the daytime too, like when they watched Saturday morning cartoons side by side on the shabby plaid couch. And when she couldn't cling to him physically because they were out in public (in the schoolyard or at summer day camp), she'd linger in

his general vicinity, only three or four yards away, in case she needed him. He never pushed her away as some older brothers do. He didn't mind her shadowing him. She was his little sister.

He let her cling to him later on as well, in college when she had her nervous breakdown, and he held her as she sobbed, his nose buried in her fragrant bush of hair, inhaling also the smell of her depression and desperation, and her exhaustion from the struggle not to kill herself. Over and over he told her as he rocked her: "I'm here. I won't leave you. I love you."

* * *

All around him, people are quietly praying. Ever since he can re-member, it was always him and Polly. They were the two younger ones. Edna, being older, was usually off somewhere with her friends. Edna was also different from him and Polly because she was Dad's favourite, and the only one he never hit. He never laid a hand on his fair-haired first-born. That was reserved for Tom, and, only rarely, Polly. Polly was a small, frail girl who had nearly died at birth, and then again a few years later, so everyone tiptoed around her as if she were a porcelain doll. Even Dad. Occasionally, though, he was so furious and out of control that he even went after her. Once when she was seven, he grabbed her by the hair, and Tom, to free her, ran over and kicked him in the shin. Dad spun around, howling in pain, and flew at Tom, while she scurried to the farthest corner of the room. There she cowered, covering her eyes with her hands and cry-ing as if she were being beaten instead of Tom. He was getting badly thrashed, but at that moment he was not a victim. An aficionado of TV cartoons, he was imagining himself a superhero with a cape, defending his younger, weaker sister. He was rescuing a fair damsel in distress, whom Oil Can Harry had tied to a railroad track in front of an oncoming train. He was proud of himself for saving her, snatching her away from the fast-approaching train—*whoosh*—just in the nick of time.

Edna, unlike him, had no heroic inclinations. She always made sure to be on the winning side—in this case Dad's—no matter what. Once when Dad was beating Tom with a belt, and Tom was down on the kitchen floor, curled up, his hands raised to shield his face, Edna looked down at him from her great height, snickering at him, and her lip was curled in a sneer as she walked out of the room. That same sneer is still on her face now whenever she talks to him, or even glances at him from across a room. As if he's total scum.

That sneer apparently is contagious because, like a plague, it has spread to Polly's face, as well. She too now snubs him. The wedding last week was only the latest of many such incidents. She and Arthur follow Edna and Jim in everything. A few days before the wedding, Polly, Arthur, Edna, and Jim returned, suntanned, from a two-week trip to Spain. The four of them (The Fucked-up Four, as he thinks of them) have, for the past seven years, been taking holidays together, and so far—not counting Spain—they've been to Alaska, Australia, St. Maarten, the Swiss Alps, Peru, and the Far East. On each trip, all along the way, they post photos of themselves on Facebook and Instagram, where you can see them drinking, laughing, skiing, dancing, schmoozing, and cruising—delighting in marvellous vacations to which Tom and Carolyn have never been invited. Expensive, exclusive vacations where the five-star hotels, first-class restaurants, exotic day excursions, nightly entertainments, and all the other "extras"—in fact, everything but the flights—have been generously paid for by Edna and Jim. They have bought Polly and Arthur.

And Polly and Arthur were willing to be bought. No, more than willing: happy. Grateful even. Polly, frightened and insecure, was flattered to be befriended by her attractive, confident, successful older sister, and accepted into her and Jim's glamorous social circle. Finally she'd made it into the "in" group, something she'd never been able to achieve before. It's like in high school, or even grade one, where the awkward, morose, dark, unpopular girl slavishly follows the glib, graceful, popular, fair-haired one. For Polly and her sleazy, social-climbing, failure of a husband, it is both a thrill and a

social achievement to hobnob with Edna the upper-class socialite, her oily-rich husband (whose father made his money in oil), and their oily, oily-rich friends.

Tom knows Polly inside out. They haven't had more than a handful of real conversations in the decades since she married Arthur, but he knows the essence of her, the innermost places in her heart, the part of her that never changes. He can picture her deliberating, making her calculations, consciously or—more likely—unconsciously. She was never one to admit or articulate, even to herself, her profoundest feelings or thoughts; in adulthood she's moved through life with a certain detachment and an emotional fogginess, so as to get by, just make it through her days. But he can imagine her deep, unspoken logic in recent years: *If getting in with Edna and Jim means selling out Tom, well, so be it. Everything comes at a price.* The main thing is to keep Arthur happy, appeased. Because without him she can't survive. Without him she is nothing. *Don't go away, Arthur. Please don't ever leave me.*

In this way she is just like Mom. And so is Edna. You'd think that Edna, always so sought-after and father-loved, would deep down be a stronger woman, more independent, than Polly. But when it comes to her man, she's exactly the same. A total wimp. If Jim told Edna to jump off a bridge, she'd comply. She might balk a bit first but in the end she'd do what he said. She and Polly are basically no different than Mom. Mom was many things, but above all she was an accommodating wife. Always acquiescing, succumbing, submitting. Poor Mom. She was—all of us were—so afraid of Dad.

RACHEL

RACHEL'S WORRYING ABOUT her honey cake again. It's a disaster, she thinks. I have only ten pans of cake for this whole gym. Ten pans at thirty servings per pan equals three hundred servings, and there are at least eight hundred people here. This is terrible.

What can I do? Nothing at this point. It's too late to do anything about this now.

Wait—what if I cut each piece of cake in half? That will stretch the ten pans further. Instead of three hundred portions I'll end up with six hundred. That's two hundred servings short of all the people here, but still, it will probably be enough. If I discount all those stupid, skinny, dieting women, only about six hundred people will want my cake anyway. Yes, with six hundred servings we can manage.

These pieces of cake will be pretty small, though—each one just a slim little sliver instead of a big, generous hunk. But so what? Nobody breaking a fast cares how big their portion of cake is; they just want to cram something into their mouth as fast as possible. Most likely they won't even notice.

I can't leave the room now, right in the middle of these prayers. But at the first opportunity, I'll scoot to the back room and start halving all the cake. Not *having* all the cake; *halving* all the cake!

She chuckles.

THE GYM / LUCY

THE LITTLE GIRL in the red dress is back. She trots over to the grey-haired man on Rachel's right, stands in front of him, and smiles. He smiles back at her, extends his hand, and she takes it. Then she nods, satisfied, and runs back to her mother. The man, who until twenty minutes ago had never seen this girl, watches her affectionately as she returns to her mother's embrace.

Lucy gazes at the grey-haired man. He looks intelligent and interesting. She wonders if he's here alone, and if he's available. Not for herself, of course—what an idea! She laughs. (Tom glances at her sharply: there she goes again!) No, she's considering this man for her friend Marilyn, who is divorced and "looking." This man has a deeply pensive expression, and she wonders what he is thinking.

EZRA

EZRA IS THINKING: I am a failure.

He knows there are people who would dispute this, but he doesn't care. To him it's obvious that by any objective measure he is a failure as an artist. Despite his sizable talent and originality, his paintings don't sell, he has never won a prize, and no gallery wants him. There are dozens of art festivals in Toronto, as well as open-air fairs, exhibitions, conferences, openings, receptions, galas, fundraisers, and parties. He's never invited to anything. On the few occasions when, at Mona's prodding, he has rallied his self-esteem and applied to take part in a festival or conference, he's never heard back from the organizers, and his follow-up emails have gone unanswered.

He is invisible online, as well. If you google either "Canadian artists" or "Toronto artists", his name does not appear. He is not part of the scene internationally, nationally, or even locally. It is agonizing. He's never wanted to be anything but an artist. At age six, when asked what he wanted to be when he grew up, he'd always reply firmly (with the lisp he eventually outgrew), "An artitht." Yet next week he'll be sixty-six and he still hasn't achieved success. And there isn't much time left. His parents both died at seventy-seven and he figures he'll probably die around the same age. That leaves only eleven years and eleven years is nothing. When his first-born, Jerry, was two, a friend instructed Ezra to shut his eyes and turn around in a circle. Ezra complied and his friend said, "You'll shut your eyes and turn around like this, and it'll all be over. Jerry will be grown

up and out of the house. So seize every moment you can to spend with your kids." He was right. Eleven years later Jerry was bar mitzvahed; and eleven after that, he got married and went to live abroad. He was gone. If I now close my eyes and turn around, Ezra thinks, I'll be seventy-seven, and that will be that. The gates are closing. I hear them creaking shut.

No one can say he hasn't tried his best. He did everything he was advised to. He set up a website, joined Facebook, Twitter, and LinkedIn, "networked" to the best of his ability, and even blogged for six months for an online art journal. (What a waste of time that was, stealing whole weeks away from his painting!) He knows these activities are a necessary part of being an artist these days, but he's no good at marketing himself and he hates doing it. It makes him feel like he's a *thing*, an object like a bar of soap or a can of soda, and of about the same value. As he recently told his brother-in-law, a mortician who was urging him to promote himself more actively: "If I were good at, or even interested in, self-promotion, I'd have gone into marketing, not art."

Nowadays, though, these two things are almost indistinguishable. Today's art schools, unlike when he was a student, include compulsory courses on "The Business of Art," where professors teach their students how to sell their work, and themselves.

"You have to develop a narrative about yourself, a compelling life story," declared a blogger in an online art magazine that Ezra read last week. This blogger, a professor at a well-known art school in Toronto, offered the example of Charma Musk, whose rags-to-riches "narrative" included being born into abject poverty in a dirt-floor shack to an illiterate, heroin-addicted mother, along with twelve other sick and half-starved siblings. "You're not selling just your art," this professor-blogger explained. "You're selling yourself."

Right, thought Ezra. *Selling yourself*—the world's oldest profession. And one I have no intention of joining.

At such moments he is proud of his integrity and disdain for self-promotion. But he also knows that this is at least part of why he is a failure, a nothing and a nobody, in the art world, whereas younger

artists like Charma are on everyone's lips. Charma is a "rising star"—no, an already-risen and ever-rising star, a shooting star who, from her place up in the stratosphere, shoots down all her competitors, picking them off like minor meteoroids, as easily as tin ducks in a shooting gallery. He has seen her paintings and they are okay but nothing extraordinary. What Charma *is* extraordinary at, though—positively brilliant at—is the online game. She grasped from the get-go that succeeding as an artist is not about the quality of your art; it's a popularity contest. So for years she worked assiduously to acquire zillions of "followers" and "friends", who now vote for her in online competitions and nominate her for conferences, juries, and sinecures. He, on the other hand, is not comfortable or skilled at the online game, and for this he is now paying dearly.

Mind you, he'd die before doing most of the things that Charma does to get ahead. He knows all her tricks and tactics because—along with thousands of other people—he is on her listserv, so he's been targeted over the years for all of her "campaigns". (This is the word she actually uses. In his mind, *campaign* is associated with warfare, and it feels like she is waging some kind of war.) At least a dozen times he—not he personally, but he as part of a mass mailing—has received requests from her for help. Just last month she begged him to vote for her in an online contest for "Toronto's Favourite Artist," sponsored by *Toronto News World* (a rag if ever there was one). Whenever he gets an email like this from her, he's so shocked by its brazenness and crassness that he laughs out loud. But then, on and off during the course of the day, he struggles with himself over how to respond. With her most recent campaign, he struggled even more than usual. It was a matter of principle: she wasn't the best candidate on the list. Also, he felt manipulated. Yet he was a little afraid not to support her. She had power in the Toronto art scene, and he didn't want to alienate her. In the end he didn't vote for anyone at all, but she won the contest anyway. And the next day, in yet another mass mailing (and all over social media, too) she boasted proudly: "Winner: Toronto's Favourite Artist, 2018! (Runner up: The Group of Seven!)"

How vulgar. How self-serving. He, in a million years, couldn't imagine doing a "campaign" like that.

All around him now, people are praying the silent Amida, confessing their various sins, large and small. In this intensely confessional atmosphere, he, for the first time, admits to himself that if he could (meaning if he were temperamentally able to—if he had more of a pushy gene or were less mortified by the immodesty of elbowing one's way forward), he too would try some of Charma's sleazy tricks. He longs for success—so passionately at times that it is a kind of sickness. Lately he's felt he would do almost anything in the world to sit with Charma on the top branch of the Canadian art tree, looking down with her at the unsuccessful artists on the ground below, all as faceless, grey, and inanimate as rocks.

His mother's brother Oscar is a bitter person. Ever since Ezra can remember, Uncle Oscar has complained about not making as much money as his brothers and of having been swindled by a business partner. Whenever he speaks, it is to vent his spleen or spew invective. When Ezra was a teenager, after one of his uncle's visits he swore to himself that he would never be like that, no matter what happened to him. He would accept with as much graciousness as he could muster whatever life sent his way, and he'd keep all bitterness from his heart and mouth. (As the machzor says, *Open your mouth only to declare God's praise*.) But lately he feels uncomfortably like Uncle Oscar. Everywhere he turns—in magazines, newspapers, blogs, flyers, on Facebook, Twitter, and LinkedIn—he sees Charma's face, her confident, smiling, thirty-something face, taunting him: "I'm better than you. I'm more successful than you. I've just won another prize (or grant, jury appointment, conference keynote, interview, great review, or honour). And not only that: I have four or five decades ahead of me to keep collecting more accolades. Whereas you are old and washed-up." And he, torn with pain and fury, and detesting her smug little face, wants to throw down his paintbrush once and for all, and scream at her and the whole world: "It's not my fault! It's not my fault what happened! It's not my fault!"

⟩~ Except that it is.

The bitterest thing of all is that it didn't have to end up this way, and the fact that it has is entirely his own fault. He could have been, like the Marlon Brando character in *On The Waterfront,* "a contender." And the only reason he isn't now, and never will be, is because he screwed up on a snowy winter afternoon forty years ago. For the past four decades he has been tormenting himself about this one little mistake. Perseverating on how different his professional trajectory—his whole life—would have been, if only he hadn't made this error, this stupid, wrong decision that ruined his career. He can't stop thinking about this mistake. He goes over it and over it and over it in his mind.

He was twenty-five years old, in his last year of art school. He and one of his classmates had each had a painting selected for a group show of "talented young Toronto artists." The vernissage took place on a Saturday afternoon toward the end of February at a small museum owned by the city. A handful of gallery owners came, among them Joe Frost. The Frost Gallery was one of the oldest and most well-established in Toronto, and Joe, the founder's middle-aged grandson, was highly respected. He stood in front of Ezra's painting for a long time and then turned to Ezra.

"This is very good," he said. "Are you submitting it for the Clifton Prize?"

The Clifton Prize! The most prestigious art prize in Canada, its winners a Who's Who of the country's most celebrated artists. The thought of submitting his painting to the Clifton, when he wasn't even out of art school yet, hadn't crossed his mind. "I didn't think of it," he said.

"Well, you should."

Frost was wearing a flamboyant bow tie—lime-green with red polka dots—that mesmerized Ezra, vaguely reminding him of measles. "I'm chairing the jury this year," Frost said, "and we're looking for not just the same old thing but some fresh and interesting work. Which yours most definitely is. You must submit this."

"Okay. I will. Thank you."

"What's your name again?" Frost peered at the brochure in his hand.

"Ezra Miller."

"Right. Okay, Ezra. I'll keep an eye out for your painting."

He strode off with Ezra staring at his back. The Clifton Prize! Winning this, or even making its shortlist, would permanently establish his reputation as an artist. No matter what he did or didn't do after that, he would always be regarded as someone significant, someone to take seriously. No one could ever take this away from him—this recognition, this anointing.

In addition, the Clifton was Canada's most generous art prize, awarding the winner one hundred thousand dollars, and each runner-up fifty thousand. Even fifty thousand dollars was amazing. Enough for him to live on—frugally, but he was used to frugal—for two years, allowing him to continue painting full-time, instead of having to take on some crappy menial job to support himself. And if he won ... A hundred thousand dollars! Enough to start a family on—maybe even a down payment on a house—if he and Mona decided to get married (something he had only just begun to fantasize about).

I'm dreaming, he thought, I'm dreaming, as he sauntered around the exhibition with a stunned smile. Near the door he saw Mike Madison, the head of the school, and told him what had transpired. Mike was thrilled: nothing like this had ever happened before to a student at their school. He was leaving town that night for a few weeks in Europe, so please follow up, he told Ezra, with Heidi Krupp, the school's newly hired Head of Marketing and Public Relations. She would do all the paperwork and submit his painting for the Clifton. Ezra couldn't do this himself, Mike explained; submissions had to go through a sponsoring institution. He brought Ezra over to meet Heidi who, looking chic in a tight yellow dress, was laughing with a slick, good-looking man, and holding a half-full flute of champagne. She was young and friendly, and excited about Ezra's news. It was important for the school to have some "big stars,"

she said. At her previous job at Darwin College, one of the students in the cooking and hospitality program won the nation-wide McCain baking competition, and that prize generated a lot of media attention for the college. Similarly, the Clifton Prize could really put Ezra's art school on the map. She told him that if she needed anything from him like a photo or a bio, she'd be in touch soon, but she assumed that his file contained all the information she'd require for the application.

"I'll leave you in Heidi's capable hands," Mike said, and hurried off to schmooze with a wealthy board member who'd recently made a six-figure donation.

ᐧᐤ For the rest of that evening and all of the following day, Ezra walked around in a daze. Then he got back to work. For the next three weeks he was deeply immersed in painting. For his final project for school, due at the end of March, he was painting the largest canvas he'd ever done, and the piece was complex and challenging. Often he felt frustrated, anxious, or full of self-doubt, but Mona was always supportive and patient with his dark moods. "I don't know if I can do this," he'd say. She would reply calmly, "Of course you can." And he'd keep going.

When he painted, everything else disappeared. Other than seeing Mona on the weekends, all he did, now that classes were over, was paint alone in the off-campus studio that the school provided for its final-year students. Sometimes he neglected to eat or sleep. He was in the throes of creativity, fully absorbed and occupied. One day, struggling with mixing just the right shade of blue paint, trying to reproduce the colour he'd come up with the day before but unable to get it quite right, it crossed his mind, like a hazy vision from a faraway world, that sometime around now was the deadline for submissions to the Clifton Prize. He wasn't sure of the exact date—he hadn't written it down, trusting Heidi to manage all these details—but something made him think of this now. He paused for a moment, his paintbrush in mid-air, while he considered whether or not to call Heidi and remind her. But cell phones didn't exist forty years

ago, and there were no regular phones in the studios. There was a pay phone out in the hallway, but it was cold there, and he hated the long, frigid wait while the students ahead of him engaged in extensive chats with their girlfriends or boyfriends. Even more than that, he didn't want to lose twenty minutes or a half-hour now from his painting; it would ruin the flow of the work when he was right in the middle of it.

He deliberated. His father, a practical man, had always advised "double sealing" when it came to important matters. An officer during World War II, he had, whenever possible, relayed his orders to subordinates not only through one channel, but two; this he called "double sealing." Ezra thought of this now. But then his eyes wandered back to his painting. The woman in it was developing a surprising resemblance to Mona, and she needed some blue or green, or maybe a greenish blue, in her skin, to offset the blue-grey eyes. He'd studied Van Gogh's use of green when painting skin, and he thought it would work well here. He lifted his paintbrush to fix Mona's cheekbones and the area under her eyes. "I'm leaving you in Heidi's capable hands," Mike had said. Then, a week after the exhibition, Ezra had bumped into Heidi in the hallway, and she'd told him she was "on top of everything." So why doubt her? She'd managed the submission for the prize that baking student had won, hadn't she? In any case, he wasn't even certain of the deadline for the Clifton. He couldn't very well call her and say, "I have this vague feeling the deadline is sometime around now." He'd look like an idiot. Tonight at home he'll verify the date, he decided, and tomorrow he'll give her a call. The woman in the painting—not Mona, he told himself; she just looks like Mona—called out to him like a Siren. He lifted his paintbrush. And immediately he was submerged again into the ocean of art, its silent, separate, subterranean world.

)— The next day he dropped by the school. The secretary handed him the dog-eared red booklet listing the application details for all of Canada's main art competitions and grants, and he saw at once that he'd been right: the deadline for the Clifton Prize had indeed

been the previous day. But he wasn't worried. He was sure Heidi had taken care of everything. Just to be on the safe side, though ("Double seal, double seal"), he knocked on her door. There was no answer, so he left her a note.

Three days later he heard back from her. She left a message on his answering machine at home, saying that in ten days she would be leaving her job at the school. She had found a new position, once again in cooking and hospitality, which was her real love. And she was very sorry, but in all the turmoil she'd lost track of time, and the deadline for the Clifton Prize had slipped her mind. "But don't worry," she told him. "For someone of your talent, there's always next year."

꡶ There was no next year. That was his one chance for the brass ring and he'd blown it. By the following year he was no longer part of the school, and he hadn't been taken on by a gallery or any other institution that could submit his painting, so that was that. Meanwhile he and Mona had decided to get married and start a family. She was an assistant librarian and her salary was very modest, so he took a job painting scenery for the Tom Thumb Young People's Theatre. Only for a year or two, he told himself. Just till we're on our feet. Then I'll return to my art.

That "year or two" became six, then twelve, then eighteen. He had time for his own painting only on the weekends, or in the middle of the night when Mona and the kids were asleep and the house was still. At the end of these eighteen years, the mortgage was paid off and he and Mona had saved enough to put their three kids through college. At last he could leave Tom Thumb and return to his art. By then he was forty-four.

He got off to a good start. He was part of a group exhibit at the local Jewish Community Centre—this centre here, where he is right now—and the review in the *Globe and Mail* singled him out as particularly worthy of praise. He even sold a few paintings. But just as he started approaching galleries, hoping someone would take him on, the recession hit, and no gallery would take a chance anymore

on an unknown artist. Everyone wanted only the big names, the prize winners—safe bets where wealthy art appreciators could be certain that the value of their purchases would appreciate with time. Even so, he continued painting, supported financially and morally by Mona. Until Toronto elected a crack addict mayor who hated intellectuals, artists, and culture. Outraged that the number of libraries in Toronto exceeded that of its donut shops, this donut-loving mayor asked, "Who reads books anyway? Who needs libraries?" and without listening to the answers, closed half the libraries across the city. One of them was Mona's. For eight months she searched unsuccessfully for another job, and when ultimately she gave up, Ezra returned to Tom Thumb. There went another six years (ages forty-eight to fifty-four).

Finally, around eleven years ago, soon after his fifty-fifth birthday, he quit that job and returned to his art. This was made possible by the unexpected death of both his parents just a few months apart. An eerie convergence for him of searing grief with the searing joy of being able to paint again. It reminded him of the last scenery set he'd painted for Tom Thumb. For their Halloween program, they'd performed the W.W. Jacobs horror story, "The Monkey's Paw." In it, a man receives a magic monkey's paw which he uses to wish for two hundred pounds, the amount he needs in order to cover his final mortgage payment. The next day his son gets killed in a machinery accident at work, and the employer, although denying all responsibility, makes a goodwill payment to the family. Of exactly two hundred pounds. The moral of the story: "Be careful what you wish for." A valid lesson, even if rather grisly for children aged nine to fourteen, Ezra thought while painting the backdrop: an impoverished, spooky interior of a Gothic house. And then he'd had his own macabre windfall.

Now here he is, after eleven years of painting full-time, and he's still nowhere as an artist. A nobody. A complete unknown. Meanwhile all these younger artists—Charma and her ilk—zoom past him in their social-media-equipped racing cars, while he, an old man, stands watching them from the side of the road.

He'll never know if he'd have won the Clifton Prize. He had a good chance, but there was no guarantee, of course. Yet even if he hadn't, even if he'd just made the shortlist (or even the longlist), everything would have gone differently for him after that. He'd have been in the game. A part of the scene. His friend Sam, a photographer, once commented that in his field you had to win a prize, or at least make a shortlist, right at the beginning of your career, because with rare exceptions, that's the pool that would be drawn on for prizes, for everything, forever after. If you didn't get your foot on the bottom rung of the ladder early on, you had no chance of ever getting even halfway up. It's the same with painting, Ezra thinks now. If I'd made even the longlist of the Clifton back then, a gallery would have taken me on, I'd have had solo shows, not just group ones, and these would have been reviewed in newspapers and magazines and online.

By now he would be on the lists of Toronto artists, Canadian artists, International Jewish artists, and maybe even the general international lists (not just the Jewish ones). He'd have been interviewed in newspapers—in the *Globe* and perhaps also in the *New York Times*—as well as on TV, radio, and blog sites. Prominent critics and pundits would have consulted with him on serious, wide-ranging questions about art and his artistic process, and listened respectfully to his answers. Afterwards, his incisive replies and clever quips would have been repeated, retweeted, and discussed, part of the national conversation about culture in Canada, and maybe even beyond. He'd have been seen and heard—he'd have been visible and had a voice—instead of being just part of the faceless masses, one of the millions who only watch and listen.

Last but not least, his paintings would have sold. They'd have been purchased by individual collectors and galleries: maybe the Art Gallery of Ontario or the National Gallery, and maybe even some galleries in the United States, Europe, and Asia. For the past forty years, he'd have been able to live, and support his family, through his art, rather than by painting witches' castles and cartoon animals for children—or mooching off Mona, which filled him with shame.

He could have accomplished so much more with all that extra time. He'd have been able to leave behind him a substantial oeuvre.

He'll never forgive himself for that mistake back then. For being an idiot and messing up his one big chance. He ruined his career, and in a way, his whole life. He can't sleep at night or properly enjoy his days, for berating himself. Hating himself.

To escape from this now, he lowers his eyes to his machzor. *God is patient, compassionate, and kind,* it says. *God loves for a thousand generations and forgives all mistakes and transgressions.*

He flips the pages, searching, without knowing for what. He stops at a prayer he recognizes:

Forgive us. Pardon us. Be kind and merciful to us.

This, he knows, is one of the many collective prayers for Yom Kippur. "Forgive *us*"—not "Forgive *me*." Over and over, everyone in this room has been saying this prayer, requesting forgiveness for the errors and wrongs committed not by them individually, but by the entire Jewish people.

Suddenly, though, this prayer strikes him as more personal than that. As a message directed specifically at him: an injunction, a plea even, to forgive. To forgive himself finally for his long ago mistake —to pardon, and be kind to, himself—and to move on. To begin, before it's too late, to live his life fully and with joy, without that old, festering grief.

"Forgive," he instructs himself in a whisper. "Forgive, forgive, forgive." And he repeats this under his breath so many times that it starts to sound like a nonsense word: *Giffergiffergiffergiffergiffergiffergiff.*

TOM

IT'S THE SILENT Amida now, the special set of prayers recited quietly, privately, and intimately, and it's the last time they'll be said on this year's Yom Kippur. As is the custom before beginning the silent Amida, Tom starts by taking three steps backwards, whispering one Hebrew word per step: "God—open—my lips," but when he tries to take the three steps forward to return to his original position—"so my lips—will proclaim—Your praise"—he can advance only two steps because of a woman hurrying by in front of him, and he misses saying "Your praise." What will my lips proclaim now, instead of God's praise? he wonders. Then it strikes him that this is just like him and his sisters: three steps backwards, only two steps forward—the relationship always receding, never moving ahead.

He doesn't feel like starting the Amida yet—he doesn't feel ready—so he just stands there for a while. And even though he's not praying the Amida prayers, he is really praying, and with all his heart and soul. He's praying that he can find some peace with his sisters, or at least some peace from the torment of his relationship with them. He is praying for a solution, or resolution, to these disturbed, disturbing relationships. Sometimes when he wakes up in the middle of the night, he can't believe that he and his sisters aren't able to have even a regular, mundane conversation with each other about work, or their kids, or the state of the world—just normal, neutral stuff like that. How could things have deteriorated between them to such an extent? Even after all the books he's read on family

dynamics and dysfunctional relationships, he still can't make sense of this.

On Yom Kippur you're supposed to search your soul, atone for your errors and character flaws, and do everything in your power to repair your relationships—not just with God but also with people. He is willing to search his soul and admit his mistakes and missteps with his sisters and their husbands, but it is not in his power to unilaterally repair these relationships. He knows because he's tried. He has tried everything he could think of for the past two decades and nothing ever works. He has attended every one of his sisters' and their families' milestone events, dragging Carolyn and the kids along with him. He has always behaved appropriately, in fact warmly and affectionately to everyone, and he and Carolyn have given generous gifts to his sisters, their husbands, and their kids for all of their birthdays, bar and bat mitzvahs, and weddings. In addition, he has tried talking separately to Edna and Polly about his relationships with them. He has approached each sister at various points for a heart-to-heart, to try and clear things up, clean things out, but to no avail. Edna screams at him every time, her face turning lobster red as she shouts at him, enumerating all the ways he is inadequate: he's crap as a brother, crap as a brother-in-law, crap as an uncle, crap as a son, and in fact, crap as a general human being. Tom, as strong and as "adult" as he tries to remain during these tirades, invariably ends up in tears, and sometimes Edna does too, but these tears never lead anywhere. There is no softening of positions or increase in mutual understanding. These conversations resolve nothing, they just flay open the old wounds, so he doesn't see the point in trying this again.

With Polly it's different, and in a way even stranger. First of all, she won't meet him alone in person. She explained to him soon after her marriage that Arthur didn't like it; he couldn't see why she would need to see Tom alone unless they were talking about him behind his back. Still, Tom and Polly have had a few one-on-one talks on the phone over the years. Each time, when he's expressed concern about their relationship, she's insisted that everything is fine between

them, and she has no idea what he's talking about. The last such conversation was a year ago, shortly after their cousin's daughter's bat mitzvah, and Tom asked Polly directly, "Are you angry at me?"

"No," she said.

"If I did something that upset you, would you tell me?"

"Yes."

Perplexed, he told her how hurt he'd been by her and Arthur at the recent bat mitzvah. He was careful not to attack Arthur or say too much. As Carolyn had suggested, he kept to "I" statements, focusing on how he'd felt when he and Carolyn were with her and Arthur, or with them and Edna and Jim, and got ignored or excluded.

"Well, over the years," Polly said, "Arthur and I have developed a friendship with Edna and Jim. We have many things in common. We share the same values."

Values. One of Jim's favourite catchwords, which in his mouth is usually preceded by the word *corporate*. A year or so before this conversation, Polly and Arthur had started adopting Jim and Edna's phrases, and sometimes even Jim's family's idiosyncratic inflections. Tom thought of replying, *What? And Carolyn and I don't?* But he knew that they didn't, actually, share the same values as the four of them—bourgeois conformity, materialism, and conservative politics —and he had no desire to. He didn't say any of this to Polly, of course. In conversations with his family of origin he is always careful not to push too hard or too far, in case he drives the relationship beyond the point of no return, like a car flying over a cliff. Though now he wonders what good it has done, all his cautious self-restraint and tiptoeing around. He and his sisters are at the point of no return anyway. There is very little left between them and they are almost totally alienated from one another.

Sobbing, he asked Polly if she still loved him.

"Of course," she said.

"I love you, too," he replied. A minute later he hung up feeling both reassured and confused. He wasn't crazy. He knew what had happened at that bat mitzvah. Polly and Arthur had treated him and

Carolyn shabbily. But he was willing to take Polly's words at face value. She had never lied to him. There was no reason not to believe her now.

But then two weeks later, at the next family event, she and Arthur snubbed him and Carolyn again.

Maybe she doesn't know how she acts toward me, he thinks now. (It is a lifelong habit for him to rush to Polly's defense, as automatic as the Babinski reflex when you scratch the sole of a newborn's foot.) Perhaps she is not even aware of her own real feelings towards me—ambivalence, or worse.

Then again, what does it really matter how self-aware she is or isn't? The way she treats him when they're together—weirdly and coldly, avoiding all eye contact with him—that's what counts. She treats him like a pariah. And each time she does this, he feels it like the lash of their father's belt.

Whap! He recoils as if he's been hit. What was that sound? The woman on his left, the laugher, is looking upwards, and he follows her gaze. A black bird has slammed into the highest window across from them, and because outside there's a ledge underneath it, the bird is splayed dead against the window, filling it like the framed picture of a mangled, bleeding bird. He doesn't know much about birds—the different species or their nomenclature. Is this a crow, a vulture, or just a plain black bird? (And is a black bird the same as a blackbird?) *Black bird singing in the dead of night.*

The thud it made when it struck the window reverberates in him, causing an inner thud and shudder, as if it's his own demise he's just witnessed, or as if this bird were a warning of some kind. Bam, thump, and it's over. What was that Monty Python routine? "This bird is dead. It's expired. It has gone to meet its maker."

What does that mean anyway, "gone to meet its maker"? The bird had a meeting scheduled with God in front of the pearly gates? Whatever it means, we'll all "meet our maker" soon enough.

Blackbird dying in the dead of night. Take these broken wings and learn to fly. All your life. You've been only waiting for this moment to arise.

THE RABBI

THE RABBI IS reciting the silent Amida but he isn't fully focused on the words of the prayers. He's lightheaded from fasting, and his body feels light, too—almost weightless, as if in a moment he will float upwards and bang his head on the ceiling. Somehow he's been emptied of all his bones, muscles and blood, and filled instead with a crazy happiness. *I am part of this community; I am not alone!* Now that he's shepherded this gym full of people, this congregation, through this year's High Holidays, he and they belong to each other.

He glances around the room. This place is so full of love, he thinks. Love, like a vapour, permeates every inch of this gym, pressing sideways against the painted concrete walls and rising to the highest rafter. He scans the people nearest him without knowing any of their names except Tom's. In the front row on his left, he examines Tom and Lucy; in the front row on his right, Rachel, Ira, and Ezra. Whom do they love? he wonders. God? (Probably not.) Their parents? Their children? Their siblings, friends, lovers, spouses? He hopes to have a spouse himself one day, a woman who will love him. So far it's been just him and Mum. She's at home now and they'll break the fast together tonight, as they do every year, enjoying her cauliflower soup. He loves that soup. It's funny what people love. Some people love cars. Others love dogs or cats, sometimes more than humans. He scrutinizes these five congregants. Apart from their families and friends, what in life do they love? Their work? Music? Movies? Nature? Politics? Clothes? Money? Sex?

Drugs? This is his people, they are his congregation (even if temporarily), and he realizes he doesn't know them at all.

Our time together will end soon, he thinks. In less than an hour. Then he might never see any of them again.

He doesn't want this to be over yet.

The U'n'taneh Tokef prayer that they read earlier today opens with: "Let us now proclaim the power of this day's holiness." He can taste the power of this special day now; he has been tasting it all day long. But for him the power of Yom Kippur—its magic even—does not derive from its being The Day of God's Judgment, but because it is The Day of God's Love. Maybe it's his lightheadedness, but it seems to him at this moment that Yom Kippur (in English, The Day of Atonement) should instead be called Yom Ahava, The Day of Love.

As if to agree with him, the words that appear before him now in his machzor are: *Your love for us is infinite.* Instead of whispering them as is customary for the silent Amida, he reads them in a normal voice, and since his voice is amplified by the microphone, some of the congregants glance up at him, startled.

It's true, he thinks. Your love *is* infinite. And how infinite are all the varieties of love. There is love unrequited and love returned. There is joyful love, melancholy love, twisted, sick and crazy love. Probably there are as many types of love as there are people in this room—for every individual, a different kind of love (and not all of them kind). For sure some people here have no love at all in their life. They are loveless, or unloved, and lonely. If he were Mr. Fantastic, he would stretch out his elastic, infinitely extendable arms and, in one huge embrace, enfold everyone in this gym. He would hold them close and keep them safe forever.

He hears a small, still voice. It is Yom Kippur whispering to him. Gradually the voice gets louder and louder until it's booming like God at Mount Sinai. This boom, this roar, must be audible beyond this building, he thinks—six, even sixteen, blocks away. Yet, oddly, no one seems to be aware of it here except him.

"Love each other!" bellows Yom Kippur. "Love each other better! Love each other more!"

His skinny heart swells with aching passion for his people, and for this whole sad, troubled, unredeemed world. He feels his heart expanding and straining inside his rib cage, pressing relentlessly against his chest. He's sure he is going to crack right open. He cannot contain all this longing and love.

TOM

AS TOM PREPARES himself to recite the last silent Amida of Yom Kippur, something shifts in him. An hour ago, if you'd asked him, he would have said he didn't believe that by the end of tonight his fate would be decided for the coming year. That's plain silly, he would have replied. I'm a physician, a scientist: I don't believe in hocus pocus.

But now something's changed. Perhaps it's the accumulation, almost the hypnosis, of hour after hour of music—all those hopeful prayer songs—together with thousands of words of poetry, stories, and homilies, either spoken or written. Or maybe it's nothing more than the disorientation and weakness that hits the body after twenty-four and a half hours of fasting. Whatever the reason, at this point nothing in the world seems more plausible or imminent to him than that his fate for the coming year will be decided in the next thirty minutes. His life—his real life, not something abstract—is hanging in the balance.

Tell the truth, Tom, he thinks. Examine yourself top to bottom. Don't skip any dark corners. It's now or never.

He begins to whisper to himself the Ashamnu prayer, and like everyone around him, bangs his right fist against the left side of his chest once for each of its twenty-four Hebrew words:

"Ashamnu" (we have been guilty)—bang!

"Bagadnu" (we have betrayed)—bang!

"Gazalnu" (we have stolen)—bang!

"Dibarnu dofi" (we have slandered)—*Yes, I have slandered. I have slandered my sisters and their husbands*—bang!

My sisters and their husbands have been assholes to me. There's no doubt about that. I have a long list of things they have done over the decades—to me, to Carolyn, to our kids. (I hate them most of all for hurting Lenny and Samantha.) All my grievances against them are legitimate. They've shat on me—on us—for the past thirty years.

"He'evinu" (we have acted perversely)—bang!

"V'hirshanu" (we have done wrong)—bang!

But the truth is, I'm not perfect either. I have done things wrong. I've done all sorts of things wrong.

I never set out to hurt my sisters and their husbands—I have never intentionally been mean to any of them—but I've hurt them just the same. If someone, say a friend of theirs, asked them about our relationship, they'd probably—no, for sure—have a list of grievances against me, same as I do against them.

What would they say exactly? Edna and Jim would go way back, starting twenty-five years ago when I didn't fly back from England the instant their first child, Gavin, was born. I was a struggling medical student and had already purchased a cheap ticket home for two months later—for my annual visit each summer, when I had no classes or internships—and couldn't change it. When in July I arrived in Toronto, bearing gifts for them and Gavin (which was a financial challenge since I was living on a tight student budget), they accused me of not caring about them or their baby. Of being selfish. And also "narcissistic"—the main word, I think, that characterizes *them*.

"If you cared about people ..." was how Edna back then started her rant, and how she has started hundreds more of them since. It's been her and Jim's constant refrain. If I cared about them, I'd visit them all the time, become an integral part of their lives, and really get to know their kids. I'd spend every possible moment, especially the weekends, at their house.

But I couldn't do that. Life at their place is one long party, and I've never been a party person. Also, I couldn't stand their friends. They were shallow, materialistic, and small-minded, and the less time I spent at Edna and Jim's mansion, the happier I was.

But they wanted me there. They longed to be conveners, and without people (like me and their friends) agreeing to be convened—flocking every weekend to their house to help fill its (and their) emptiness—they couldn't fulfill their fantasy about themselves and their home as a social hub. In that house, though, I was uncomfortable. I always felt like nothing but a prop in a play—performing as "Edna's brother, the one who studied medicine in England." Yet I know, if I look at it from their point of view, that they wanted, maybe even needed, me, and I let them down. I wouldn't play the part in their life that they'd assigned me. This infuriated them. And yes, hurt them, too.

"Zadnu" (we have acted arrogantly)—bang!

"Hamasnu" (we have done violence)—bang!

Polly I hurt in a different way than Edna. I abandoned her. I went off to grad school in England and left her on her own. Within weeks of my departure, she found Arthur. An asshole, but at least someone to cling to. If I'd stayed in Toronto, I'm sure she'd never have ended up with such a shmuck. A man in numerous ugly ways a carbon copy of our dad. But she was desperate. I wasn't there. And she couldn't bear to be alone.

"Tafalnu sheker" (we have practiced deceit)—bang!

"Ya'atznu ra" (we have counselled evil)—bang!

I disappointed my sisters in these ways. But to them my greatest crime—what was unforgivable and ultimately split us apart—was that I didn't like their husbands. I didn't think they were good enough for my sisters (how ironic in retrospect!) and didn't try to disguise this. I was never overtly rude to either of them—I'm Canadian: I'm polite—but I also made no effort to engage with them or win them over, which I realize now is what you're supposed to do when someone new enters your family. I trusted too much in the bedrock-bond between siblings. It never occurred to me that not accepting their husbands would cost me my relationships with my sisters. That they'd dump me like a sack of garbage on the curb.

What I wouldn't give to be able to go back now and do all that differently. Like that time, early in our relationship, when Jim and

Arthur invited me to go with them to the gym. To this exact gym, actually! Here at the downtown Jewish Community Centre! I refused. It wasn't anything against them; I never go to the gym. I'm self-conscious about my body and am not athletic, so I was afraid that, being out of shape, I'd embarrass myself in front of those two jocks. I wouldn't be able to climb the ropes, catch the ball, do push-ups or pull-ups. So I said no. Now I wish that instead of simply refusing, I'd proposed an alternative, made some sort of counteroffer. Suggested we all go out for a beer, for instance, or to a baseball game—something male-bondy like that. Instead I just mumbled some lame excuse that, even to my own ears, sounded phony, and which I'm sure they took as a rejection of them. They never invited me out again—not to the gym or anywhere. Well, why would they? I turned them down the first time they asked. It's my own fault.

If only I could rewind the tape of that conversation, and this time tell them, "Sure, I'd love to go to the gym with you guys." I'd swing from the ropes like a monkey if it would bring me back my sisters.

"Kizavnu" (we have spoken falsehood)—bang!

"Latsnu" (we have scoffed)—bang!

We have fucked up. We have made a mess of things.

Bang! Bang! Bang!

THE RABBI / THE GYM

ALL FIVE OF them hear the crash at the same time, but like Tom, they are beating their breasts, immersed in the Ashamnu, so they don't look up from their machzors. Tom distantly assumes that a second bird has smashed into the uppermost window of the gym, splashing its soft, wet innards all over the pane. To Lucy, the crash sounds like Larry tumbling out of bed last week, bruising himself all over. Rachel, who is imagining the crucial delicate step of assembling a Religieuse à L'Ancienne (which she thinks, with her poor high school French, means "Ancient Religion"), feels her cake collapse from the inside. Ezra hears a framed painting clatter to the ground. Ira experiences the noise as something soft, like the crumpling of clothes.

It's the rabbi. He's lying face down on the floor, totally still, as if dead. Rachel has seen scenes like this only on TV. In murder mysteries, where a body (a corpse) is sprawled in an awkward position on the carpet of a study or the pavement of a parking garage, while a detective barks orders to his staff about where to search for clues. This rabbi on the floor of a community centre gym can't be real.

Tomorrow people will argue about what happened next. Some will say that the prayerful, whispering room fell completely, eerily, silent. Others heard a woman scream. The little girl for the rest of her life will dream of grownups running madly around in circles, so confused and hysterical that they're no longer adults; just three-year-old children, the age she is now.

One thing that happens for sure is that five people—Tom, Lucy, Ira, Rachel, and Ezra—converge simultaneously on the fallen body. What makes these five people, out of the whole eight hundred in the room, rush forward, nobody knows. Maybe they don't know themselves. But without exchanging a single word, they all crouch or kneel around the rabbi in a circle. Tom and Lucy, who approached from the podium's left, are on his left side; Ezra, Ira, and Rachel, who approached from the right, are on the other.

Tom quickly takes charge. "I'm a doctor," he says. He leans over the body, checks for vital signs, and points to Ira: "You in the green shirt, call 911."

Ira doesn't have his phone on him; he jumps up and runs out of the room, hoping there will still be someone at the front desk. There is. After he's delivered his message, he thinks: I'm so stupid. I could have just stood up and shouted: "Who has a phone?" Probably half the people in that gym have phones on them today, even though it's forbidden on Yom Kippur.

Tom, so concentrated on his task that he hears only silence, sweeps his fingers through the rabbi's mouth, lifts the chin, pinches the nose, affixes his lips to the rabbi's to form an airtight seal, and begins blowing. Rachel, watching with fascination, thinks, It's the same as blowing up a balloon! Ira, hurrying back to the gym, stops and stares. It looks like Tom is deeply, intimately kissing the rabbi. The little group turns expectantly to Ira. Confused, and embarrassed by the attention, he tells them an ambulance has been ordered. "Good," Lucy says, and Tom nods. Ira, as he kneels again, is warmed by their approval.

A dozen or so individuals, including three doctors offering their help, have clustered near the little group. Ezra rises as its self-appointed spokesperson, and replies to the same queries over and over: "What's wrong with the rabbi? Will he be all right? When are we going to finish the service?" After a couple of minutes he ascends the podium and addresses the whole congregation. "Please, everyone, remain calm."

This isn't really necessary: there is no pandemonium. Most of the people are still sitting, frozen in their seats, anxiously asking their neighbours what has happened, and assuming somehow that the five people who have formed a circle around the rabbi know what to do and have the authority to do it.

Ezra says: "We are fortunate to have a doctor here who is administering CPR to the rabbi, and an ambulance has already been called. We expect it will arrive soon since the nearest hospital is only three blocks away. We plan to resume services shortly, but in the meantime, please stay in your seats. Thank you for your patience."

As he descends the podium, the noise level surges in the gym, with almost every congregant present breaking into conversation. A few frown up at the clock. It's late. Yom Kippur will be over in forty-eight minutes. They are hungry, thirsty, and tired after this long day of praying and fasting, and they want to go home. But how can they slip out now, with the rabbi lying in the middle of the floor? They can't very well just step over his body and leave.

Ezra returns to his spot, crouching like a cougar. What a sweet-looking face this young rabbi has.

Why did he collapse? Did he have a prior heart condition? It must be a heart attack if this doctor is doing CPR. How could something like this happen on Yom Kippur?

After each sequence of two breaths that Tom's been blowing into the rabbi's mouth, he has been forming his fingers into a "steeple," intertwining them tightly, and pressing, quickly, rhythmically, into the rabbi's chest. Every time he does this, he counts aloud: "One, two, three ..." up to thirty. At thirty, he again sweeps out the rabbi's mouth, tilts back the head, lifts the chin, pinches the nose, covers the mouth with his own, and blows twice. Then he returns to pumping the chest, counting from one to thirty. Then two more breaths. Then more pumping.

Lucy gently grasps the rabbi's ankles and slightly raises his legs, looking questioningly at Tom. Tom nods. She continues holding the legs in this position.

Ezra stands up again to wave more people away from the rabbi. He answers their questions as best he can, repeating numerous times, with patience, but wearily: "We don't know anything yet. We're still waiting for the ambulance to arrive. It should be here soon."

Rachel says quietly to Tom, "I know CPR. I can relieve you." Tom, straddling the rabbi, one knee on either side of the body, shakes his head. To Rachel he looks exhausted. Unlike her, he has obviously been really fasting, and she's worried that he won't be able to last until the ambulance and medics arrive. "I can do the breathing," she says. "Let me help." He doesn't reply. Then he nods. He continues pumping: "... twenty-four, twenty-five, twenty-six ..." At "twenty-seven" he glances pointedly at her, and before he's reached twenty-nine, she's already scrambled into position, kneeling to the left of the rabbi's head. Immediately upon hearing "thirty," she does the mouth sweep and gives the rabbi his two breaths. On each one, she gratefully sees his thin chest rise. Then Tom starts pumping again: "One, two, three, four ..."

Thirty pumps by Tom, two breaths by Rachel—this cycle continues dozens of times. To Lucy it seems to be going on forever. Sharply she asks Ira, "When is the ambulance coming?" He stares at her blankly. "Go check," she says. "Tell them to hurry." He leaps up and runs out of the gym.

Tom is pumping, pumping, pumping hard. He's totally drained but he can't stop—if he stops, the boy will die. He keeps pumping as if he's pumping his own heart to keep himself alive.

Then, across the room, there's a vision: a flash of his sisters and, a little away from them, Carolyn with his two kids. This young rabbi on the ground is as pale and fragile as a girl, he thinks; it could be Polly, or Samantha, down on this hard floor. *Save her, save her. Save her life.*

PART TWO

THE GYM

THE AMBULANCE HAS come and gone. Five minutes ago two white-coated men gently lifted the rabbi onto a stretcher and carried him away. The congregation watched in respectful silence, worried for him and hoping he'd be all right, but also relieved that the ambulance had finally arrived. Now they could finish the service and go home. But then they heard the heart-rending wail of the ambulance's siren—a tragic wail like you'd hear at the Wailing Wall—and they listened anxiously until it faded away. A minute later they began murmuring among themselves, the room hummed like a beehive, and soon people were speaking in full voice as if they were in their own homes. A few people are still silent, though—like Tom, Ezra, Lucy, Ira, and Rachel, assembled at the front of the room. Even after the rabbi was carted off, none of them returned to their original seats; they all stayed together—bonded to each other by some mysterious glue—close to where the rabbi collapsed. Tom, since the paramedics arrived and took over, has been sitting on the floor with his eyes closed, breathing heavily.

"Are you okay?" Ezra asks him for the second time, crouching beside him.

"Yes. Just tired," Tom says, panting.

His face is dead white. "You don't *look* okay," Lucy says.

"I'm fine," Tom says testily, struggling to catch his breath. "I'm a doctor." As if doctors can't be sick. Or maybe as if doctors always know best, including about themselves. His eyelids flutter.

"You need a drink," Lucy says.

A nearby congregant, a fat man with a green tallis, overhears this and objects: "A drink? It's Yom Kippur!"

Ignoring him, Lucy pulls a bottle of water from her bag and offers it to Tom. He hesitates. "It's over in less than an hour," she says. He accepts the bottle and takes a sip. The man in the green tallis frowns. First the rabbi collapses mid-service and gets dragged away; now, at the front of the room, right next to the prayer podium where everyone can see him, some guy is guzzling water. Everything is wrong at this Yom Kippur service. "Who's in charge here?" he asks belligerently.

"Me," Tom says. "I'm on the board of the shul. I'm its representative here." The water seems to have revived him a bit; his breathing is less laboured.

"Well, when are we going to finish the service?" the fat green man demands of Tom—and then (as Tom, feeling weak, closes his eyes for a moment) of Ezra. Lucy and Rachel he disregards as if they aren't even there. "Some of us want to get home before midnight."

Ezra scans the gym. It's only been about twenty minutes since the rabbi fell but it feels like an hour and a half. Some people have left, but the room is still about two-thirds full; there are around five hundred people here, waiting to complete the service.

"Was there any backup for the rabbi?" Ezra asks Tom. "Do you know if there's anyone here who can lead the rest of the prayers?"

"I can," Lucy says.

Ezra looks at her, surprised. "You know how to lead?"

"Yes."

Tom's voice is hoarse: "You know the right tune for Neila?"

Lucy nods.

"Start from the repetition of the Amida," Tom says.

"I know."

"All right. Go." Tom tries to stand up. "Rest some more," Ezra says to him, pressing lightly on Tom's shoulder, and Tom sits back down. Ezra and Ira stand on either side of him like two flanking angels, and Rachel is in front.

Lucy ascends the podium, conscious of Tom sitting near the bottom stair, inches from where the rabbi lay. Silently she faces the ark, her back to the congregation. An expectant hush fills the gym. Paging backwards through the rabbi's machzor, she finds the right place, and for a few moments just breathes, preparing herself to begin. But she can't. She descends the podium, to the consternation of the congregation—What is happening *now?*—and returns to her little group.

"I want to do something before the repetition of the Amida," she says to Tom. "A prayer for the rabbi—a misheberach."

Tom is startled by the request. A misheberach, the prayer for the sick, is not normally a part of Neila. But then he says, "Sure. Under the circumstances, that's a nice thought."

"Go, girl!" Rachel says, grinning.

Ira, who hasn't said a word since the rabbi was taken away, has been watching all this closely. He didn't like Tom when he first saw him—a smug bastard with a perfect life, he thought—but now he feels a grudging respect for him. Tom probably saved the rabbi's life. Not that a life is worth a whole lot, really. But still. He's a sort of hero. And now that Tom is down on the ground and vulnerable, he elicits a flutter of empathy from Ira. When Tom drank the water just now, Ira could feel the cool water trickling down his own parched throat, refreshing it. Now he has an impulse to stroke Tom's arm the way his own mother did when he was sick as a boy. But he doesn't dare. And anyway, Tom doesn't need any comfort from him. For that he has the strawberry blonde who gave him water, probably his wife. Lucy her name is. The one who's about to lead the service. He's never seen a woman do this before. This didn't happen back in small-town Manitoba. He wonders what it will be like.

At the podium, Lucy faces the congregation. "Before beginning the repetition of the Amida," she announces, "we're going to do something a little unusual." She smiles wryly. "Though in any case, as we all know, this is already an unusual Yom Kippur." She has the shadow of an accent. Her father came from Edinburgh, and the faint

echo of a Scottish lilt slips into her speech whenever she feels emotional or stressed. "I know everyone is upset and worried about the rabbi. So instead of just picking up where he stopped—"

She herself stops. To her surprise, she is all choked up. She sees the rabbi tumbling to the floor. He keeps doing this over and over again, like a clown repeating his tumbling trick five, ten, fifteen times. She can't get this image out of her mind. But the rabbi she sees isn't just the rabbi. His face, when he hits the floor, alternates between his own and someone else's. On one tumble she sees the rabbi's face; on the next, it's Larry's. Then the rabbi's again. Then Larry's. It takes Lucy a while to pull herself together (eighteen seconds, Tom notes, gazing alternately at her and at the wall clock). A long time when five hundred people are watching, and waiting for you to finish your sentence.

With an effort, she says: "We'll start with a prayer for him. A misheberach, the prayer for sick people. We'll pray for his quick and full recovery."

"Ah-*meyn*," shout a few people.

But the fat green man, back at his seat, scowls. You don't say a misheberach during Neila. It's not done. But what can you expect from a woman leading the service? And a woman who gave someone a drink on Yom Kippur, at that. She doesn't know a damn thing. Probably doesn't even know right from wrong.

LUCY

TODAY SHE'S HARDLY sung along at all with the rest of the congregation. She's been feeling separate from the people and prayers around her. But now, as she opens her mouth and starts to sing, she feels the air rising into her chest and a peacefulness filling her. This happens to her often when she leads services. Until her mother died fourteen months ago, Lucy was a volunteer prayer leader at her nursing home, and there she sang the misheberach (among other prayers) dozens of times. Sometimes the Hebrew prayer and other times the English-language version written by Debbie Friedman. Now she attaches Friedman's tune to the Hebrew words, knowing, because she's done this before, that the words and music will perfectly mesh.

"May the One who blessed our forefathers and foremothers,

"Abraham, Isaac, and Jacob; Sarah, Rebecca, Rachel, and Leah,

"Bless and heal everyone who is sick."

As if these were magic words, something clicks in her and open-sesame's a door inside of her that was locked. All through Yom Kippur, God has been so far away as to be nothing but a theoretical concept. But now she feels an invisible presence near her, inside her even, that is realer and more intimate than anything in the world. This presence, this God, she thinks, was known also to Abraham, Isaac, Jacob, Sarah, Rebecca, Rachel, and Leah, and was in existence even before them—before there was even a planet Earth or a universe. God is the one constant, and has always been guiding and directing everything, including all of human history. You've been

with us all along, she muses with surprise, and you're still here with us now. Like that prayer we said this morning: "God reigned, God reigns, and God will reign forever." (*Reign*, not *rain*; I hope it doesn't rain forever!) But it's true. There is something, God, that is bigger and stronger than me. An enormous, kind, and benevolent force that will help me through what lies ahead. I will not be alone with all that.

She continues singing:

"May the Holy One's compassion flow out toward all who are sick,

"And restore them, heal them, and strengthen and revive them."

She is crying now. Her back is to the congregation so almost no one can see this, but Tom can, and from his vantage point on the floor he watches her, astonished. An hour ago, sitting on his left, this woman laughed her way through the service. Now on the podium, in front of hundreds of people, she is crying. What a strange person. But then he thinks more charitably, Maybe she's not that strange. Perhaps something is hurting or worrying her—possibly a sick friend or relative. Conceivably he is not the only one here who is struggling with something.

In any case, this Lucy sure can sing. Her voice rises and falls as naturally as the water flowing in a pebbly stream, and its sound is as pure, transparent, and refreshing. Listening to her reminds Tom of a Hasidic story. There was a boy who didn't know the words to any of the prayers, but still longed to pray on Yom Kippur with the rest of the congregation. All this boy knew how to do was play the flute, so in the middle of the Yom Kippur service he pulled out his flute and played the prayer that was in his heart. The congregation was horrified. People yelled at him: "Don't you know anything? It is forbidden to play an instrument on Yom Kippur!" But the Baal Shem Tov silenced them and thanked the boy, explaining that because of his purity of heart and sincere, passionate desire to pray, the prayers of the whole congregation would now reach up to heaven.

Lucy is no longer weeping. But as she continues to sing, her grief is subsumed into her voice. There is a deeper timbre to it and a

subtle ambiguity as if she's simultaneously singing in both a major and a minor key.

"May the Holy One send complete healing to all who are sick,

"Healing of the body, and healing of the soul."

Her voice is shadowy yet also back-lit—like sun filtering through a thick curtain of dark honey—and it's so beautiful that for a moment Tom almost believes that a wounded soul like his can heal.

"Send healing," she sings, "for the Jewish people and for all humanity,

"Speedily and soon. And let us say: Amen."

Joining her on the last word, the congregation cries out, "Ah-*meyn!*"

And Lucy, her face streaked with tears, smiles.

RACHEL

LUCY BEGINS THE repetition of the Amida and Rachel watches her with admiration as she sings:

"Praised are You, Lord our God and God of our fathers and mothers,

"God of Abraham, Isaac, and Jacob, Sarah, Rebecca, Rachel and Leah,

"Great, mighty, awesome, exalted God, who bestows loving-kindness and creates all things."

You never know what's inside a person, Rachel thinks. You'd never guess by looking at Lucy—a plainly-dressed middle-aged woman—all the beauty inside her. Her voice has the richness and smoothness of honey cake batter when you lick it off a spoon. What's weird, though, about honey cake batter is that once it's baked, it changes entirely. Not just in texture—from raw gloop to solid, like any cake—but even in flavour. Actually, its texture is strange, too. Honey cake is the stickiest cake in the world. It adheres, glutinously, to everything. To the pan. To the palate. To lips. The way the rabbi's lips stuck to hers when she gave him those two breaths at a time. His lips were soft. Like William's. She can still feel how William's mouth felt and tasted, even though it's been nine years. She'll never forget his smell or his taste. She'll never forget *him*.

They loved each other in so many ways: physically, spiritually, and culinarily. (Not to be confused with cunnilingously!) Though with her and William, food and sex, and sex and food, intermingled

constantly. She loved cooking for him and prepared elaborate, scrumptious, sumptuous meals, plying him with all her favourite recipes. Some of these he'd never encountered before, and after tasting them he begged for them again and again. As with sex. She was more adventurous and unconventional than him, and he was always asking her to introduce him to new sexual positions. They experimented and explored together both sexually and gastronomically. He licked from her fingers her homemade pâté de canard en croute and devoured her boeuf bourguignon, quiche Lorraine, and key lime pie. But still he left her.

A little girl in a red dress marches up to the podium and stands near the bottom step, scrutinizing Lucy. That's what I looked like at that age, Rachel thinks. She has a clear image of her appearance back then, thanks to pictures in the family album. Her hair was curly like this little girl's, and in almost every photo she was eating. A lollipop. A cookie. An ice cream. Always something sweet, never an apple or celery stick like they give kids nowadays. She can't imagine life without sweets. God forbid she should ever get diabetes. Cirrhosis, thrombosis, tuberculosis—no problem. But diabetes, where she wouldn't be allowed to eat any foods with sugar for the rest of her life? What would be the point in living?

Here last week on Rosh Hashana, someone out in the hallway told a joke about diabetes. Four Europeans go hiking together and get lost. First, they run out of food, then out of water. "I'm so thirsty," the Englishman says, "I must have tea." "I'm so thirsty," the Frenchman says, "I must have wine." "I'm so thirsty," the German says, "I must have beer." "I'm so thirsty," the Jew says, "I must have diabetes."

Rachel smiles, but it vanishes quickly—last night's dream has returned. In this dream, she'd been on holiday in Morocco, and when she returned to Canada, she discovered there were no more sweets in the whole country. Not a single cookie, cake, candy, or chocolate bar. Canada was utterly devoid of sweets. This disaster, she knew in her dream, was the result of the scurrying, rat-like activity of the health food nuts. She'd grown up believing that "a spoonful of sugar helps the medicine go down," but nowadays the acolytes

of the health food religion see a spoonful of sugar as equivalent to cyanide. They actually call sugar "poison"! And they condemn it not only in terms of its health risks, but in moral terms. It is "bad," and so, by extension, are the people (like her) who consume it.

A group of these anti-sugar fanatics is also ruining her job at the shul. Starting in two weeks, she will have to abide by the new guidelines they've pushed through: to omit sugar from all her desserts. She's supposed to substitute grape juice, honey, or date syrup instead. Yuck!—the mere thought makes her gag. This self-righteous gang at her shul is led by her ex-friend and one-time roommate Algae. (Algae was born Amanda but at some point turned flaky and adopted a more "natural" name.) Algae and her cadre of followers are, to Rachel, a wolf pack devouring her pleasant, peaceful, grazing deer of a job. Because of them and their latest decree, she's been seriously considering quitting her position as the shul's cook and baker, but she needs the income and currently has no other prospects.

In last night's dream, her first reaction to the disappearance of sweets from Canada was to plan a trip to the States, where she could get her fix and stockpile supplies against any such calamity in future. But it turned out that the situation was much more dire than she'd realized. The health food lobby, with the support of the World Health Organization (one tentacle of a corrupt United Nations), had vanquished all its opposition, and now there was not one single sweet—not even a lone surviving chocolate chip cookie—in the entire world.

Standing in the gym, surrounded by prayers, she is stabbed by a sense of loss and sadness. She pictures a barren landscape: pitted, uninhabited, and uninhabitable, like the moon. She saw a poster like this once; its caption read, "Life Without Mozart." She chuckles ruefully. Some people experience desolation when imagining life without music or art; she grieves over the lack of a chocolate chip cookie. What a shallow person she is.

She glances down at Tom. He is still sitting on the floor, but he appears better than before: some colour has returned to his face. He is loyally flanked by Ezra and Ira. Good people, she thinks, and

scans the gym. There are so many serious, praying people here. Almost all the adults are fasting (she can tell from their pallor), and so are even some older children. Yet she is not. She, out of this large, jam-packed gym, is practically the only person who is not fasting. Why is that? Why can't she fast for even one day a year?

Usually she tells herself, and others, that she can't fast because she has low blood sugar. Blood *sugar*, she thinks now. Does low blood sugar mean that your body lacks—and therefore craves—sugar? Could this explain her desperate love of sweets? She has no idea. But she does know that there is no bona fide medical reason preventing her from fasting. The real reason she doesn't fast is that it makes her too sad. Horribly, agonizingly, almost unbearably, suicidally, sad. Food is her comfort and joy. Its colours, textures, smells, and flavours all cheer her up and encourage her to go on. For her, a day without food is a day without sunshine—a day without any pleasure or happiness at all. It is a day of abject misery and loneliness.

Lucy is singing: "God, hear us today and forgive us."

Will God forgive me for not fasting? Rachel wonders. Not that she thinks God really cares one way or the other. Most likely God has more important things on his mind. But probably he will.

Or maybe he won't.

Maybe he will.

Maybe he won't.

This is like that game where you pluck the petals off of daisies. He loves me. He loves me not. He loves me. He loves me not. William loved her not. Or maybe he did. Or maybe he didn't. She'll never know for sure.

Such deep sadness. But no. She's not going to let it engulf her. She is not going to allow the beginning of this tsunami—these first, dangerous drops of despair—to penetrate the thin cracks in her sea wall. Think sweet thoughts, she instructs herself. *Think. Sweet. Thoughts.*

A beautiful, a magnificent, cake. For the bar mitzvah next week at the shul—the last event where she'll still be allowed to use sugar —she will make a splendid Three-tiered White Chocolate and Raspberry Cheesecake. Maybe she'll even add liqueur—a dribble

of Kahlua, Cointreau, or Grand Marnier. She'll have to be careful with the liqueur, though—you don't want all those little kiddies staggering home soused! She grins, picturing this. Then she remembers the main challenge of this recipe. The trick with this cake—as with cheesecakes in general—is making sure you cool it very gently. Otherwise you get cracks in the surface, and that will ruin your whole presentation. You want to keep your surface smooth and pretty and all internal cracks invisible. Same as when you present yourself to the world.

Contentedly she runs through the recipe in her mind:

Melt the butter and chocolate, stir in the crushed biscuits, divide this mixture between three baking tins: one large, one medium, one small. Press the mixture evenly over the base of the tins, and then chill. Make sure that the base covers right up to the edge of each tin, or the topping could leak through.

For the filling, melt the white chocolate, stirring occasionally. Make sure it doesn't become too hot. Then beat the cream cheese and eggs together. Add the sour cream and vanilla and whisk again until completely smooth. Stir in the melted chocolate and mix. Divide half of this mixture between the three chilled bases. Scatter the raspberries over the mixture in each tin and cover with the remaining mixture, spreading evenly.

Bake the three tins of cheesecake (for different lengths of time, depending on their size), till they are all firm around the edges and just set in the middle. Remove from the oven and leave to cool at room temperature before transferring to the fridge to chill. Don't rush them into the fridge.

To decorate, pulse the raspberries with the icing sugar in a food processor, making a purée. Pass this through a sieve and discard the seeds.

Remove the cheesecakes from their tins. Place the largest one on a serving plate and the two smaller ones on cake boards. Cut a cake dowel to the height of the largest cheesecake. Press down into the centre of the cheesecake and place the middle-sized cheesecake on top. Repeat the process with the medium cheesecake, and place the

smallest cheesecake on top. The dowel helps support the cheesecakes and prevents the lower layers from getting crushed.

Whip the cream and spoon it into a piping bag with a star nozzle. Pipe rosettes of cream close together around the top edge of all three cheesecakes and top each rosette of cream with a raspberry. Pour the raspberry coulis onto the top tier. The piped cream should prevent it from dripping down the sides.

Make the white chocolate curls by placing a chocolate bar on its side, then dragging the blade of a long sharp knife at a slight angle towards you. For easier, shorter curls, you can use a vegetable peeler, but for this great, final cake, make the longer curls. Arrange the curls over the top tier.

Wow! What an impressive, gorgeous cake this will be!

And mmmm, so delicious! Mmm mmm mmm! She can't help smacking her lips.

TOM

IT'S THE AMIDA now and Tom knows he should be standing for it like everyone else, but he doesn't feel up to it yet. Though he is doing better even than a few minutes ago. Gradually he is coming back to himself. He smiles wryly: Coming back to your self. Returning to your soul. The essential requirement of Yom Kippur.

I'll be all right, he thinks. I just overdid it a bit with that CPR. All that pumping was strenuous. But what could I do? Let that kid die?

Now he's a doctor again, scanning himself clinically: his heart rate, breathing, perspiration. Yes, he'll be fine—thanks at least in part to the kindness of strangers. He glances up at Ezra, Ira, and Rachel, all standing around him like a triangle of protective trees, and Lucy nearby. Actually, they're not really strangers anymore—not after what they've been through together today. Slowly he tries to stand up. A mistake—he feels dizzy and confused, and quickly sits back down. They're almost like family, he thinks. Look how they've been guarding me. Ezra on my left, Ira on my right, Rachel in front of me, Lucy close by on the podium. Four angels. Like four cousins; family.

Family. My sisters. *Oy.*

All that endless crap with them and their husbands—why do I even continue to care about it? What do Edna, Polly, Jim, and Arthur really matter anymore? They don't care about me. And they're not even my real family at this point; that's Carolyn, Lenny, and Samantha. They're the ones who matter to me now.

Yet they're still not completely irrelevant, my Family of Origin. (My "F of O"—very close to F.O., isn't it?—as in Fuck Over or Fuck Off?) Because my sisters and their husbands have fucked over not only me, but also Carolyn, Lenny, and Samantha. And in a way, that's hurt even more than what they did to me—hurting the people I love.

Hurt—what a strange word. Probably the only verb in the English language that is the same in the past and the present. They hurt me (past). They hurt me (now).

With hurt, the past never ends.

Carolyn has tried to make light of it for my sake, but she has been so hurt by Edna, Jim, Polly, and Arthur. They never accepted her. Even before meeting her, they decided she was inadequate because she wasn't Jewish. As if it were her fault what religion she was born into! And it made no difference, as they got to know her, that she always showed the greatest respect for Judaism, that from the get-go she agreed our kids would be raised as Jews, and that once she converted, she was far more religiously observant than I, or than any of those four. Nothing she did was ever good enough.

In addition to the sin of being born a Christian—a sin not listed among the ones we've been pounding our chests over all through Yom Kippur, such as being (like my sisters) haughty, judgmental, and hard-hearted—Carolyn didn't "know how to dress." She came to one of Edna's fancy, sophisticated parties in a dress she'd sewn by herself specially for that event. Proudly she told me the night before, "I got the fabric on sale; this whole thing cost only $29.99!" I thought that was cool, particularly since the slinky fuchsia tube dress she'd sewn fit her perfectly and looked fantastic. But Edna was first scandalized, then insulted. She took it as a sign of disrespect that Carolyn had come to her party in a homemade "schmata," rather than a new outfit purchased for the occasion, preferably something with a designer label.

But Carolyn never wore designer labels. To her, they seemed obscenely overpriced and a waste of money. Why spend eight hundred dollars on a dress, she'd say, when you can make a reasonable

facsimile for thirty? She was at home with the kids back then, and seldom wore anything but jeans and t-shirts. For theatre and concerts, she had some nice slacks and a couple of jackets that she threw over plain black or white tops. My lovely, relaxed, warm, ample, soft-skinned Carolyn looked beautiful in everything she put on. And in nothing at all.

Edna and Polly couldn't (or wouldn't) see Carolyn's natural beauty, but Jim and Arthur recognized it right away. From the moment they met Carolyn, they had their hands all over her. There was far more touching of her smooth, rosy flesh than was warranted by the usual polite family kiss or hug. All that evening Jim and Arthur told dirty jokes, glancing at her to gauge her reaction. At one point, near the buffet table in his home, Jim's hand wandered down Carolyn's back and, as if by accident, grazed her bum. She didn't say anything; just frowned and moved away. The next day, Jim and Arthur agreed with Edna and Polly that Carolyn didn't fit in with our family.

The main reason they decided this wasn't her unwillingness to flirt or flatter; it was her loyalty to me. Even at that first meeting with them, when she wanted them to like her, she refused to join in when my sisters and their husbands made fun of me or put me down. "We're only teasing," they said, but she didn't fall for that. She was staunch and didn't laugh along. Not then, or anytime afterward. Of course, not playing the Mishivitz scapegoating game meant she was rejecting the essence of our family's culture and traditions, so to pay her back my sisters completely marginalized her. "We thought she'd be another sister to us," Edna said to me once at a party when she was drunk, "but she isn't." This was true but, as so often with Edna, she didn't grasp the full meaning of her own words.

A prayer sung by Lucy is floating flute-like on the air:

"Open for us the gates of righteousness; then shall we enter, praising the Lord.

"We knock at your gates, merciful God; please do not turn us away empty-handed."

Do not turn me away empty-handed.

This Lucy is a nightingale singing her heart out. Probably as she leads these prayers she's thinking about something elevated—God, or Truth, or Righteousness. While I am still steeped in my family shit.

Carolyn never stood a chance with my sisters. By definition she was unacceptable because she was associated with me. If I'm a piece of crap, and Carolyn chose freely to attach herself to me, then she must be a piece of crap, too. If she were even just an object—a red belt strapped around my waist, for instance—they'd have to despise that belt because it was attached to me.

Their despising of me and Carolyn increased over time, but the relationship between us and them reached a new nadir about three years after Carolyn and I got married. Everyone had gathered in Winnipeg for a reunion with our father's side of the family, and all of us were staying at the same hotel. As it happened, Carolyn's and my room overlooked the hotel garden, and on our second day there, on a warm July morning, lazing in bed after sex, we overheard through an open window Edna, Polly, and their husbands planning a night on the town for that evening. Just for the four of them. Pointedly leaving us out. Carolyn, usually even-tempered, was incensed. Not for herself; she couldn't have cared less about bar-hopping with my sisters and their husbands. She didn't like bar-hopping and she didn't like the four of them. But she was cut to the quick by what she saw on my face.

"Let me go down and talk to them," she said, a soft hand on my arm. "I'm sure they won't mind if we ask to join them tonight."

"No," I said. "Never mind. It doesn't matter."

"It matters," she said. "It does."

I stared up at the ceiling, not agreeing but also not disagreeing. She tramped downstairs to the garden and gave the four of them a piece of her mind. I didn't hear what she said—as soon as she left, I stepped into the shower, hiding like a coward in the foggy steam. But by the time she returned to the room, she and those four were enemies for life.

I should never have let her go down to that garden. I knew she could be a lioness in defense of those she loved; I'd seen her stand up

for her mother against half the bureaucrats in the department of Disability Services. It's my fault, not hers, that as a result of that incident, our relationship with my sisters and their husbands took a nose dive from which it's never really recovered. Winnipeg was the beginning of the end.

But no, that isn't true. Because three months before this "family reunion" (family *dis*union, more like), I accidentally received an email that Arthur had meant to send only to Polly, Edna, and Jim. Somehow my name had been added erroneously to the list. In this email, Edna called Carolyn "that fat, stupid shiksa." Carolyn! My beautiful, wise Carolyn! I scrolled down and read the whole two-day thread. The four of them mocked and derided Carolyn, their animated email exchange triggered by what she had worn to a family bat mitzvah the weekend before. At first I was wounded. Then astounded by their meanness and cruelty. It was a revelation to me how much hate they had in them, even now, as adults, when they were living apparently happy, pleasant, privileged lives.

I pretended, of course, not to have seen that email, and I never showed, or mentioned, it to Carolyn. But it turned out to be useful. It was, for the detective in me, always trying to uncover the truth (or is it an archaeologist, scratching at the earth to tear away the layers of hidden history?) proof, undeniable physical evidence, that Carolyn hadn't "started it." "It" being the open hostility, maybe even warfare, that came to exist between those four and us.

But anyway who cares who "started it"? This isn't grade one, with two kids pointing fingers at each other and yelling to their teacher: "He started it!" It doesn't matter who started it. The start of this in any case goes way back, to before we were born, to our parents, and their parents before them, and all the way back, back back back, to the beginning of time. To Cain and Abel. To the first spawnings of love and hate in the world. And all that matters now is the people I love, who also love me: Carolyn, Lenny, and Samantha, plus a couple of lifelong friends. These are the blessings of my life. And everything else amounts to just a hill of beans.

Everyone is singing now. Where are they in the machzor? Oh, here—still on the same page. Lucy is singing one line of the prayer, then the congregation is repeating it. This prayer is familiar. And what a wistful, pensive melody . . .

From his low place on the floor, he joins in loudly:

"Open the gates, Lord, and show us the way to enter."

LUCY

LUCY LOVES TO sing, and as she sings these prayers now, she's filled with elation, even ecstasy. She feels like she's flying, as weightless as an astronaut floating in some upper celestial sphere, a place of zero gravity. And indeed she does not feel grave at all. Serious yes, but not grave as in death. It's the euphoria of singing, she knows, but also the special rapture experienced on Yom Kippur. One of her favourite stories is about a rabbi who always led Yom Kippur prayers using joyful melodies. A guest visiting his town found this surprising and asked him why he did this. The rabbi replied, "A servant cleaning the courtyard of his king—if he loves the king and wants to give him pleasure—is happy to clean the garbage from the courtyard, and therefore sings joyful tunes." In another version of this story—with these old parables, there is always more than one version—the rabbi replies, "While the servant is cleaning the courtyard, he is not thinking about the filth all around him, but of how beautiful the courtyard will be when it's clean." Now, in this spirit, the prayers rush through Lucy like a happy, powerful river, emptying out everything inside her, cleaning her, cleansing her. They flush away all the lies, pretenses, and foolishness inside her—the usual assortment of petty thoughts and emotions, deceits and self-deceptions, that all human beings engage in every day. Instead of these, in Lucy now there is a shimmering light, a glowing, womb-shaped space with room in it for something new, alive, and as yet unknown to grow and emerge.

She cries out, "God, awesome and holy, we have no God but you!"

She is alone on the podium, but she is not alone. She is praying on behalf of the whole community, representing it to God. To her, this is a great honour and responsibility. She is a petitioner, not a performer. Unlike one of the prayer leaders at her mother's nursing home, Marsha, who always led the service as if it were her operatic debut at the Met. Lucy, as she leads now, is aware of the hundreds of people with her in the gym, each with their own problems, fears, hopes, and dreams, and for all of them she sings:

"Lord, have compassion on us!

"Pardon us, forgive us, take pity on us, and grant us atonement.

"Open the gates for us, even as they are about to close.

"The day is waning, the sun is low, the hour is late.

"Another year has slipped away.

"Let us enter the gates at last."

The congregation, listening, hears the joy in her voice, but also the sense of urgency and the hint of a sob. To them, this seems fitting. With the room darkening around them, she, the voice of their community, is begging God to forgive all their flaws, failings, and imperfections. There are abundant, well-known stories about prayer leaders who have burst into tears on the podium, sobbing and wailing loudly, unrestrainedly as they asked God to pardon, help, and save the Jewish people (and this not only in times of historical crisis, such as the Holocaust or the Inquisition). A prayer leader's anguish is to be respected. It is evidence of her sincerity and suitability for this role, and it is what one should expect when a community's representative is pleading with God for the well-being, indeed the lives, of hundreds of souls. As Lucy beseeches God for mercy and a good year for everyone present—a year of health, peace, and prosperity between now and next year at this time—the people in the gym listen to her warble, whisper, shout, moan, groan, and hit high, piercing notes. Her voice, now booming, resounds throughout the room, bouncing off the basketball nets, the white concrete walls, the hanging ropes (which, tied into nooses, look to Ira like suicide

invitations), the old-fashioned, ever-ticking black clock, and the far-thest corner of the upstairs running track.

Lucy is focused entirely on the prayers she is singing, on pro-nouncing the Hebrew words perfectly and applying to them the correct traditional tune. But after a couple of minutes, she is dis-tracted by an image partway between her eyes and the top right-hand corner of the machzor. At first this image is vague and hard to identify; it is a mere flickering that is slowly taking shape, like mol-ecules gradually assembling themselves when they "beamed up" someone on *Star Trek*. She is startled and wonders if there is some-thing wrong with her eyes, but she keeps on singing, and little by little this image assumes a form and becomes recognizable.

It is Larry's hand. Just his hand, nothing else—cut off from the rest of him, dismembered, something out of a horror movie. This hand is trembling uncontrollably, the way it did last night when he reached for her breast. This horrible, greyish, gruesome, severed hand—still in a way the hand she loves and intimately knows—ob-scures some words in the machzor while it continues to shake. For a moment she has the illusion that it isn't his hand that is shaking; it is the room itself, in fact the entire building—that underneath the floorboards of this gym, an earthquake is beginning. Then this impression passes and she knows it is only this hand that is quak-ing. But now she is quaking, too, and so is her voice as she sings. Meanwhile this eerie hand, like a memento of Banquo's ghost, does not depart from her. She keeps having to move the machzor this way and that, in order to see the words this hand is blocking.

She sings, "We recall how our great cities were devastated in the past: Jerusalem a desolation, Zion a wilderness." Now the hand undergoes a change. The skin disappears from it, melting away in seconds, leaving behind nothing but bones. A skeleton's hand. It trembles halfway between her and the machzor. Dry bones, she thinks. Dry bones that God will bring back to life in a thousand years when the Messiah finally comes. But not in my lifetime. Not in time for me.

The skeleton's hand hovers translucently over the words of the prayers, and her own hand trembles as she shifts the machzor so she can continue praying. She must continue, for the sake of all the people here.

A few pages later, this bony, fleshless hand metamorphizes again. This time, it floats in front of the podium, between her and the congregation, and the thin, fragile bones transform into wood. Into a tree branch, a leafless, skeletal branch, protruding from the left side of a verdant, vibrant, healthy oak. This branch is swaying back and forth gently in the wind. Then she sees it is not just swaying; it's waving. Waving at her, waving to her in a friendly, familiar way, still recognizably in the shape of a hand. It is trying to tell her something, send her a message; she can feel it whispering to her, but can't grasp what it is saying because she doesn't understand the language of trees. Suddenly, though, she feels terribly sad. She sings, almost sobbing, "Our days are a passing shadow. Yet You are eternal, You have years without end!" The final words of this sentence she sings so loudly she's almost yelling, as if to drown out the vision of the uncanny dead branch hanging from the Tree of Life.

Numbly she progresses through the rest of Neila. The congregation joins in the prayers at all the prescribed moments. And all the while, the bony, leafless branch-hand is waving to her, wanting to communicate something, a truth that it is important for her to know. It waves to her prettily, beckoningly, on a lovely spring-like day, against the background of a blameless blue sky.

EZRA

EZRA, WATCHING LUCY, observes her glazed, inward-focused stare and strange half-grimace, half-laugh. He wonders what is going on inside her.

Hail explodes against the upper windows of the gym. It crashes down, attacking the glass loudly like mini bullets. People glance up, startled. Then, as with so many things in life, they get accustomed to it. In less than a minute, the steady pelting has become inoffensive, even comforting in its rhythm, numbing them, lulling them into a deeper level of trance. Already they were entranced, thanks to hour after hour of prayers, music, and the exhaustion of fasting, not to mention the urgent claims of their inner worlds, since they've been living for the past twenty-four hours mainly inside their hearts, minds, and souls. In addition, they have been standing now for a long stretch, as this part of the service requires. Only a handful of congregants, the very old or infirm, have claimed the right to remain seated. Tom among them, Ezra notes; in fact, Tom is the only one sitting on the floor, but at least he is no longer deathly pale or panting. Hopefully he will be all right.

Bam! Bam! Bam!—the hail pounds down. There are flashes of lightning. Then, like the lightning, come flashes of memory.

His and Mona's first baby: a miscarriage. The yellow room they'd painted in anticipation, with a line of waddling baby ducks encircling the walls.

His first orgasm (or anyway the first he can remember). Alone on his bed with the plaid coverlet, a week before his bar mitzvah.

The fragrance of his mother's cooking on holidays: the mingled aromas of brisket, kugel, tzimmes, and coffee cake.

The smell of Mona after sex. Spicy, musky.

The silky feel of the linens on his father's bed where he lay dying, when Ezra smoothed the sheet for him.

The wall of acrid cigarette smoke he always had to walk through when visiting his father at the factory where he worked.

The rich deep green of the forest in a fairytale backdrop he painted for Tom Thumb. The exact same green as the real-life forest bordering the cottage his parents rented once for a family vacation.

The rhythmic pounding of the skipping rope—*bam bam bam*—when his late sister Leanne played skipping on their driveway as a girl.

His oldest child, Jerry, yelling at him: "Why can't I have a new bike like everyone else? Monty Heller just got one. Why can't I?" Because there was no money, that's why. The guilt of his art. Later that afternoon, he and Mona made love. Afterwards she held him, stroking his head while it nestled between her breasts. His wracking guilt. "Never mind," she said. "You have a gift, and a gift like that exacts a price. He'll understand when he's older."

But did he? Does he even now? All these years later, there's still a wall between him and Jerry. He tried to paint this wall once, to give it form and thus lessen its torment. But he couldn't.

Another year gone by. Another mile advanced in his march toward death.

No—don't think that way. There are things to look forward to still. Philip's wedding. And then, if all goes well, grandchildren ...

And paintings, of course. There will always be more paintings. He'll paint until he dies.

All around him congregants are pounding their breasts, doing the Ashamnu. It's the last one for this Yom Kippur, so there is urgency on their faces as they make their final confessions. The gates will be closing soon. It's now or never to face the truth about yourself.

And what is the truth about *him?* Right now, the truth about him is that he needs to go to the bathroom. This is *his* urgency. But he's holding it in, the way he held in, for all those years, his desire to paint. He had no choice then but to wait, and he has no choice now. You can't walk out of a Yom Kippur service a quarter of an hour before the end.

The gym is warm and smells of unwashed bodies and angst. Almost everyone is praying, but not Rachel, who is frowning in the direction of the back room. Maybe she's worrying about her honey cake, he thinks. She mentioned before that there might not be enough to go around. On his right, with Tom seated on the floor between them, stands Ira who, with his sallow complexion, looks like he hasn't eaten a proper meal in months. Tom is trying slowly to stand up. Ezra offers a hand and, when Tom is upright, pats him on the back avuncularly. He is relieved; Tom gave him a bit of a scare. All they needed here today was a second heart attack. What a Yom Kippur this has been! A Yom Kippur from hell. Yet in a way a comforting one, too. People came together. Like when it rained at his and Mona's wedding. The ceremony was held outdoors in a park, and when the rain started, everyone scurried under the green-and-white striped awning of a nearby kiosk, rushing then crushing each other and laughing. In that moment (a friend said later), an "instant community" was created, and even people who'd never met before were included in its warm embrace. Someone else, while still under the awning, said that rain at a wedding is good luck. Probably bullshitting to make them feel better. But it's true—he and Mona *have* been lucky. And happy, too. Luckier and happier than most.

His art, though, has been neither lucky nor happy. This was rubbed into his face yet again when he escorted the paramedics, who were carrying the rabbi on a stretcher to the front door of the community centre where their ambulance awaited. On his way back to the gym, Ezra passed the lounge-cum-gallery, and wanting a few quiet minutes to himself, stopped in to glance at the latest exhibit. It was atrocious. Displayed on three walls were tacky, imitative paintings, and on the fourth was a Bristol board poster with a glowing

review by Charma Musk. The paintings were terrible, total crap, so why was she praising them? Then he saw who the artist was. Her last name belonged to one of Toronto's wealthiest Jewish families. A ubiquitous name: he'd seen it on university buildings, hospital wings, museum atriums, and concert halls. Of course Charma would gush over this new young artist.

When did he last see Charma? It was about six months ago. They were attending the same vernissage, and she arrived late, smack in the middle of the speeches, and (typical for her) made a grand entrance. Down the main aisle she swaggered with her two young daughters in tow, both of them ridiculously overdressed with crinoline dresses, elaborate bows in their hair, and lipstick. Charma, making a lot of fuss and displacing several other people, organized adjoining seats for herself and her daughters. Not long afterwards the speeches were over, and she was immediately surrounded by admirers. Ezra watched as people dashed over to shake her hand, congratulate her on her latest prize, and compliment her on her daughters.

Remembering this now, though, oddly he doesn't feel the usual stab of pain. Most likely he will again at some point—there is an ebb and flow to this anguish of his—but at this moment he doesn't envy Charma or anything she has. And he couldn't care less about where he is situated on the tightrope continuum stretching between failure and success. It seems absurd to him, almost comical—it would actually be funny if it weren't so tragic—how many hours (no, days, weeks, months) during the past three decades he has spent agonizing over this, green with envy and black in mood. So he hasn't won a prize—big deal. So he's sold x number of paintings and not ten or a hundred times that. So what? An hour ago a young man nearly died right in front of him. This wasn't a message from God—he doesn't believe in that nonsense—but it sure does put things in perspective. He is alive. And he is a lucky man. He has Mona and three terrific kids. Jerry is doing brilliantly at his PhD. Philip and Loretta are in love, happily living together with their cats, and planning a destination wedding. And Carrie's depression has abated. They finally found meds that work for her, she recently returned to school, and she's

smiling again and going out with friends. So what does he have to grouse about? Look around this room. So many sad, troubled faces. Sick people, lonely people. People going through divorces or mourning the death of someone they loved. People who've been laid off and don't know how they'll make it till the end of the month. Is he really going to whine away his remaining two or three decades because of a prize he didn't win and some paintings that didn't sell?

"You have a great talent," Mitch Smolensky told him once. This was years before he became a famous art critic in England, where he died in the late '80s, but it still comforts Ezra on his dark days to remember this praise, along with other accolades he's received from people he respects. Even without all these, though, he knows how good his paintings are. He knows. And knows, too, that this private knowing may have to suffice.

How much longer is this service going to take? He wants to pee, and he's tired. Tired of standing. Tired of his thoughts. Tired also of the bitter, unhappy man he's become. Or anyway, is in the process of becoming. He doesn't want to end up like Uncle Oscar. Oscar the Grouch, he and Leanne nicknamed him. A puppet of a man who was controlled and manipulated by his puppeteer, Resentment.

I could be a happy man, Ezra thinks, as prayers swirl around him. It's all a matter of attitude, of approaching life in a certain way. "Happiness is a habit," Aunt Evelyn used to say. When he was younger, he never knew what she was talking about, but now maybe he does. She married an Argentinian man whose father and sister, back in the late 70s, "disappeared." There was plenty of darkness in Uncle Emanuel and Aunt Evelyn's shared life, plenty to be unhappy about. Grief and terror in his homeland, and then their son Ernesto being diagnosed with cerebral palsy. But Aunt Evelyn was always cheerful. She shone, exuding an inner radiance. She smiled easily at everyone, even the mailman and complete strangers. She gave little gifts to her nieces and nephews, just to see them beam. She made peace between warring relatives and convened the whole extended family for delicious multicultural meals. Always with that sunny smile of hers.

People all around him are still pounding their breasts repent-antly, and here he is, thinking about happiness. He must be really shallow to be pondering happiness on Yom Kippur, instead of Guilt or God. But no. Yom Kippur is not about self-flagellation—even the rabbi said so. (He hopes the rabbi will be all right. The paramedics who took him away seemed optimistic. After Yom Kippur he or Tom should give the hospital a call.) No, happiness is important. It's his own lack of happiness—his unhappiness, actually—that more than anything else he feels guilty about. It has hurt not only him but those he loves most. When Carrie, in high school, first became de-pressed, her psychologist told him and Mona that Carrie was "very affected by her father's moods." He never forgot that. He never will.

No, happiness is everything. Yesterday morning, as a kind of pre-Yom Kippur gift, Philip emailed him a quote from Reb Nachman that he'd encountered online: "Joy is not incidental to spiritual quest; it is vital." Was Philip dropping him a hint? Probably not. That is not Philip's way. But anyway this adage is true. You can't spiritually grow when you're depressed. You can't do anything when you're depressed. Look at Carrie, who did nothing for a year but lie on her bed. Happiness is the bedrock of any good life.

He sees himself now as in a movie, mooning about for days or weeks on end, full of self-pity: "I haven't received the recognition I deserve. My dream has not come true." He feels ashamed and also stupid. Out of the billions of people on this planet, how many of them have gotten what they deserve (or think they deserve) and had their dreams come true? One in a hundred thousand? One in a mil-lion? How many charmed Charmas are there in the world, or can there be? After all, if everyone were famous, then there would be no such thing as fame. And who knows if even she is satisfied with her lot? He saw her interviewed once, and after replying to a question about all the prizes she'd won, she said impulsively to her interviewer, a sympathetic man with warm brown eyes: "But it's never really enough, is it? There's always another, bigger prize you could win, another honour or accolade to strive for. You're never really there."

That's it exactly. You're never really there. You spend your whole life chasing success, running after the iridescent, dancing, elusive, illusive bubble, and when you finally reach the magic glade, you discover it's empty. There's nothing there.

Suddenly he wants to paint that. That precise image. The magic glade that, like Arden Forest, contains nothing and everything. Only hopes, fantasies, and dreams. He laughs with pleasure. He won't leave this service yet; he'll stay till the end. But he's excited now, and—yes—happy. He can't wait to get home and start painting. He'll paint this happiness. He'll paint his joy.

RACHEL

OH GOD, WHAT if there isn't enough honey cake? I really need to take all three hundred servings and cut each one in half. This is going to take a long time, too, twenty minutes at least, because I'll have to rinse, and then dry, the knife after almost every single slice, honey cake being so sticky. And when am I supposed to do all this? I can't leave the room right now in the middle of the service. But how much longer do these prayers go on for? (It already feels like forever!) And I can't ask anyone; they're all praying. Maybe, to be on the safe side, I should head to the back room now. Because what if all of a sudden Yom Kippur's over and I'm only halfway through dividing up the cake? I could end up with five pans that each contain thirty generous portions and five pans each containing sixty teeny-weeny ones. That would be a disaster. No. I must get to the back room ...

Stealthily, aiming to be inconspicuous—but not unnoticed by Tom, Ezra, and Ira—Rachel slips out of the gym.

IRA

WHERE IS RACHEL going? Why's she leaving? Perhaps I should go now, too. What am I even doing here? What difference does it make if I stay till the end or just leave? Leave this room, and then the world? No one will miss me when I'm gone. No one will care one way or the other.

Tonight's the night. I could walk out right now, return to the dorm, swallow the pills on my desk, and that would be that—all over and done with inside of an hour. So why wait till this service finishes? Just because one isn't supposed to leave a service in the middle? That's stupid. Why worry about being polite and "socially appropriate" when in an hour or two I'll be dead? What difference could it possibly make whether I do, or don't, complete this Yom Kippur service before I die?

It doesn't. But wow, this voice is beautiful. I want to hear more of her singing, this Sad-eyed Lucy of the Lowlands. And it feels good, warm, to be standing here with Tom and Ezra, as if, because of what happened with the rabbi, there is a connection between us and now we all belong together in some way. It isn't true, of course. That's a lie, false comfort; the usual kind of weak, human self-delusion. The real truth is that each of us is alone. Always, and terribly, alone. But still, maybe I'll stay a little longer. Why not? It will all be over soon.

TOM

THEY'RE DOING THE Ashamnu now, one of his last opportunities this Yom Kippur to ask, and get, forgiveness. Striking his breast and reciting the final verses of the prayer, Tom reviews all the wrongs he has committed, either intentionally or unintentionally, during the past year. He has—in both small and not-so-small ways—hurt people: Carolyn, Lenny, Samantha, friends, relatives, colleagues. He feels small and contrite. He does not know if God will forgive him. But he is very grateful that Carolyn has, and so have his kids. Every year, between Rosh Hashana and Yom Kippur, the four of them formally request forgiveness from each other. This is no perfunctory ritual. The apologies are specific and heartfelt, and sometimes hard to make. But it's never happened (so far, anyway) that one of them has rejected another's apology and withheld forgiveness. We are not only forgiveness-seekers, he thinks; we are also forgiveness-granters. In the image of God, The Great Forgiver. What a terrible thing it would be to not be pardoned by—or to refuse to pardon—Carolyn, Lenny, or Samantha. How cruel, and how ... *unpardonable* that would be.

Yet he has never really pardoned his sisters and their husbands, or his father, has he? Why exactly is that? he wonders. Deeply immersed as he is now in the spirit of Yom Kippur, it seems rather strange to him, and unkind. But there's no comparison, he tells himself, between his sisters and Carolyn, Lenny, and Samantha, because Edna and Polly would never dream of apologizing to him

for anything or requesting his forgiveness. If they did, maybe he would grant it. But they never will because they don't believe they've done anything wrong. And even if he spontaneously offered them his pardon, without it being solicited, they would probably reject it. He smiles wanly, remembering how, as a college student, he did Werner Erhard's personal development workshop, "est," and on one of the breaks phoned his father and told him, "I forgive you."

"I don't need your forgiveness," his father said and slammed down the phone.

At the time he was shocked; he'd expected his father to be grateful. He'd even imagined they might finally have their first honest conversation about the past. But afterward he could see how telling his father he forgave him was, in a way, just another, subtler, form of the old accusation. "I forgive you" was merely the spoken, first half of the sentence; the implicit second half was: "For what you did to me."

Still, he did make this one attempt. And there would be no more of them now that Dad was dead.

Lucy is singing in her golden voice: "God, accept our sincere repentance. We confess our sins to You so we may cease doing violence to our lives."

Violence. Yes. He still remembers the exact moment when he decided never to forgive his father. He was nine. That morning Dad had beaten him for maybe the hundredth time, and after supper when Dad asked him if they were okay now, he nodded yes as usual but swore in his heart never again to forgive him or really make up. Make-up was the phony layer of paint that Edna had recently started smearing on her face. Like the war paint he'd seen in westerns on TV. From now on he would only do a phony make-up with Dad; from this point forward, it was war between them. He vowed he'd never forgive Dad as long as he lived.

But now, here in this gym, he asks himself: In that phrase—*as long as he lived*—who is the *he*? Is he himself the *he*, or is Dad the *he*? If it's Dad—well, he's no longer living, so now he can forgive him.

Not so fast, as the cowboys used to say. Grammar games aren't everything in life, and he's nobody's sucker. Whoever he'd originally

had in mind with the pronoun *he,* he is not going to forgive his father today just like that, with a snap of his fingers. This would be, in a way, a betrayal of the child he once was. It would mean breaking a vow that he made to himself.

Vows. Last night, the Kol Nidre prayer annulled all the vows of everyone in the congregation that were made under coercive or oppressive circumstances. His was made under that kind of circumstance. And vowing never to forgive Dad saved his life. It kept him from being nothing in his own eyes but a helpless, battered victim. From this vow flowed a lifetime of self-respect, first gushing through him as soon as he made this promise, as miraculously as the water that spurted from the rock when Moses hit it with a stick. If he reneged on this promise now, what would happen to him? What would he have left? Who would he even be? It would be like yanking out the cornerstone that holds up a building. His whole inner structure would collapse.

Or would it? He's fifty now, not nine. He has resources and options that he didn't back then. Forty-one years ago he made a pledge, but today he can choose how he wants to relate to that. If he decides, at some point, to forgive Dad, he can. It's his decision. His life.

He glances up—a woman is watching him from across the aisle. Tentatively she smiles, and vaguely he smiles back. Does he know her? Is she one of his patients, perhaps? She reminds him a bit of Carolyn, even though she doesn't look anything like her. It's that gold scarf she's wearing, similar to Carolyn's favourite one. Then again, all women remind him of Carolyn. She is, to him, the only woman in the world.

Lucy cries: "Seek God while God may be found! Call out to God while God is near!"

He is not ready to forgive Dad yet, but it intrigues him that he's even entertaining the possibility that one day this might happen. And if this is possible, perhaps another day will come when he can forgive Edna and Polly, as well. Though this is hard to visualize. It would have to be very far off in the future. Right now they are so estranged.

Estranged. He likes this word. As a sociological concept it has dignity, and it lends normality to the severance between him and his sisters. It's not so weird that he and his sisters don't get along. Lots of siblings don't. If he Googled the term *Estranged siblings,* it would probably turn up millions and millions of views. There might even be a Google group for estranged siblings. And that is only talking about nowadays. In the past, too, siblings were a problem for each other. Look at the Bible. Joseph and his brothers, Jacob and Esau, and worst of all, Cain and Abel. At least he, Edna, and Polly aren't physically killing each other—or anyway not yet!

Still, it's sad how far apart they've grown. He didn't realize until recently how great this distance is. There were signposts, of course—milestones and warning flares all along the way—but somehow he missed their full significance. He recognized the chipping off of hunks of bark from the tree trunk, but never doubted that the tree itself would remain standing. Now, in the months since Dad's death, he's seen, as if suddenly waking up, that the tree has been felled to the ground, and is lying there dying, gasping for breath.

He himself is still standing, though, along with the rest of the congregation. The people around him, despite their exhaustion, are praying feverishly, murmuring with their eyes closed or open, and rocking back and forth. Maybe some of them, like him, are struggling with estranged siblings, or estranged parents or children. How do family members actually become estranged? he wonders. The physician-scientist in him considers studying this sometime. He could conduct research on the disease of sibling estrangement and publish his findings in a refereed journal. It could be fascinating to generate a taxonomy of all the various forms of alienation between brothers and sisters, and examine the different ways this pathology originates and develops, one cancerous cell at a time.

He doesn't need, though, to do this research. He already knows how sibling relationships deteriorate. With him and his sisters, it wasn't instantaneous like an electric saw dividing conjoined twins, quickly and efficiently sawing its way through flesh. It took time.

Like building a wall, one brick after another. With those rough grey bricks his father used in his construction projects. Each brick in the wall between him and his sisters was a hurtful incident that never got cleared up between them when it occurred, and before you knew it, another one got piled on top of it. One more brick. One more brick. He remembers the bricks in *The Crucible*. There was one good man who refused to give false testimony against an accused innocent woman, and to try and persuade him, they piled bricks onto his chest, one after another—one more, one more, until the final brick crushed his inner organs, killing him.

So many bricks. So many incidents. What happened in that hotel garden in Winnipeg was just one of hundreds. These bricks piled higher and higher until they reached the heavens, blotting out the sky. A Tower of Babel, where suddenly he and his sisters could no longer understand each other's languages.

He can recall each incident-brick in minute detail—each one a complete story, maybe even a novella. He knows his litany of grievances so well that if you woke him up at three in the morning, he could immediately recite it for you. For years he has nurtured these grievances and wounds, counting and recounting them like a miser his gold. They are as familiar to him as his own body, as his own physical wounds and blemishes. But out of all these stories, there are six that stand out, like six broken commandments. For easy remembering, he has abbreviated each of them into a single sentence, a sort of story title. For example:

Polly and Arthur Making Me Share A Bedroom With Aunt Elsie At Their Out-of-town Wedding

Polly and Arthur Giving Everyone An Honour At Their Daughter's Bat Mitzvah Except Me And Carolyn

Polly and Arthur Not Inviting Lenny and Samantha To Their Grandson's Bris

Edna Walking Out Of The Room When Dad Was Beating Me

Edna Not Letting Me Be Alone With Mom In The Days Before She Died

Edna Telling Me The Last Time We Met, "I Love You But"

"I love you but …" What does that even mean? What is the second half of *that* sentence? I love you but *I don't like you?* If so, this is true also of his feeling for Edna. And Polly, too. Maybe he still loves them, but he doesn't like them anymore.

Stop. If he's not careful, these six stories will suck him down like quicksand, and it will take him hours, perhaps days, to clamber his way out. Lucy's voice, calm, warm, and beautiful, helps him balance safely on the solid surfaces of these stories, as if they are nothing but their titles. Now, for the first time, he reviews them coolly, almost clinically. Oddly, most of them—almost his entire precious collection of insults and hurts—now strike him as rather petty. Sure, they demonstrate his sisters' and brothers-in-law's insensitivity, selfishness, meanness, narcissism, and in some cases deliberate cruelty. There is no question about how much they have hurt him and the people he loves most. But how would their crimes be assessed in a court of law—or even, on this Day of Judgment, in a "Yom Kippur court of law"? Would they be considered relatively minor misdemeanours, or serious crimes justifying a life sentence?

Not a life sentence. Definitely not. And not even a life sentence of him refusing to forgive them for the rest of their lives. After all, God pardons everyone: murderers, rapists, pedophiles. So who is he, a mere human being made of dust and ashes, not to forgive his sisters? Besides, they are not such terrible people overall. They are not murderers, rapists, or pedophiles. They pay their taxes and even donate to charity; they are decent citizens. There are lots of worse people in the world. True, he doesn't especially like, or trust, Edna and Polly anymore, and he has no desire to spend much time with them. But this has nothing to do with forgiveness. Who was it who said, "You only make peace with your enemies; you don't have to make peace with your friends"? Ditto with forgiving. You only need to forgive the people who have hurt you; it's not necessary with those who've treated you well.

Also, Carolyn wants him to forgive his sisters—and even his father, too. She's been saying this for years. After Dad died, she

intensified her efforts, bringing home yet another book for him from the library, this one called *The Life-Changing Magic of Forgiveness.* Hokey title. He threw it on the coffee table and told her he'd never read it. But two weeks after the end of shiva, he irritably skimmed it and got the main gist. Not forgiving someone—holding on to a grudge, resentment, anger—poisons you and can taint your whole life. Forgiveness is not only, or even mainly, for the other person; forgiveness is a gift to yourself.

Fine. Okay. But how can he ever forgive Edna for walking out of the room, sneering and laughing at him, while he was being beaten as a child? She abandoned him in his time of need. And she betrayed him by siding against him with Dad.

But what was she then? pipes up an unfamiliar voice (the voice of Yom Kippur, perhaps?). *Eleven? Twelve years old?* He pictures Samantha around that age, then Lenny. They were only kids. Edna, when this happened, was only a kid, too. How could any child have stood up to a big, beefy bully like their father? Maybe Edna's laughter back then was actually nervous laughter, rather than laughter of contempt as he thought. Perhaps she cared about her little brother and fled the kitchen because it hurt too much to watch him getting battered yet again. Or, less generously, maybe she fled fearing that if she stayed, she'd get bashed around, too. Who knows? He probably never will, and most likely even she does not know herself. (How true that is about Edna: she does not know herself.) In any case, all this was a long time ago. Is he really going to hate her for the rest of her life because of one minute in 1977?

He remembers her at the age of eleven, watching TV next to Mom on the couch, with a far-off look in her eyes and the exact same body position as Mom's. A wistful, hopeful girl full of dreams.

He was observing her from the rust-coloured love seat. On his left, snuggled against him, Polly was curled up, with her thumb in her mouth, rocking slightly.

Around the same time, when he was seven and she was six, they were sitting back to back, leaning against each other in perfect balance. "We're holding up the whole world," Polly said. "If one of us moves, the whole world will fall."

He can't help it—he still loves them, in spite of everything. One day maybe he'll even be able to forgive them. But whenever that is (probably a long time from now), he'll make sure not to tell them he has forgiven them. He doesn't want a repeat of what happened with Dad. He will forgive them silently, just inside his mind and soul. And even though he won't say a word to them, perhaps just the same they will notice.

He is not yet ready for this, though. It still feels as if forgiving them and their husbands would be like saying it was okay what they've done to him, Carolyn, and the kids, all these years. And it isn't. But at some point he may be prepared to forgive them. Perhaps even in the not-so-distant future. In five years, or even three.

Something lightens in him now, in his heart and belly. He sees again the good man in *The Crucible*. The grey bricks stacked high on his chest are lifting off one at a time. One brick gone. Then another. And another. All of them flying upward—flying up, up, and away.

SHUL

LUCY IS APPROACHING the end of Neila. Accompanied by the congregation, she sings the last line of the prayer Our Father Our King: "Treat us with justice and mercy—and save us."

A little boy runs up to the open ark; his father lifts him so he can shut its door.

Alone Lucy sings, "Hear O Israel, the Lord our God, the Lord is One," and the whole room repeats this. Then, together with the congregation, she says three times, "Praised be God's glorious sovereignty forever and ever," and seven times, "Adonai is our only God." Now she begins the Kaddish Shalem, the final prayer of Neila. Tom removes a typed page from his jacket pocket, scans it, and confers in a whisper with Ezra. Ezra ascends the podium and stands next to Lucy. She sings the last sentence of the Kaddish Shalem, "May God, who makes peace in the heavens, bring peace to us and to all of Israel." Ezra shakes her hand and she descends the stairs, pale but radiant. On the way back to her seat, people stop her several times to shake her hand and wish her a "Yasher koach" or its English equivalent, "Well done." From the podium Ezra calls out, "Yasher koach, Lucy!"

"Yasher koach!" the congregation echoes.

Lucy blushes. Ezra says:

"Thank you, Lucy, for leading us so beautifully in Neila, and especially when you were pinch-hitting. We are all very grateful.

"Now the time has come to blow the shofar. Tonight we do just one long blast, the tekia gedola, and this will conclude Yom Kippur. As we all know, the sound of the ram's horn is meant to awaken us spiritually, jolt us from our stupor, and inspire us to be better people. This morning the rabbi—"

Sensing that, by referring to the rabbi, he may be injecting into the room a note of melancholy or even anxiety, he switches gears. "You were invited, if you had a shofar, to bring it here this evening and join our shofar blower in the tekia gedola. So if you have a shofar with you now, please assemble near our shofar blower, over there."

He points to a second podium, directly across from him on the other side of the gym, where Mickey Samuels, a ponytailed college student at the Conservatory specializing in the trumpet, is waiting with his long, twirled shofar. A dozen congregants from all parts of the gym form a horseshoe in front of him. Two of their shofars, like his, are long; the others are all short, each just a single curl, and therefore much easier to blow. Many people have left their seats to cluster as close as possible to the group of shofar blowers. Young children run up to them, too, some grasping plastic toy shofars, and trailed by tired, anxious parents. A couple of fathers hoist toddlers onto their shoulders to give them a better view. The gym vibrates with excitement and anticipation.

"Tekia gedola!" Ezra shouts.

The thirteen shofars shriek, howl, and wail cacophonously, each in its own pitch and for as long as it can. This is a great caterwauling, not a melodious symphony. A ram's horn is not a musical instrument like a violin; it is the horn of a male animal—smelly, primitive, and crude—and the sound it makes is startling, harsh, primeval. It shocks you, shakes you, wakes you up. And thirteen of them all together sends the gym's high windows trembling and its basketball nets swinging. Some children, hearing the shofars' raw, protracted blasts, laugh with delight. Others become frightened and start to cry. Parents comfort, or laugh with, their children, remembering their own childhood reactions when they first heard the shofar: how they

clung tightly to their father's large hand or buried their face in their mother's skirts.

The shofars that people brought from home last ten, maybe fifteen, seconds before tapering off. But Mickey's tekia gedola goes on and on and on, lasting an astounding thirty-five. It's those young lungs, Ezra thinks, strengthened of course by his practicing the trumpet every day. Ira, standing off at a distance all by himself, hears Mickey's tekia gedola and shudders. Rachel, in the back room cutting cake, stands at respectful attention for the duration of the tekia gedola, as if for a national anthem or for Remembrance Day in Israel when the siren sounds for a full minute across the whole country. As she listens, she tries to imagine eating a tekia gedola, taking it into her body, stuffing in through her mouth that enormous, magnificent sound. Lucy is certain that this tekia gedola is the longest one she has ever heard. It seems to persist forever, crying, screaming, and praying all at once—for her, for Larry, for everyone in this gym and the entire world.

"Next year in Jerusalem!" Ezra shouts.

"Next year in Jerusalem!" the congregation shouts back.

The gym is full of happiness now. Neila is over, they've all completed another year's High Holydays, and it is a relief and a physical pleasure to be able to walk around freely after a day of being restricted to their seats. People mill about, laughing, chatting with friends and wishing strangers a happy new year, a shana tova. Dozens of congregants start for the door.

"Please don't leave yet!" Ezra exhorts from the podium. "I know we're all tired and hungry, but it'll take just ten more minutes to do Maariv (the evening service) and Havdala (the prayer to separate Yom Kippur from the rest of the year). And for those of you who stick around until the end, we have delicious honey cake!"

Reluctantly, sheepishly, about a third of the people lined up at the door return to their seats. Ezra does a quick Maariv, and when he starts Havdala, someone switches off the electricity. Now the gym is in darkness, with the only light for hundreds of people emanating

from a single braided candle, flickering on the podium, that Ezra is holding high. The congregation is hushed and still while Ezra continues reciting the prayer. But when he reaches the part that is a song about Elijah the prophet, they join in singing, slide their arms around each other's waists, and begin swaying together to the rhythm of the tune. The music, like a breeze animating the leaves in a tree, sweeps across the entire gym. There are human chains of four, ten, twelve, or twenty people all undulating to the music. Even Ira, who was standing off by himself, got pulled in by a yellow-haired woman, and finds himself rocking back and forth, back and forth, part of a warm, accepting community.

Suddenly the song is over, the prayer is just plain words now, and almost immediately the swaying comes to a halt. Still, people keep their arms around each other's waists for another minute, as if unwilling to relinquish this closeness and return to their individual separateness. But when Ezra begins the Aleinu prayer, people drop their arms and the human chains dissolve.

Ezra completes the Aleinu. Now all that's left in the service is the final Mourners' Kaddish. The congregation gazes sympathetically at the seven mourners. Among them, Tom—tired, dazed, almost not knowing what he is doing, and with a numb feeling of Why Not?—recites Kaddish for his father.

After this prayer is finished, Ezra yells out, "Shana tova!"

"Shana tova!" replies the congregation.

People embrace and wish each other a good year. Now into the main aisle of the gym struts Rachel, pushing a food trolley bearing ten large pans of honey cake. Behind her, with head bowed, follows a pimply teenage girl who was hiding in the back room and agreed to help cut and distribute the cake. Rachel, without realizing it, parks the trolley on the exact spot where the rabbi lay an hour ago. Precisely on top of where his body was, as if to say: Food, pleasure, or life itself outweighs, overrides (as literally as a trolley) morbidity, disaster, and the shadow of death. She and the girl remove eight of the pans from the food cart and set them down on nearby chairs. People swarm the cake like locusts, as though they haven't eaten not

just for the past twenty-five hours but for the past twenty-five weeks. Rachel couldn't be happier. She is feeding the world. She is a good, bountiful person. Everyone here is eating her cake. They are loving her cake. They are loving her.

Exactly as she feared, some of the portions are twice as big as others. Even with her volunteer helping, there wasn't time to cut all of them in half. But what she has presented to the congregation seems perfect to her now: two sizes—one large (for large, or especially hungry, people) and the other small (for people who are smaller, less hungry, or even not fasting). Each individual can take whatever they need. ("From each according to their ability, to each according to their need"—the credo at the Socialist Zionist summer camp she attended one summer.) Three boys near her are stuffing cake by the handful into their mouths. Her rich, sweet cake is disappearing rapidly from all the pans. Even so, she can see that everything is going to be all right. There will be enough to go around. Like the oil in the story of the Chanukah miracle, her cake will last as long as it is needed.

Tom, Lucy, and Ira are standing in a loose cluster near the podium. From the bottom shelf of the trolley, Rachel lifts a half-empty pan of cake and brings it to them, placing it on the edge of the stage. Lucy, Tom, and Ezra (returned now from the bathroom) help themselves and thank her. But Ira, hungrily eying the cake, asks Rachel in a tone like Oliver Twist's, as if she really might say no: "Is this cake for anyone who wants it?" "Of course," she answers, and holds out the pan to him.

The five of them sit on chairs and eat their cake a little apart from everyone else. They have been through something together: they were the first ones to rush over to the rabbi, and they cared for him until the ambulance came; in this way, their Yom Kippur has been different from that of the rest of the congregation. Now this day is almost over, soon they will go home, and suddenly they are all hit by exhaustion and by the magnitude of what happened here. They eat the comforting, sticky cake in silence. Ezra circulates a bottle of water: one after another they drink from it and hand it

wordlessly to the next person. There is a ritualistic feeling to this, like the passing of a peace pipe.

When the bottle of water has circled its way back to Ezra, he says, "Rachel, this cake is terrific."

"Thanks," she says, smiling.

"It's really excellent," Lucy says with her mouth full. "Can I have the recipe?"

"Sure. It's really easy to make."

Tom is studying Rachel with a frown. "Aren't you the baker from the shul?" he asks.

"I am."

"You looked familiar," he says, "but I wasn't sure from where. I'm not a weekly shul-goer, I'm afraid, even though I'm on the board. Which is why I didn't recognize you. Sorry."

"It's okay. Even if you were there every Shabbat, you'd barely see me. I'm nearly always in the kitchen. It's the volunteers of the Kiddush Committee who serve the food."

"I see. Well, I must say, when I have been in shul—like for the Steinhauer bar mitzvah last month—your kiddushes have been sensational. I loved your butter cookies."

"Well, you can kiss those cookies goodbye."

Tom, startled by her truculence, asks, "What do you mean?"

"Didn't you hear? They've outlawed sugar at the shul. There are new food regulations coming into effect in two weeks."

"You're kidding."

"No."

"You mean no sugar at all?"

"None."

"How are you supposed to make cookies and cakes without sugar?"

"Search me. With grape juice, they say. They want me to use grape juice, or date syrup." She can't keep the bitterness out of her voice.

"Sounds disgusting," Lucy says.

"I agree," says Tom. "We should do something about this."

"Yes, but what?" Rachel asks him. "They've already decided on this policy."

"I'm not sure, but let's talk about it. Give me a call tomorrow or the day after, whenever suits you. Shoshana in the shul office has my number."

"Okay, I will. Thanks."

"No problem. Oh, my phone! Excuse me ..." Tom swivels sideways, pulling a vibrating phone from his pants pocket, and puts it to his ear. "Hello?" He listens for a few seconds, then says, "Thanks for letting me know," and turns back, smiling, to their little group. "Good news! That was the hospital. The rabbi isn't out of the woods yet—there are still some more tests to do—but he's made it to first base. His condition is stable."

"Thank God," Lucy says.

"Hallelujah!" Rachel punches the air.

Ezra says, "Phenomenal." Then he asks Tom: "Is there anyone we should notify?"

"Good point. I left a message for the president of the shul after the ambulance came, but I should probably give her another call now. I think the rabbi has a mother."

"Everyone has a mother," Ira says.

Tom stares at him.

By now the gym is almost empty, but to the fifteen or twenty congregants still present, Ezra calls out joyfully: "The hospital just called—the rabbi's condition is stable!" A white-haired couple and their son hurry over for more information. Ezra chats with them briefly, then watches them leave and contemplates the remaining people in the gym. He recognizes only one grouping: a family of two parents, two teenage daughters, and a son—all of them plump, robust, and cheerful, and loud, enthusiastic singers. They sat across the aisle from him last night and he couldn't help noticing their exuberant participation. Now they are teasing each other, joking around, feasting on Rachel's cake, guzzling pop, and appearing overall triumphant to have made it to the end of Yom Kippur. Ezra, too, feels triumphant. Although he knows he hasn't yet vanquished his demons, and that the pain over his lack of artistic success will almost certainly strike again at some point, at this moment it is completely

gone and he feels totally free. What does it really matter, he thinks, how famous I am or am not? So what if I don't get my five minutes in the sun. Who cares? What I've been a part of here today has been so much realer and more important than any of that. This is what life is truly about.

Ira, like Ezra, has been observing his surroundings. First he watched Ezra chatting with an old couple and their son. Now Tom is on his phone, chuckling with the president of the shul. Lucy is complimenting Rachel on her baking and Rachel is complimenting Lucy on how beautifully she led the prayers. On the opposite side of the gym, a dozen congregants are talking and laughing either in pairs or groups. Everyone in this place is with someone else, and soon they will all go home to break the fast together with their families and friends. Everyone here belongs somewhere and with someone; only he belongs nowhere and with no one. It's always been this way and always will be. He, the outsider, l'étranger. Alone.

Well, at least this won't go on forever. Tonight's the night. Everything is ready. Before coming here, he laid out all his options on the desk in his dorm room. It'll just be a matter of choosing: the red pills, the green, or the yellow. Or some colourful combination of them all. He'll have his own personal smorgasbord one hour from now. His own last supper. He rises to leave.

Tom, pocketing his phone as he turns around, notices Ira. What an awkward and strangely intense young man, he thinks. But he—along with Ezra and Rachel—stayed with me the whole time I was down on the floor during Lucy's Neila. He didn't leave my side. And now he's the one who looks unwell. As white as the plaster Dad used in construction or that I use for building arm casts. He looks frightened, too. And lonely.

"Are you leaving?" he asks Ira.

Ira nods, avoiding Tom's eyes.

"Are you okay?" Tom asks.

"I will be," he says.

Some undertone in these words sounds not quite right to Tom. To delay Ira a little longer, he asks, "Do you have somewhere to break the fast?"

Shame flits across Ira's face, as if not having somewhere to break the fast were a sign of failure: proof that he is unwanted and unloved. He shakes his head. Then, picturing his laid-out pills, he says with a sardonic smile, "I'll have something at the dorm."

"You're a student."

"Yes."

"From out of town?"

Ira nods.

Tom thinks: He's so fragile. He has that same lost, vulnerable look that Polly had during her breakdown. And his eyes: as green as a swirling sea.

"Come break the fast at my place," he says. "It's just me and my wife, but you're really very welcome."

Ira hesitates, dubious.

"In fact—" Tom scans their whole little group—"you all are. Why don't you all come over to my house to break the fast, if you don't have other plans? I live just across the street, two houses down. And my wife, Carolyn, is a marvellous cook. We can eat something together, unwind a bit. You don't have to stay long."

Lucy, Rachel, and Ezra exchange glances. "All of us?" Lucy asks. "Are you sure?"

"I'm sure. The more the merrier."

"Your wife won't mind?" Rachel asks.

Tom laughs. "You don't know Carolyn. She'll be tickled. She loves having people over."

Ezra is unsure. He was planning to go home and paint. But then he thinks, What's an hour? He can start painting one hour later. And he's tired and hungry, and wouldn't mind a hot meal with friendly people. "I'm game," he says. "Thanks, Tom. My wife's in New Hampshire visiting her mother, so I'm on my own tonight."

"Great!" Tom says. He looks questioningly at the others.

"This is lovely of you," says Lucy, "but I'll have to check first what's happening at home." She pulls out her phone and sees a text there from Larry, sent an hour ago: *I'm tired. Going to sleep now. See you in the morning. Love, Lar.* "Okay," she says to Tom. "I can come. Thank you."

He nods with a smile.

"I wish I could join you," Rachel says, "but I have to clean up here, and this is going to take a while."

Tom, Lucy, Ezra, and Ira survey the gym. Hundreds of congregants scurrying home like mice have—like mice—left the place dirty. In addition to the pans on the chairs, trolley, and floor, there are crumpled, soiled napkins, crumbs, morsels of cake, empty water bottles, juice cartons, used straws, and all sorts of other detritus strewn throughout the room.

"You don't have to clean all this," Tom says to Rachel. "All you're expected to do is stack the pans on the trolley and leave the trolley in the back room. Tomorrow the community centre staff will come in and take care of everything else. It's in their contract with the shul."

"Really? I assumed I had to wash all the pans and tidy up," Rachel says. "What a relief! And now I can break the fast with you all."

Tom smiles, then turns to Ira. "What about you, Ira? Will you join us, too?" Ira doesn't answer. Tom says quickly, "Whatever you had planned for tonight can probably wait until tomorrow. Am I right?" He hears himself pleading with this young man, and he doesn't know why. But it feels important to persuade him to come.

Ira, watched by Tom, Lucy, Rachel, and Ezra, deliberates. When Tom asked him just now "Am I right?", his eyes were both eager-friendly and impatient-pushy. He seems to really want me, Ira thinks.

"You're right," he says to Tom. "What I had planned for tonight I can do anytime."

"So you'll break the fast with us?"

Ira nods.

"Excellent!" Tom beams.

"You're sure it's okay, bringing us all home?" Ezra asks.

Why do they keep asking him if he's sure? He's sure. He's never been more sure of anything in his life. "It's more than okay. It's fantastic," he says. He feels buoyant and strong; the world has never been better. "Let's help Rachel with the pans, so we can get out of here."

Rachel, Ezra, and Ira start collecting the cake pans from the chairs and floor while Tom calls home. As they load the pans onto

the trolley and head for the back room, Tom gets the answering machine and leaves a message.

"Hi Carolyn, I got your text and I'm glad your migraine's gone. I'll be home soon. I'm bringing a few people with me to break the fast. I'll explain later—it's a whole story. But don't worry about the food. I'll manage everything when I get home. Love you."

He smiles, hanging up. He knows his Carolyn. By the time he gets home, the table will be beautifully set and all the food laid out. Pocketing his phone and turning around, he is surprised to see Lucy on his left. She seems to have been waiting for him. "Who did you lose?" she asks.

"Excuse me?" He doesn't understand.

"You were saying Kaddish."

"Oh, I see. My father."

"I'm sorry," Lucy says.

I'm not, he wants to say, but restrains the impulse. "Thanks."

After a pause, she says, looking down, "My husband has Parkinson's."

Now it's his turn to say "I'm sorry." Then, "How far along is it?"

"It's just beginning. One month old."

"Ah, a baby."

"Yes. Me, too, I'm a baby at this."

"You'll find your way. Everyone does. Is there anything I can do to help?"

"We have a doctor, but I don't know if she's any good."

"Who is it?"

"Dr. Calderone."

"Maria Calderone? At Toronto General?"

"Yes."

"She's very good. Your husband is in capable hands."

"Thank you."

"I didn't do anything. But I know it's … very hard with Parkinson's."

"Yes." Lucy's eyes fill with tears.

"You'll be okay," Tom says. "I know from hearing your Neila how much strength you have inside you." He feels stupid saying this;

it sounds so banal, and maybe even patronizing, to tell someone they'll be okay—because after all, how can one ever really know? Yet as soon as the words were out of his mouth, he knew they were true. She's a strong person, Lucy. She'll be all right.

Ezra, Rachel, and Ira return from the back room and, together with Tom and Lucy, exit the gym. The passageway leading toward the lobby, though, is so narrow it forces them to divide into a pair and a threesome. That's like a full house in poker, smiles Ezra, strolling with Tom ahead of the others.

After a while Tom asks, "What do you do for a living, Ezra?"

"I'm an artist. I paint."

"No kidding! What kind of paintings?"

Ezra dislikes classifying or describing his creations. "I'll show you," he replies. Still walking, he pulls out his phone, fiddles with it for a moment with both thumbs, and holds it up to Tom. Tom takes the phone from him and halts, scrutinizing the photo.

"This is beautiful," he says.

"Thanks."

"I mean it. It's fabulous."

Ezra blushes with pleasure. Tom hands back the phone and they resume walking. A few moments pass. Then Tom says thoughtfully,

"You know, my partners and I—I'm in a practice with four other doctors—we're renovating an old house in Yorkville to use as our new office starting in January, and we were just talking about how we need some original artwork for the walls. There'll be five consulting rooms, plus two waiting rooms and a reception area that we need artwork for. Do you have any paintings we could look at?"

Ezra smiles to himself. Hardly any: only about sixty canvases leaning against the four walls of his studio, all unwanted and unsold. "I do," he says.

"Have you got a catalogue or website I can share with my partners? Or better yet, maybe we could stop by your studio sometime?"

"Sure." Ezra feels a little dizzy. "That would be terrific!"

"You have no idea how grateful I'd be," Tom says. "We've been struggling with this for months. Just last week we were discussing how

we can't open a new office with nothing on the walls—it'll look like a monastery!—but none of us had any idea where to start or the time to do research on this. And your work, if this painting you showed me is any indication, is tremendous. It would be perfect for us."

"Thanks." Ezra can barely speak. Eight rooms at two paintings minimum per room: that's sixteen paintings that Tom and his partners would buy. He can't believe his luck.

Tom keeps talking, as if he has to sell himself to Ezra rather than the other way around. "We have a lot of traffic coming through our front door. Between us five doctors, we get over a hundred patients a day. This could give your art some serious exposure, Ezra. And if you like, we can keep your brochures or your card at the front desk, in case people ask about your work."

"Thanks," Ezra says again. He can't think of anything else to say. Then, a few steps later, he hears Mona's voice: *Follow up, Ezra. Get his phone number.*

"How can I contact you tomorrow?" he asks Tom.

"My office is at Bay and Wellesley, but in a minute we'll be at my home and I'll give you my card. How fortunate that we met, Ezra!"

"Yes. It is."

They continue walking, with Ezra feeling emotional, through the cramped corridor. This passageway, he thinks, is as narrow as a birth canal. At the end of it, he and Tom, as if synchronized, turn around at the same moment and wave to Lucy, Rachel, and Ira. Rachel waves back and the threesome catches up. The group of five emerges from the unlit corridor into the bright, spacious lobby, quickly traverses it, and a moment later is standing outside in the chilly darkness. This, Lucy thinks, is the story of a human life. We come from darkness, have a few seconds in the light, and then return to darkness again.

"Look!" Rachel cries, pointing. "So many stars!"

They all look up. The sky is twinkling with millions of stars, and inside the Milky Way—swirling, it seems to Rachel, like icing smeared on a cake—there are trillions more. Pausing on the front stoop of the community centre, all five gaze in silence at the endlessly vast, beautiful, incomprehensible cosmos. To Tom, the heavens

seem impossibly far away, yet so close he can almost reach up and touch the stars. Like God, he thinks: at once a distant, inaccessible king and an intimate father whose warm hand you can grasp whenever you want. Lucy is laughing now, contemplating the sky: We are so insignificant! But no, that's not exactly true. At least in this little corner of the universe, there is nothing more important than people. Important to ourselves, of course, but also to God. After all, where would God be without humans? Who would God speak through, or speak to, if not us? Talking animals, like Balaam's ass? *Balaam's ass*—she pictures both Balaam's donkey and Balaam's bum, and laughs and laughs, wiping the tears from her eyes. Tom notices this but, no longer dismayed by Lucy's intermittent, inexplicable laughter, just smiles. Ira is staring at one particular star that he feels a kinship with. It is fine, he tells his star, that I am going to break the fast at Tom's house, but this is obviously only a detour. Sooner or later I'll take those pills. In the meantime, though, I might as well enjoy what I can. In spite of himself, he is cheered by the prospect of being a guest in someone's house—the first home he has been invited to (not counting Ken's) in his three and a half, mostly lonely, months in this inhospitable city. And he won't be going there alone; he'll be accompanied by these other people he sort of knows. Rachel, excited about the tasty hot meal awaiting them at Tom and Carolyn's, happily surveys the faces of her four comrades. She smiles at Ira and he smiles back. Then she slips her arm through Lucy's.

"Come, friends," Tom says. "Let's go home." They walk out together into the cold, dark night.

About the Author

DR. NORA GOLD is a prize-winning author. Her first book, *Marrow and Other Stories*, won a Vine Canadian Jewish Book Award and was praised by Alice Munro. Her second book, *Fields of Exile*, won the inaugural Canadian Jewish Literary Award for best novel, and was acclaimed by Ruth Wisse and Irwin Cotler. *The Dead Man* was honoured with a Canada Council translation grant and published in Hebrew. Her recent book, *18: Jewish Stories Translated from 18 Languages*, which was praised by Cynthia Ozick and Dara Horn, is an anthology of translated works that originally appeared in the prestigious literary journal that Gold founded and edits, *Jewish Fiction .net* (www.jewishfiction.net).

Gold has a PhD in social work and, while a tenured professor, she conducted research on illness/disability, sexism, and antisemitism. After leaving her academic position to write fiction fulltime, she spent six years as the Writer-in-Residence at the Centre for Women's Studies at OISE/University of Toronto, where she created and co-ordinated the Wonderful Women Writers reading series.

Gold also co-founded three progressive Canadian organizations, all devoted to strengthening democracy, civil rights, and social justice in Israel. She is active on social media, posting regularly on LinkedIn, where she has over 100,000 followers. For more about Nora, visit www.noragold.com.